the named

marianne curley

BLOOMSBURY

First published in Great Britain in 2002 by Bloomsbury Publishing Plc
38 Soho Square, London, W1D 3HB

Copyright © Marianne Curley 2002
The moral right of the author has been asserted

Quote on p.7 from *Images and Inscriptions* by Maurice West
published by HarperCollins (Australia) © Maurice West
Reprinted by kind permission.

A CIP record of this book is available from the British Library
ISBN 0 7475 5764 0

Typeset by Dorchester Typesetting
Printed in Great Britain by Clays Ltd, St Ives plc

10 9 8 7 6 5 4 3 2 1

This book is dedicated to my mother
And to the loving memory of my father

History is always written by the victors,
and the defeated create a new set of myths
to explain the past and gild the future.

Morris West

Prologue

Her hair is black and thick with bouncing curls that bob around her shoulders. Her eyes are blue, deeper than his, a much more attractive child, he knows. She is their parents' favourite but he doesn't care. Her name is Sera, and at ten she is the driving force of his life.

'Hurry!' Sera turns back once, urging her little brother forward. 'It's going to bloom for the first time ever. I can't miss it!'

The boy hurries as fast as his short legs can move. 'What's going to bloom?'

'The flower, you idiot. The one I've been waiting for. The giant black iris!'

He stamps his left foot and stops still. 'Don't call me an idiot.'

She turns, impatience making her eyes widen. 'I didn't really mean it. Now come on!'

He follows and asks in youthful innocence, 'How do you know it's going to bloom?'

Sera pauses long enough to give her brother an exasperated look. 'I've been watching the bud form for the past three months. Today is the first day of the spring equinox.

Don't you know anything?'

The boy takes off again, struggling to keep up. He wants to see the black iris bloom – an event that will occur for the first time this morning, apparently – but not nearly as much as his sister does. It's Sera's excitement and the privilege of sharing it that propels him over the grassy hills and into shrub and bushland at the first stirring of a misty dawn.

Sera stops suddenly, collapses on her heels and moans in relief. 'We didn't miss it! Look, there it is.'

The boy finally catches up, and, standing beside his sister, glances at the long green stalk supporting a perfectly formed black bud. His head tilts sideways. 'Is that it?'

'Of course it is!' Sera snorts without taking her eyes off the bulb. Now shut up and watch! It's going to be spectacular.'

For all his short life the boy has been aware of his sister's love for all things strange or extraordinary, like unusual flowers, orphaned woodland creatures, vivid sunsets. And many times he would simply sit in awe of her adventurous spirit, wishing that he too were old enough, or large enough, to swing down those cliffs with only a single rope tied around his waist. He shrugs and sits on the moist grass beside her, content in the knowledge that he won't always be four years old.

A sudden snapping of twigs nearby to their right has both their heads swivelling sharply towards the sound.

'Whatwasthat?'

Sera swallows around a sudden lump in her throat, the hairs on her slender body standing on end. She turns to the boy with a brave face. 'It was nothing. Don't be such a baby.'

Another twig, this one closer, startles the boy again. 'Is something coming?'

'Shhh! How should I know? But if you're very quiet, whatever it is will surely go away.'

But it doesn't go away. A moment later, a hideous creature of enormous size, in human form but with only half a face, appears through the mist to stand before them. The children scream and stumble backwards, grasping each other. Sera starts shaking. 'Wh-who are you?'

The creature appears to grow before their eyes as he straightens his broad back. 'I am Marduke.'

Sera gasps as if the name somehow explains the giant creature's presence. Her frightened eyes grow as wide as cannonballs and she flicks a look at her brother. He pulls on her arm. 'What did he say?'

Sera squares her shoulders. Brushing her brother's question aside, she turns and asks the monster, 'What do you want?'

In a guttural voice the creature with half a face replies, 'I want to take you to a place where it is midnight every day and black irises glisten under a bleeding moon.'

Shaking her head, Sera takes a tremulous step backwards. The half-faced creature stretches out one hand, the largest hand the boy has ever seen. He watches as the hand curves around his sister's face, and in that moment his heart is stricken with the certain knowledge that this monster is out to harm. But the boy finds himself unable to make the slightest motion, not even to lift a finger to his trembling lips.

The monster's hand shifts; the boy's eyes move with it to the top of Sera's head. The monster catches his eye and smiles with half a mouth, then squeezes his fingers. Sera screams, loud, long and in agonising tones that reach far into the surrounding woodland. When her body goes limp,

11

the creature lays her down on the grass, where she moans and grasps her head with both hands, her eyes open wide and staring. The creature stretches his massive arms into the air, making him appear even larger in the boy's eyes, and releases an almighty roar that has the surrounding trees shaking to their roots. And within that roar the boy hears his father's name called for all the world to hear, but his thoughts become confused as terror rages through him.

Cowering and trembling at the power in the giant's hands and rough voice, the boy's eyes shift to his sister squirming and groaning at his feet. But he feels the monster's eyes on him and looks up. Staring down with one golden-coloured eye, the creature slowly and horribly smiles. As suddenly as he came, and without another word, the monster disappears, leaving the boy to gaze at an empty space.

Suddenly Sera hisses, clutching her brother's ankle with a feeble hand.

Released from the creature's spellbinding hold, the boy gathers his much larger sister into his arms, cradling her black curls against his chest. 'Who was that, Sera? What's happening? What's wrong with you?'

She tries to speak but blood trickles from her mouth. This scares the boy half to death. 'Sera!'

Sera screams again and blood begins to seep from her eyes and ears. The boy becomes frantic, his whole body rocking and shaking with tremor after tremor. Tears form a crooked path down his face. He tries to rise in search of help, but Sera's grip on his ankle momentarily tightens. Her eyes begin to lose their vivid colour. 'Wait,' she says with enormous effort; and as he leans his ear down to her mouth, she whispers her last ever spoken words, 'Remember the name.'

'The creature's name?' the boy asks, glancing up as if the strange-sounding word still lingers in the mist-filled air before him. But all he sees is a scrawny green plant that has now collapsed and withered, black petals fluttering slowly to the ground.

With nothing but pain in his heart, the boy screams.

It's the scream of the boy child that finally wakes Ethan. Sweat pours off his bare shoulders, quickly chilling him in the crisp night air. He wraps his quilt around his shivering limbs as his bedroom swims into focus and his heart rate starts to slow. A strange sense of relief fills him as he slowly understands: the dream is over, and he has at last woken from another of his vivid recurring nightmares.

Chapter One

Ethan

I wake with the heavy feeling that my brain turned to lead during the night. It was the dream again. Well, what else is new? For twelve years now I've dreamed of that hideous monster. You'd think now I'm sixteen those childish nightmares would leave me be. If they had some meaning, shouldn't I have worked it out by now? Surely.

A sound penetrates the dull throbbing of my head. At first I think it's Dillon. Sometimes he drops in before school and we get the bus together. But then I realise that today is Sunday and my slowly awakening mind begins registering that this mournful sound is coming from my parents' bedroom. It's Mum. She's crying, her sobs growing more intense, even while it's clear she's trying to muffle them with her pillow.

I drag myself out of bed, groaning, and pull on a pair of jeans. At Mum's door I breathe in deeply. The last time she cried like this she couldn't stop for three days. Pushing open her door, I glance around for Dad, but I'm not really surprised when I see no sign of him. When Mum's depression kicks in, he's usually the first to run.

She sees me and attempts to dry her face using a corner of her sheet. And through the tears and red eyes she smiles, but she can't hold it for more than a fleeting moment before her face tumbles again. 'Cup of tea?' she whimpers. I nod and back out quietly, relieved to be doing something useful.

Dad's in the kitchen, sitting at the table with his legs folded one over the other, staring into an empty coffee mug. His apathy hits somewhere deep and I turn on him. 'What happened to set Mum off this time?'

He continues staring into his mug; I don't move either. The silence takes on an ear-shattering dimension. Finally he replies, 'Does there have to be a reason, Ethan?'

He's right, there doesn't, but I'm not about to tell him so.

'For what it's worth,' he goes on, 'she had a disturbing nightmare.'

'What, her too?'

Dad's eyes flicker once in my direction and I think, great, a reaction, but then he goes back to staring into his empty coffee mug again. I try to remember the last time we had a normal conversation, but of course I don't have to think hard to figure it out. My sister Sera's sudden death was the start of all our problems. But where will it end?

Mum is waiting. So I make her cup of tea just the way she likes it, with a touch of honey, and take it in to her. She looks better and offers me a small brave smile as she takes the cup from my hands. We talk about this and that for a while and when I'm sure she's OK I leave her.

Back in my room I find myself standing and staring

15

at my bedside clock like it has all the answers my family needs to repair its broken soul. I know it's only a clock, made of wood and glass mostly, but I picked it up at a junk market a couple of years ago, struck by the idea that it had had a whole life before I found it, in someone else's home, waking someone else up every morning.

I don't realise I'm staring so hard at the clock until its hands start going crazy, rotating faster and faster as I unconsciously offload some of this frustrated energy pent up in my head. Suddenly the entire clock starts to move, lifting off the table and spinning in midair. I've done this before a couple of times – moving objects is one of my skills – but never with so much force. Straight away I realise I'm losing control, so I'm way unprepared when the clock starts turning somersaults, rising almost to the ceiling. Finally it explodes. Splinters of wood, metal and glass shower over me. I start clearing it up before Mum or maybe even Dad comes to take a look.

Mum is first. 'What happened?' she asks from the doorway, sliding an arm through her dressing gown. 'It sounded like a bomb went off in here.' Her eyes take in the debris littering the floor. 'It looks it too. Are you all right, Ethan?'

I glance down at the broken pieces of my clock gathered in my hands. 'Ah, sorry, Mum, I dropped my clock.'

Her eyes narrow slightly as she pointedly takes in the multitude of small pieces. 'Were you standing on the ceiling?'

I shrug and give a lame smile.

'All right, just make sure you don't leave any sharp

bits lying around.'

I assure her I'll clean it up before I go out, and she leaves me to take a shower. At least she's looking brighter now. I tidy up the rest of the mess and finish dressing, all the time wondering how my father can stay seated at his kitchen table, staring into an empty coffee mug, when an explosion rocks his son's bedroom only metres down the hall.

Minutes later I'm out. Relieved, I head straight for the mountain, to a place that has become a sanctuary to me. To say this place puts me in another world is understating the reality. It is another world.

The first time I walked into the mountain I was four years old. I don't remember much of that day except the long rocky climb, and trying to get away from Dad, who wouldn't let me out of his sight in those early days. But it wasn't long before a numbness set in, a numbness which hasn't lifted off him since.

It was in these hills, buried deep within the southwestern slopes of the Great Dividing Range, that Arkarian found me. For days he spoke to me of challenges, great adventures and powers beyond my imagination. Then one day this strange man with bright blue hair and really weird eyes took my hand and led me inside the mountain.

Of course Arkarian is not really that strange, once you get past the superficial oddities. His electric-blue hair and violet-coloured eyes are that way only because such things as hair and eyes change colour over time. A long time. He never seems a day older, though I've known him for twelve years. His body stopped aging the moment he turned eighteen.

Arkarian is still taller than me, though now the

17

difference is not so noticeable. He has an aura about him. I still feel it, even after all this time. Part of it is in the way he speaks, in soft tones that demand without arrogance. Part of it is in his violet eyes and their ability to communicate without the need for speech. Over the years we've formed a friendship. For the first five years of our relationship I was his Apprentice, and he's still my immediate superior. But he taught me more than I ever learned in all my years in a mortal classroom.

The rock wall disappears as I stand before it, re-forming the moment I step through the opening. As soon as I make my way down the softly lit hallway, I hear Arkarian call, 'Ethan, I've been searching for you.'

The hallway has many doors: some rooms we use for training, some I've never been inside. Arkarian says they change often so there's no point to looking unless I require that particular room's service. And I learned early that curiosity is not necessarily a good thing.

I get to Arkarian's main chamber, and as always, the incredible high-tech equipment that doesn't exist in the mortal world yet, floors me. 'Very funny, Arkarian, you knew I was coming. You know everything.'

He glances up at me from across the room and gives a little laugh. 'You flatter me, Ethan, but you must remember, to know everything is impossible.' His eyes remain on mine, assessing me. It doesn't take long to notice my dark circles. 'Did you have another nightmare?'

I shrug, glancing purposefully at the 3-D holo-graphic sphere in the centre of the octagonal cavern which, at the moment, suspends a perfect image of the Palace of Westminster, London, in, if I'm not mistaken, the 1300s. My nightmare is still too raw and I'm not ready to talk about Mum. Her depression is getting worse, a thought that makes my heart sink. I nod my head towards the sphere. 'What year is this?'

Arkarian comes over, tactfully dropping the subject, and flicks a backhanded wave at the sphere. 'It's 1377. Your next assignment. But that's not why I summoned you. Sit down, Ethan.'

He sounds serious. I know this tone of voice.

'Stop worrying! It's good news.'

An antique wooden stool appears before me at the point of his finger. I take the hint, straddle it, fold my arms across my chest and wait, wondering, as I often do, at the passion Arkarian has for all things ancient.

He stares at me for a minute, his head slightly angled. Today his blue hair is contained in a band at the base of his skull. It has the effect of making his eyes appear deeper violet. 'You're being promoted.'

I jump off my seat, leaping into the air. 'Yes!' This is fantastic news. It's more than that really. The Guard has been my life for as long as I can remember. Most times it's also been my home and haven. It's not that my mortal home isn't safe, it's just … uncomfortable and, well, just plain morbid.

Arkarian grins, knowing how much I've wanted this recognition. No one works harder than I do. I would give the Guard my soul.

'The Tribunal is so pleased with your work, you're to be made a full member at a ceremony to be held in Athens next month.'

The reality of his words are hard to grasp. '*Full* member?'

He nods, still grinning at me, pleased with my reaction. 'But hold on, Ethan, there's something else.'

19

What else could there be, except maybe …? I reach across and grab his shoulders as if to hold him steady when I'm the one that needs holding up. 'Arkarian, are you saying I'm going to be awarded the power of flight?'

He glances briefly away, and instantly I understand that his words are going to disappoint. His eyes come back to mine and he says gently, 'You're not getting your wings yet, Ethan. Have patience.'

But the disappointment, coming after the nightmare from last night and Mum's depression this morning, hits me like a flood surging through the lower valley. My hands fly up in the air as I demand an explanation. 'Oh, come on, Arkarian! I completed my apprentice-ship years ago, and I've been an active member of the Guard for ten years at least.'

'Yes, but you started when you were a mere infant.'

I nod, admitting this. 'But I've heard of others who've received this power years ahead of me.'

He puts it simply. 'They were ready; you are not.'

I groan and slump, realising that there's nothing I can do. Nothing beyond what I do already, that is – keep trying to prove myself. 'So what's this other news?'

He releases a soft sigh, produces a matching stool for himself and sits opposite me so that we're on eye level. 'You're to be given an Apprentice.'

It takes a full minute to register. The impact of this honour finally hits and has me springing up again and pacing the windowless underground room, punching the air with my fist. 'An Apprentice! Of my own?'

Arkarian's eyes follow me. When I stop and search his face for confirmation, his eyebrows lift with a gentle nod of his head.

For the Tribunal to give me this responsibility must surely mean my wings are almost assured.

'Almost,' Arkarian confirms, reading my mind as usual. 'All you have to do is train your Apprentice, complete your next mission successfully, and you'll have your wings by your next birthday.'

'*Yes!* This is brilliant, Arkarian. How did you swing it?'

He gives me a tolerant grin. 'I'd like to take credit for your promotion, Ethan, but you did this yourself with your own good work. Now that I've admitted that, don't let your advancement go to your head as I'm inclined to think it might.' He looks at me hard. 'You want to prove you're worth entrusting with this ultimate power, don't you?'

I nod fiercely. 'Oh, yeah.' I come back to the old wooden stool and try to sit still long enough to make sure I understand it all, but my right leg can't stop jumping up and down. I put my hand on my knee to hold it still. 'So you're saying, if I successfully train this Apprentice, I could have my wings within three months?'

His lips don't move, but his eyes are saying heaps.

'There's a catch, isn't there?'

'Not at all,' he quickly assures me. 'But there is a certain urgency developing ...' He nods towards the circling holographic sphere of Westminster Palace. 'You don't have a lot of time before your next mission.'

'How long?'

'A few weeks.'

Weeks? What could Arkarian, or the Tribunal for that matter, be thinking? To train a small child would take years. It did with me. I remember some of those early lessons – Arkarian was patient ('cause I had two left feet in those days) but relentless. We trained here in a variety of rooms, learning skills most people wouldn't learn in a lifetime, from self-defence to self-existence. But it was years before the Tribunal thought me skilled enough to handle my own mission.

'I only have a few weeks to train an Apprentice?'

Arkarian nods. 'But it won't be as hard as you're thinking. Remember, you were an infant when you came to me, an unusual occurrence. Your new Apprentice is more adept than you imagine. She's skilled in her own right.' He chuckles, glancing down at his slender, ageless hands. 'Quite surprisingly so.'

I'm still taking in the part where he uses the word 'she'. 'I'm going to be training a *girl*?'

'Correct.'

'How old is this girl?'

'Fifteen.'

Suddenly the idea of training a girl takes an interesting spin. 'Oh, really?'

His head tilts with a small smile.

'What's her name? Do I know her?'

He remains silent and my body hair starts to prickle all over my skin with a sense of foreboding.

'Her name is Isabel,' he says softly.

Even though it's an unusually old-fashioned name, it draws a blank. Arkarian keeps looking at me as if I should know this name, or this person at least. Slowly a recognition somewhere deep inside my head starts happening. *Isabel*.

'I think I do know that name. Remember, when I was younger I had a best friend called Matt? His kid sister's name was Isabel. But you said my Apprentice wasn't a child. And anyway –' I dismiss this crazy idea quickly – 'the Isabel I remember was a wild little monkey, a nuisance to society, always tagging along with Matt and Dillon and the rest of us guys when we had important things to do, like build fortresses in the woods, scour the dump for motorbike parts, play rugby. Stuff like that. It couldn't be her.'

Arkarian stares at me stubbornly, a funny knowing smile tugging at his lips.

'No way, Arkarian. I'm telling you it can't be her. Isabel's a pest. She'll only get in the way. She couldn't possibly be right material for the Guard. You have to believe me. This girl is nothing but a headache. You must go back to the Tribunal and tell them. They've got it wrong this time.'

'When was the last time you saw Isabel? The last time you exchanged words with this girl?'

I glance away as I think, trying to recall. We have mixed-age classes at school, so it's possible we have a lesson together, but surely I would have noticed her? I do remember, though, a couple of years ago, when Matt was still my best friend, a few of us guys went down to Devil's Creek for a swim. It was a hot day and we'd stripped to our underwear. None of us knew Isabel had tagged along. When Matt spotted his sister halfway up a tree, he told her off for following us. The rest of us laughed and teased her about perving on us until she went beetroot red in the face. She clambered down that tree faster than a Ferrari in a drag race, disappearing into the woods. We went back to jumping into the river from the rope we'd fixed to an overhanging tree. None of us realised until hours later, when we were ready to go home, that the little pest had taken all our clothes. Matt was mad as hell, and Dillon went feral, calling Isabel every swearword he could think of until Matt got so defensive that Dillon finally shut up. We had to ride our bikes twelve kilometres in nothing but our wet underwear.

Arkarian is waiting, and for a second I have trouble recalling what he'd asked. 'Oh, yeah, I haven't seen Isabel for a couple of years.'

He gives me one of his superior knowing smiles. 'That's what I thought.'

Chapter Two

Isabel

I'm late. Of course this is nothing unusual. But if I hurry I could still make the bus, otherwise I'll be walking again. School is such a waste of time. I'd rather be on a mountaintop, abseiling down a hundred-metre cliff.

'Isabel!' Mum's voice rings out from downstairs. 'Ten minutes! Can you make it?'

My brother Matt surprises me at my bedroom door, leaning his back against the door jamb, shaking his head and looking superior and smug as usual. He's fully dressed in school uniform, backpack slung casually over one shoulder, towering over me. When did he grow so tall?

'Yeah, sure,' he says sarcastically, knowing Mum won't hear a word. 'She'll make it, Mum.'

He just wants to annoy me.

I shove him backwards into the hallway and slam the door in his face, grab my uniform in bits and pieces from my wardrobe, glance quickly around the room for my shoes, throwing everything on as fast as I can. With my blue shirt half hanging out, I spin towards my dresser mirror, quickly brushing my hair into a ponytail high at the back.

When I open the door, Matt's still standing there. He startles me into taking a step backwards. Regaining my equilibrium, I push past him. 'You need a life, brother.'

He follows me down the hallway. 'I'd have a better one if you could look after yourself for a change.'

This comment has me spinning round. But I shouldn't be surprised, really. For as long as I can remember, Matt's taken his 'big brother' role way too seriously. When we were little and our father walked out, Matt decided to take over the parental role. At first I didn't mind, but hey, we were only kids then, and I loved the attention from my one year older brother. But it soon grew annoying, and now that I'm fifteen, his dominance is just interference, and I can't stand it.

I glare at him, but my grumbling stomach helps me decide to drop the subject. I jump down the stairs two at a time, running straight into the kitchen. He follows and stands at the doorway. 'You haven't time for breakfast. I'll give you some money so you can pick something up at the school canteen. Something healthy.'

I cringe, muscles tightening all over, and throw him the most evil look I can manage over my shoulder. 'I have my own money, thank you. Now get lost before I dice you with this paring knife.'

He starts to turn away, but can't hold back a cautionary. 'Watch that knife, it's new and way too sharp.'

Oooh, he drives me crazy! 'Yes, *Dad*.' The second I say it, I wish I could take the word back. Matt looks at me, his eyes dark and disturbed; and it's as if the earth suddenly stops spinning, time hanging motionless between us. I don't remember my father, but from what

Mum says, Matt both hated and adored him. Dad would get drunk often, and violent, and afterwards he'd always go to Matt and cry like a baby on his shoulders. Matt would instantly forgive him, even while strap marks scarred his little ankles. I swallow hard and take a deep breath. 'I didn't mean anything.'

He nods. 'Just watch that knife, OK?'

He walks out and, half in a daze now, I grab an apple and go to cut it into two halves, the idea being to take the halves and eat them on the bus. But Matt's reaction has unsettled me. The apple slips, shifting sideways, and the knife slices through the top of my finger. Blood spurts over the knife and on to the chopping board. I can't help squealing.

Of course, now that I really need him, Matt is nowhere in sight. I grab a paper towel and wrap it around my bleeding finger, taking a quick look at the cut. It's deep. 'Great, now I'll probably need stitches.' I hold the towel tightly, trying hard not to focus on the sharp pain darting from my sliced fingertip right through to my palm. 'Heal, you stupid thing. Heal, heal, *heal!*'

'What's wrong now?' Matt suddenly asks from the doorway.

I drop the paper towel and hold out my hand. 'I cut my finger, OK!'

He comes straight over. 'Here, let me see. You're probably making a fuss over nothing.'

'I know when I've cut myself. Tell me, were you born this arrogant?'

He takes my hand, becoming singularly focused on examining my finger. He takes it between two of his and turns it gently, making sure to view it from every angle.

27

'What are you doing?' I realise that Matt's frown is not one of concern but more of amusement. 'What's that look for?'

He snorts and peers at me kind of weirdly. 'Are you playing some sick game with me or something?'

'Huh?' I snatch my finger back and glance down at it, suddenly stunned. Lifting my hand to face level, I examine the fingertip from all angles. 'I can't believe this,' I mutter. There's no blood any more, and more amazingly, there's no sign of a cut either.

Nothing.

I realise the sharp pain's gone too. I lower my hand, still examining it with disbelief. 'This is impossible.' My voice is just a whisper. I glance up at my brother. He has to believe me. 'I tell you, Matt, I cut myself.'

His head shakes while he laughs at me like I'm some dumb airhead trying to get attention. 'You know, sometimes I think you're as weird as Ethan.'

This has my head snapping back up to his. 'You're not going to bring Ethan up again, are you?' He does it all the time, knowing full well how I've felt about his best friend (ex best friend, I should say) since we were little children. No matter how hard I try to convince Matt I'm over all that now, he still teases me endlessly. My only consolation is that Ethan – hopefully – has no idea how I felt as a kid when I tagged along with Matt and his friends looking for something interesting to do. I've never been a stay-at-home child. I hated 'tea parties' and 'dressing Barbie' games. Those little doll clothes that never fit properly made me want to scream. I wanted to climb and jump and run, and still do, but confine myself to organised sports these days. And I didn't tag along with Matt all those years just

28

because Ethan was with him, although Matt insists I did. I just loved doing things guys did. That's all there is to it.

Not that it would make any difference today. I haven't hung around Matt or his friends for a couple of years now, and Ethan no longer knows I even exist. He's in my history class and I swear he doesn't even know who I am. Never once has he acknowledged my presence.

A loud rumble outside has Matt tugging on my arm. 'Come on! It's the bus.'

Quickly I look for where I put the apple. I grab it off the chopping board, find where I dropped my bag and make for the front door. Just outside I glance down at the half-carved apple in my hand. What I see gives me such a start that the apple flies from my suddenly trembling fingers. But even on the moist grass where it lands, I can still see the rich red stain of blood on its shiny skin.

My blood.

From the cut that doesn't exist.

Chapter Three

Ethan

Isabel Becket is going to be my Apprentice. What lousy luck! And it's not that I mind because she's a girl. No way. Sure, at first I was a little surprised, but only 'cause I always imagined myself training an excited and willing child, who would be in awe as each new facet of this other world was revealed. But Isabel Becket?

I walk into my history class, quickly scouring the back row, checking for a vacancy. I chose history six weeks ago, thinking I could breeze through the course, what with my personal knowledge of the subject, but I never counted on Croc-face Carter taking the class. He's had it in for me for years, I don't know why. I never did a thing to him, not that I recall. I only started calling him Croc-face after he put me on detention for not having my shirt tucked in three times in a row. How pathetic! I was punished because I'd grown too fast for my uniform. After that, well, the name just seemed to fit. It's not my fault he has an enormous jaw full of huge white teeth.

The man just hates me.

Out of the corner of my eye I see some girl diving for the last vacant seat in the back row. A quick look around and I realise the only other seats in the class are either right up front under Carter's nose, or worse than that, right next to Matt's girlfriend Rochelle, second row from the back. But she was the cause of our friendship bust-up.

Definitely no way.

I just have to have that back-row seat, so I take off down the centre aisle as if I'm suddenly in a race to save my life. But the girl stays ahead of me, and if I don't do something drastic, I'll end up sitting so close to Carter I'll be able to smell his body odour, or trying hard not to make eye contact, or any kind of contact, with that she-devil Rochelle. The thought of these two scenarios has me pushing roughly past the girl making for the seat with my name on it. She falls to the side, right on top of Leanie Hall's lap, just as I slam down in the seat, claiming ownership.

'Hey!' Leanie calls out while helping the girl up and giving me an irritated look. 'What's with you today?'

'Sorry,' I mutter. 'I have to have the back seat, Leanie. You know how Carter hates me. If I'm in his direct line of vision, he'll hound me for the entire lesson.'

'That's because you're always ticking him off.'

'No way.'

She gives a little disbelieving laugh.

'Are you all right?' I ask the other girl, who's now standing and looking around for somewhere else to sit. 'I'm sorry, I didn't mean to shove you over like that.'

She nods and kind of gulps, her eyes flicking away across the room.

'Here,' Leanie suddenly says to the girl, offering up

her prime back-row seat. Then, looking at me, she says, 'I don't have the same hang-ups as Ethan. I think Mr Carter's sexy.'

I feel my jaw drop so low it's a wonder it doesn't hit the floor. I can't believe she just said that. Carter sexy? No way.

Leanie takes off and the girl sits in the seat across the aisle. Carter walks in and starts muttering something, but I can't focus on the man. My mind's doing a double take on the girl beside me. She's sitting examining a finger held up right in front of her face like it's the first time she's ever seen it. As she does this, I recognise something familiar about her. She realises I'm staring, drops her hand and goes red in the face.

Apparently Carter's noticed my preoccupation too. He comes down the centre aisle, stopping about midway. 'Is there a particular reason your interest in the opposite sex is far more obvious this morning, Mr Roberts? Did you wake up and suddenly realise you're of the male persuasion?'

The class sniggers.

'No, sir,' I mutter, hoping to get him off my case.

He looks at me as if I'm a pathetic excuse for a human being, then finally backs off, starting to talk about our lesson today – Alfred the Great and what a superb ruler he was, explaining how in his twenty-eight-year reign this king exhibited incredible military skill, excellent government and the ability to inspire and motivate armies of men. Carter's actually doing a pretty good job until he starts describing King Alfred's appearance, the clothes he wore and stuff like that. The descriptions are straight out of a textbook, which is, as usual, mostly inaccurate and definitely biased.

And much I would love to correct Carter, and the textbook for that matter, I keep quiet. I have to, or I could be punished with expulsion and memory erasure for breaking one of the Guard's three vital codes.

To get my mind off the inaccuracies of history, I sneak another look at the girl by my side, searching for that something about her that's triggering my memory cells. She notices and glances at me briefly before dropping her eyes to her desk. But it's all I need. Her eyes are brown and big and just like Matt's.

It's her – Matt's sister Isabel! My new Apprentice. Well, what do you know?

I take another look – for scientific reasons, of course. I mean, this is the girl I'm going to be training. I really have to size her up, assess her strengths, for instance; and, well, I haven't seen her for a couple of years. Except for the last six weeks, I guess, if she's been here in my history class all that time.

As I scrutinise her appearance, I wonder what happened. She looks so different from the scrawny little monkey I remember. She's still pretty small, but she's filled out a bit. In places, I mean. And her hair is lighter now, much lighter than Matt's. A real sun-kissed blonde, like she spends heaps of time outdoors.

I glance down at her legs and realise straight away I'm being too obvious. She notices. 'Are you finished?'

But I can't help staring at her, suddenly seeing the training of my new Apprentice in a different light. This could be fun. Hell, all those long days and nights working together, teaching her new skills like personal combat, sword fighting, bush survival and how to harness her inner psyche …

I don't realise I'm smiling at thin air until Carter

points it out to the rest of the class. It's their laughter that brings me out of my daze. 'Huh?'

The class just laughs harder, girls exchanging funny little looks with each other.

'Mr Roberts,' Carter calls out, his voice filled with mock wonder. 'How is it that you spend half your lesson either daydreaming or disrupting the class with your antics, and still manage to sustain a straight A-plus grade in this class?'

Uh-oh. Arkarian's always warning me not to give away clues. It's dangerous, he says, for anyone to suspect. And that means anyone from the Guard or the Order. Should my true identity be revealed, my life could be at risk.

Maybe I'd better start getting some answers wrong. Of course I don't have any problem failing tests in my other subjects, but after living history for twelve years, it's hard to mistake the facts.

Carter's still looking at me, waiting for an answer, one thick eyebrow raised. 'Uh, it's just you're such an excellent teacher, Mr Carter.'

This has the class in stitches. Everyone knows I hate this man's guts. And I don't intentionally set out to be a disturbing influence in any classroom, but as I see it, there's enough sadness at home, why carry it around with me all day? Although sometimes I have to force myself to remember my personal motto: enjoy what I can, when I can. At least the Guard gives me a purpose beyond this mortal existence.

'It would be a good idea if you remembered that, Ethan,' Carter says softly, spinning away. But his tone has a threatening edge, leaving me with an uneasy feeling in the deepest part of my stomach.

Appearing cool and detached, Carter nears the whiteboard at the front of the classroom and starts talking about King Alfred's introduction of the penalty system, a modern form of today's courts; and I brush the eerie sensations aside, joining in the discussion of what effect this penalty system had on the people of the time. But halfway through the discussion he loses me again, my mind unable to stay focused on something I've experienced first hand, with so many other ideas to occupy it. Training Isabel will be the most challenging thing the Guard has thrown at me so far. I have to prove I can do this. I want my wings above anything else in my life to date. This is one way I can prove I'm worthy of the responsibility. Worthy of the reward.

An idea hits me and starts taking shape in my mind. The most difficult aspect of my own training was getting past my inner disbelief. The amazing things Arkarian told me about, I had to see for myself. And I was only four, an age when imagination and reality run a fine line. So I decide, as long as I'm careful no one's watching, to show Isabel a little of what I can do. Just something trivial but enough to spark her interest.

Casually so as not to attract attention, I push my pen to the edge of my desk. Glancing around, sure that no one is looking, I will the pen to spin. For a second Isabel keeps staring straight ahead, but then her eyes shift. She sees the pen spinning by itself and her mouth drops, colour draining from her face. *Yes!*

This is exactly the reaction I want and I can't help grinning. But just then I notice a pair of trousered legs in my vision. I raise my eyes and see Carter standing before me. The look on his face causes heat to flood every cell of my body. His head shifts slowly from side to side as if he can't believe my stupidity, while his eyes squint into narrow slits, staring at me. *Oh, hell!*

Suddenly Isabel's reaction pales into insignificance. I've just made a huge mistake, and it's really going to cost me.

I've just broken a vital code – never to reveal one's powers in public.

Chapter Four

Isabel

He rushes out of class so quickly I have to run to keep up, struggling not to lose him through the narrow corridors and students changing classrooms. He runs right to the front gates and goes straight through without even stopping for breath.

'Hey, wait!'

He turns around, looking surprised. He didn't even know I'd been pursuing him for the last five minutes. 'Isabel? What are you doing here?'

I try to stop panting long enough to explain, secretly pleased that he knew my name, but still feeling like the world's biggest fool. 'Ah, I was just … sort of wondering, that's all.'

'Wondering what?'

'Where you were going. I mean, you're leaving school grounds and it's only third period.'

He walks the few steps back to where I stopped at the front gates. 'There's someone important I have to talk to and it can't wait till the end of the day.'

'Oh. Who is it?'

He doesn't say, just kicks a stone. Obviously it's none

of my business. Why would he tell me anyway? We haven't spoken before today for two whole years. 'Sorry, I shouldn't have asked.'

His hands come down on either side of mine on the iron railing. Suddenly I have to concentrate hard to force my breathing to sound normal. Feelings I thought were long dead, or at least deeply buried, claw their way back to life again.

'Look, I want to tell you, but I'd have to start at the beginning and I don't have time right now.'

'What beginning? You're not making any sense.'

'Yeah, well, I just did something I shouldn't have.'

'That thing with the pen?'

His eyes roll. 'Yeah. I have this habit sometimes of doing stuff and not thinking through to their consequences.'

'You know when I said you weren't making any sense?' He cocks an eyebrow. 'You're doing it again.'

He starts to laugh and his weirdness reduces slightly. 'Why did you chase after me?'

My pulse starts racing, but what happened with the pen made me think of my magically healing finger. Matt didn't believe me. 'Well, you see, something weird happened to me this morning, a bit like your rotating pen.'

'Really?'

I have his undivided attention and for the first time I realise just how deeply blue his eyes are.

'What was it?'

I take a step back, his presence overwhelming me for an instant. It could be because I'm about to say something that could make me appear a complete psycho case. 'I was—' I start and stop quickly. 'Um, well …'

He nods at my hand. 'Has it got to do with your

finger?'

This takes me by surprise. 'How did you know?'

'I saw you examining it this morning as if it had suddenly grown a ten-centimetre nail or something.'

His words relax me for a minute. 'I cut my finger.'

'Yeah, and?'

I flick a quick look around to make sure no one is within hearing distance, then hold up my hand. 'A few seconds after I screamed at it to heal itself, well, it did.' He stares at me for a second, his eyes narrowing slightly. 'It healed itself,' I repeat clearly in case he didn't get it the first time around.

'Well, well, Arkarian wasn't exaggerating, was he?'

'Excuse me?'

'Nothing. Look, you must be *so* confused.'

So he doesn't believe me either. 'You guys are all the same, aren't you?'

'What?'

'I told Matt, and he had the same reaction as you – total disbelief.'

'Oh, wait a minute, Isabel, don't get me wrong. I do believe you.'

His words shut me up fast. 'You do?'

'Yeah, I do, but I haven't the time to explain anything right now. I have this problem I've just created for myself. But don't worry, I'll be back. I promise. Can your curiosity hang on a couple of hours?'

'Well, yes, but –'

He turns to run off again, spinning around briefly for a final word. 'Don't tell Matt anything, OK? He won't understand.'

I agree about Matt not understanding, but I need more. My self-healing incident, Ethan's spinning pen, both on the same day, have completely freaked me out. And now he's rushing off to see someone who can't wait till school is over. Well, honestly, I can't wait either. It's all too mysterious for me.

Glancing around again I see no teachers in sight, just a couple of kids lingering between classes. One of them is Dillon Kirby, a friend of Matt's and of Ethan's too, I think. But he quickly moves off to wherever he's going, and now there's no one around. As fast as Ethan, I take off in the same direction and run hard until I glimpse him up ahead. I keep way back, hiding behind trees and boulders and scrub whenever he turns around, which he does often as if on the lookout for me or anyone who might be following.

I trail him for what seems like ages, right to the top of Angel Falls. It's quite a climb, almost straight up. Most people around here call it the mountain. I start wondering if it's worth ditching class for when suddenly he stops directly in front of a rocky wall. Just as suddenly a hole the size of his body appears in the rock and he walks inside – right inside the mountain!

I rub my eyes and move closer. But there's nothing there now except the rock wall. Going right up to it, I touch the place I saw Ethan walk through, but it's hard and solid, jutting out sharply here and there. There's a spot where some dirt has lodged and grass has started to grow with even a small tree taking root. I run my hand over the area I swear I saw Ethan just disappear into, but nothing seems out of place, nothing comes loose in my hands.

I take a step back and try to focus on breathing slowly.

This is all too weird.

Chapter Five

Ethan

'Arkarian!' I call for the fifth or sixth time, pacing his main chamber over and over, searching for a clue to his disappearance. 'Arkarian, where the hell are you? *Arkarian!*'

Finally his body forms before me, and even though I've seen him do this a thousand times, I still step back in awe as he uses his wings and resumes his physical form. He gives himself a small shake, brushing a speck of dust from his caped shoulder. 'What's the problem, Ethan? Whatever's got you in such a rush?'

'Something horrendous has happened. Where were you?'

He gives me a look bordering on intolerance. 'I don't live here,' he mutters. 'Much as it may appear that way sometimes.'

'I'm sorry, Arkarian. Did I disturb you?'

'Quite. Now tell me what's wrong. Your thoughts are too jumbled for me to make any sense out of them.'

I take a deep breath while Arkarian points at my feet. Producing two wooden stools, he sits on one. But I can't possibly sit still, and start pacing the room. 'I used a very small ...' I hold up my hand with thumb and first finger a centimetre apart. 'The tiniest, miniaturest amount of power –'

Arkarian's eyes follow me around the room. 'Were you seen?'

'Yes.'

'By Isabel?'

'No. I mean yes. I mean, I had intended Isabel to see, but my history teacher happened to –'

'Ah, Mr Carter.'

'You know him?'

He nods but won't elaborate. 'How did he react?'

Remembering Carter's face brings me back to the stool. I sit and try to explain. 'His eyes went hard, his mouth drew tight as a string. He was angry, Arkarian. I don't get why, really. It was strange.'

'He was angry, Ethan, because you revealed your powers, and he understands the consequences of your act.'

'But how could he, unless ... Is he ...?'

'Ethan, what possessed you?'

A mental image of Isabel sitting there flashes through my head. What exactly made me take such a risk? Did I really want to convince Isabel before I'd even talked to her? In the middle of a room full of people? The thought that maybe I was simply trying to impress her crosses my mind, but I push it aside. I'm not that stupid. Not that irresponsible. Surely.

Arkarian looks at me with raised eyebrows.

'Oh, hell, Arkarian, I can't believe I did it either. I'll be more careful next time, I promise.' I'd better be more careful at home too, I remind myself, recalling the exploding-clock incident the other morning. What if my door hadn't been closed and Mum had been walking past? 'What's going to happen to me?'

'A breach of security is punishable, Ethan. I'm sure you'll hear from the Tribunal shortly. I can only assume you'll be called to explain yourself at a trial before the Tribunal in Athens. But remember your good work for the Guard. And your upcoming mission will be a further chance to prove your talent and loyalty. I'm sure the Tribunal will balance it all out in your favour.'

I nod, slightly relieved. 'What should I do now?'

'Nothing.'

'But Carter?'

'I'll speak with him.'

'He's one of the Guard, then?'

Arkarian, obviously disturbed at having to reveal the identity of another of the Guard, reluctantly nods. 'He's a coordinator in the Citadel.'

'No way!'

'He's been with the Guard for twenty years. And now, his position is exposed.'

'Well, I won't reveal his identity to anyone. I swear!'

'There are two problems here, Ethan: Carter's position is now revealed to you, and your position must be revealed to him, or he'll suspect you could be a member of the Order.'

I groan at how my simple thoughtless act has started snowballing into an avalanche already.

'He's probably right now working out a plan to have you eliminated.'

'You have to tell him!'

'And then there's the fear that others may have seen you. Isabel did, Carter did. Who else was in that classroom?'

I really don't want to say this out loud. I know Arkarian knows my thoughts as I think them, and right now I haven't the concentration to shelter anything from him; but he's making me voice these next words on purpose. 'The whole class,' I mumble.

He groans softly. 'It's dangerous, Ethan. You must see this. If anyone from the Order happened to witness you use your power—'

'I know, I know.'

'And even if there was no one from the Order in that classroom today, it's just so easy to arouse suspicion. People talk, and unusual actions attract attention, creating a lot of gossip.'

'I thought I was being careful. What are the chances someone else saw me?'

'I don't know. Think.'

'A girl called Leanie, maybe; but no, she was right up front. Rochelle, Matt's girlfriend, was in that class, but I have no idea if she was looking.' My head suddenly feels enormously heavy. It drops into my hands. 'What do I do now?'

'My advice is to do absolutely nothing.'

My head lifts to meet his violet eyes. 'Why nothing?'

'It's simple. Your breach will be dealt with when the Tribunal is ready. And if you keep acting normally, especially in front of Marcus Carter, anyone else who did see your little stunt, may assume it was a trick of their own eyes. Maybe no one else saw anyway and we're concerned about nothing. So, especially at school, act as you normally do, whatever you call that.' He looks at me and grins. I don't acknowledge his humour and simply stare back. 'That will be the best way to avoid arousing anyone's suspicions. I'll talk to

Marcus before he jumps to the wrong assumption.'

'Promise me you'll speak to him quickly.'

Arkarian pats my shoulder comfortingly. 'I will. But he's not going to be pleased with you.'

'I can't wait for history class tomorrow.'

'Don't let fear consume you. Your work for the Guard has hardly begun yet, like training your first Apprentice. Trainers are selected carefully and are looked upon with honour and pride. In your case, you've been given only three weeks to train your Apprentice for the first stage of her initiation. She'll be accompanying you to England, to the year 1377, to aid the future King Richard II. But as an observer only. This mission will break the ice for Isabel, prepare her mentally to tackle her own mission in the weeks following. So she must observe carefully.'

'I understand.'

'Good. There are some dangers, though.'

'Isabel won't be in any danger, will she?'

His pause is lengthy; his words, when they come, are carefully selected. 'Not if you train her well.'

Chapter Six

Ethan

I have to see Isabel. We have to get started on the training programme. Quickly! But first she has to understand all that's happening around her and to herself. Arkarian advised me not to explain everything in one hit. The Prophecy, for example, is probably the hardest to absorb and can wait. Sure, it's to be an observation-only mission, but mentally she'll have a lot to do, mostly in accepting this complete other world that works within our mortal one, the only one she understands right now.

It's not going to be easy.

Especially since Isabel is Matt's sister, and he's as protective as a father. More so, I think. How am I going to get around him to even speak to Isabel? It's not as if he trusts me any more, not after what happened with Rochelle, which is why I haven't hung around his place for the last eighteen months at least.

My mind drifts back to when Rochelle first came to Angel Falls. Both Matt and I were attracted to her on first sight. Who wouldn't be? She was so … exciting and, well, just beautiful, with long, shiny black hair, startling green eyes, skin like molten gold. She had the most amazing laugh, and when she threw you a smile you thought it was just for you. At first I thought – *I could've sworn* – she was interested in me. I felt something between us, some deep, inexplicable connection. It hit me like a bulldozer, deep in my stomach. But her signals quickly became confusing. Was she playing on both our feelings? To this day I really don't know. But she knew right from the start that Matt and I were close friends. The strain between the three of us grew heavy, and as Matt became more serious about Rochelle, I decided to back away, sensing that our friendship was being jeopardised. I guess I thought if Rochelle wanted me, my pulling out of the race would force her into choosing. But she let me walk away. And my friendship with Matt never recovered.

Eventually it became easier not to see Matt at all. My presence was like a thorn in his side, and then one day he went off at me, telling me how he couldn't trust me any more, that I had to stop coming on to his girlfriend. I didn't know what he was on about. I never tried to win Rochelle away from him, even though sometimes, even today, when we meet accidentally, I sense something … I don't know, probably just my bruised ego thinking I could still have her if I tried hard enough. Not that I would. No way. Rochelle played with my mind once already, ruining my friendship with Matt. I'm not an idiot.

And now I have to spend time with Matt's sister. A lot of time.

I get to the Beckets' front door and notice the fine cracks in the timber boards and the peeling paint around the edges. Otherwise the house looks much the same as I remember – a quiet two-storey white house at the very end of a lonely unlit country lane that borders national forest land.

Taking a deep breath, I pull on the slightly rusted brass door knocker twice.

After a minute Matt opens the door. He sees me and raises his eyebrows. He's grown; I have to look up to meet his eyes. Well, it's been a while since we stood this close to each other. But other than by a few centimetres, he's not changed much at all. It's his intense brown eyes I remember mostly, windows to his feelings. And now he's staring at me with an expression that makes me want to look away – quickly. I swallow. 'Hey, Matt. Been a while.'

He stares for a second longer than is considered polite. 'What are *you* doing here?'

'Ah –'

'Heard you did a runner at school today. Carter was looking for you. Are you in trouble or something?'

A rock forms in my dry throat. I try to appear unconcerned. 'No, I'm not in trouble. Carter's just …' I grimace. 'Carter. Everyone knows he's got it in for me. He doesn't need an excuse to come looking.' And quickly, before I lose my nerve, I add, 'Is Isabel home?'

Matt goes dead still and says slowly, 'Yeah. Why?'

'I wanna talk to her.'

His jaw does this funny sort of slide left, then right. 'What for?'

Thankfully Isabel makes an appearance, pushing Matt aside far enough so she can see who's at the door. She jerks back just slightly. 'Ethan.'

'Can we talk?' I ask while trying not to drown in the hostility flowing off Matt's body in pulsating waves.

Isabel flicks a quick look at her brother that obviously says, 'You can leave now', but he doesn't take the hint.

An awkward silence follows. Matt breaks it. 'You got something to say to my sister?'

Isabel groans like she can't believe how much of a moron her brother is being. Quickly I decide to get it over with. 'Yeah, I do.' I turn to face Isabel. 'Wanna go for a walk?'

'With *you?*' Matt says and laughs.

Isabel sends her brother a look that could boil him in oil if she had that particular paranormal talent. A thought hits me: maybe she has. It will be fun to find out. But right now I have to get past Matt. 'Yeah, with me. What's so funny?'

He laughs so hard he has to grip the door jamb with one hand for balance.

Frowning, Isabel looks from her brother to me, then back to Matt again. 'Oh, I get it. This is some sort of joke you two have conjured up.'

Uh-oh. Now she's got the wrong idea altogether and she's starting to look really annoyed.

'Is that it, Ethan?' she demands, staring at me hard. 'Or are you asking me out …?' She pauses, her face going a brilliant shade of red.

But now I'm getting annoyed. My first instinct is to lay Matt flat to the floor with my fist, but I understand that action won't win me any bonus points. I need Matt on side so he won't give Isabel a hard time, 'cause she's going to be spending heaps of time with me from here in. So asking her out as if on a date obviously isn't going to wash with him. And I don't want to give Isabel the wrong idea either. I recall something about how she used to have a crush on me when we were kids. I'm sure she's not interested in me like that any more, but all the same, I don't want to risk hurting her feelings. I need another excuse. Fast.

'He's not asking you out,' Matt says sarcastically, quietening down at last.

She looks at me expectantly. I'm not sure what that look means. Does she *want* me to ask her out? We haven't spoken for years so I don't really know her any more. Suddenly I think of a reason that just might work. 'It's the history project.'

'What?' Isabel frowns again.

'You know, the assignment.' With my eyes I urge her to play along. 'We have to work in pairs, remember? Probably why old Croc-face was looking for me today. We've got heaps of work to do on it. I just thought we could get started on some strategies early, seeing Carter paired us up together.'

Her frown deepens but she doesn't call me an outright liar. Matt's jaw does that funny sideways slide again. 'How long are you going to be?'

Isabel glances at me for the answer, starting to look amused. 'Ah, an hour or so,' I say vaguely. I don't want Matt coming looking for us on the dot of sixty minutes. 'History, it's a big subject.'

Matt looks unimpressed but beaten. 'Has anyone ever told you you have an unhealthy interest in the subject? There's a rumour going around you get nothing but straight A-pluses.'

'Yeah, well, I think that's going to change.'

Matt gets defensive. 'What are you insinuating? Working with my sister is going to lower your class average?'

50

I really need to learn to think things through before reacting or opening my big mouth. Isabel saves the situation. She whacks her brother's arm with the back of her hand. 'Don't be a jerk.' And to me she says, 'Give me a minute while I get my *notebook*.'

Chapter Seven

Isabel

For a minute there I think Ethan is actually asking me out. But it doesn't take long to see through his stupid little game. How can I think he's really interested in me? I have to be careful not to let him think I'm interested in him, either. I'm not, anyway. Not at all.

What I am is curious, and confused and freaked out. My finger healing itself this morning was a really strange phenomenon. I can't explain it. I'm hoping Ethan can. Although why he should be able to, I don't get. But he did do that thing with the pen this morning, and walking straight into the mountain was strange too. Not that I'm going to tell him I saw him. What would he think if he found out I stalked him? It might just remind him of how I used to follow him around when we were children.

What on earth am I thinking here? Did I wake up this morning in a parallel universe or something? Of course, Ethan is not remotely interested in me. And the part about him walking through a rock wall has to have some simple explanation.

With these uneasy thoughts swimming around in

my head, I watch as Ethan suddenly pulls out a torch. I glance at the sky. It's blue, late afternoon, but there's still plenty of daylight. What is it with this guy? Is he nuts or something? 'What do you need that for?'

'It's going to get dark on our way.'

This makes me stop. 'You told Matt we'd only be an hour.'

'Actually I told Matt we'd be an hour or "so". The "so" lets me off the hook.'

'Not Matt's hook.'

He snorts a kind of agreement. 'Why is he so …?'

'Paternal?'

He shrugs a yes.

'When I was little, I mean really small, my dad … Well, Dad's last words to Matt were to look after his mum and his sister in the way that *he* never could. Matt took those words literally.'

'I didn't know your father died.'

'He didn't, he …' I don't usually like talking about this subject. It makes me uncomfortable. But talking to Ethan right now feels strangely natural. 'He walked away 'cause he was a drunk and, well, he reckoned he had to leave so he wouldn't hurt us any more.'

'But he hurt you more by leaving, didn't he?'

My fingers grow restless suddenly, as if irritating fleas have found their way under my skin. I stretch my hands out and crack every knuckle. 'Not at all. I was too young when he left.'

Ethan slides me a look like he's not real sure he believes me. I ignore it, looking straight ahead, and he says, 'Was he abusive?'

'So they say.' An uncomfortable silence follows. I don't want to talk about this topic any more. 'Look, my

father was a drunk and he beat my mum and sometimes …' I stop myself before I tell him of Matt's expe-
riences beneath Dad's leather strap. Matt wouldn't want
Ethan to know. He has such a low opinion of Ethan
these days. As kids they were inseparable, but now
Matt says Ethan's changed, become self-involved and
full of himself. Ethan starts whistling a lively tune;
completely tactless, I think, considering the topic we're
discussing. Quickly I decide Matt's probably right. I
mutter so beneath my breath.

He hears me. 'I don't know anything about the pain
of living in an abusive house, Isabel –'

'I'm not in any pain,' I fervently assert.

He gives me that funny disbelieving look again, but
chooses not to comment. 'But I do understand the grief
of separation, of losing a member of your family,
whether through divorce or …'

His words surprise me, and then I remember the
story of his sister's death. I was too little to be aware of
it at the time, but Matt and Mum have mentioned her
over the years. 'How did your sister die?'

I think at first he's not going to answer, then he says
with a small shrug of his shoulders, 'It's a bit of a mystery.'

'Really? I thought Mum said she'd been ill.'

'The autopsy stated a massive brain haemorrhage,
caused by a rare aneurism she'd probably had since
birth.'

'That's terrible.'

'But she was only ten and had never shown previous
signs of illness. Not even one headache.'

'How did you all cope?'

He pushes aside a half-fallen log that blocks the

path. 'I don't remember a thing,' he says quickly.

'You were probably too young.'

'Four,' he says and shivers suddenly.

I start wishing we'd never got on to this subject. 'I don't remember much from when I was four,' I reply softly. That was about the age I was when my father left.

He gives himself a thorough shake as if shedding the memory. 'Well, anyway, I think Dad took it the worst.'

'Oh?'

'Yeah, he's never been the same since.'

'How so?'

'Mum reckons he used to be more outgoing, adventurous. A risk taker. Someone you just wanted to be around. Someone I would have been proud of.'

I think about what I know of Mr Roberts now, selling his leatherwork from one of the craft workshops at the Angel Falls Café. A quiet, modest man who hardly speaks. 'He's a talented craftsman. His leatherwork is just beautiful.'

'Mum reckons he could have been anything he wanted.'

'Maybe this is what he wants.'

'If it is, then why does he never smile? My house is like a morgue.'

As I wonder what it would be like to live with a person who never smiles, Ethan grabs my arm and tugs me down behind a thick flowering bush.

'What is it?'

He pulls me down lower to the ground, putting a finger to his lips, frowning in uncertainty. His reaction makes me think we're doing something we shouldn't. Like when he took off this morning, always peeking over his shoulder. Cautiously he reaches up for a peep, then breaks out in a wide and relieved smile. 'It's nothing.' He drags on my jumper sleeve to keep going.

Peering over my shoulder, I see a photographer snapping shots of the valley beyond the ridge. But Ethan's uneasiness arouses my curiosity. 'Tell me why you dragged me up here.'

'There's a cabin I want to show you. It's not a real cabin now, just the remains of one. We can talk there.'

'A deserted cabin? Deep in quiet bushland? I wonder why you didn't tell Matt our destination?'

Ignoring my sarcasm, he keeps going, heading into deeper scrub. After a while he turns his torch on as the thickening canopy overhead blocks out the remaining afternoon light. I start getting the creeps and tug on Ethan's arm. 'Ah, I think we should turn back.'

Ethan stops and turns round. 'Why? We're nearly there.'

With a wide sweep of my arm I indicate the surrounding deepening woodland. 'It's just bush. And it's getting darker the deeper we go into it. It's creepy.'

But then he says, 'What happened to that pesky little monkey I used to know who couldn't stop climbing trees and jumping down cliffs and getting into trouble?'

My head tilts to one side. He's appealing to that part of me I've always found difficult to deny. 'How much further? Exactly?'

'Ten more minutes, I promise.'

'And when we get to this half-standing deserted cabin you're going to tell me how I managed to heal myself this morning?'

'Absolutely.'

He has me now completely hooked, and he knows it.

He doesn't even wait for a reply, but starts jogging off in a general forward direction. I run to catch up. After ten or so minutes he stops, and starts pulling vines down out of his way. I follow and before I realise it, we're standing beneath a couple of old wooden cross beams.

'We're here,' he says.

I do a full circle and wonder where the rest of the cabin is. After a few minutes of pulling vines down, the remains of a brick chimney and part of a decayed wall are revealed. That, apparently, is all there is left of the cabin, other than the two overhead beams and a couple of rotting timber posts on the other side.

'This is it?' I ask.

He nods proudly. 'What do you think?'

I'm starting to think this guy is way too weird. 'I swear you don't really want to know.'

He walks around, stopping occasionally to describe the room – two rooms, he says. 'The divider ran along here.' He draws a line in the air with his hand about two-thirds across from the remaining beams, then points across my shoulder. 'Over there was a small window. I remember it clearly. It had calico curtains held back by two bright-yellow ribbons Rosalind made herself. She made everything, come to think of it, including the family's clothes.' A warm, fuzzy expression slides over his face. 'She liked to add a splash of colour every chance she got.' He looks at me. 'Their clothes were really drab. Half the time she made them out of old hessian bags.'

He walks to the other end of the imaginary room and runs his hand down an imaginary object. 'This is where the wood stove sat. The damper she made in here was the best I'd ever tasted.'

These words strike me as a little odd. A nervous flutter starts up in the pit of my stomach. How on earth could Ethan have tasted this damper, or seen the calico curtains for that matter?

'You see over there?' He points somewhere over my left shoulder. I turn to look. 'That's where Rosalind hung the family portrait. It was a hand-painted gift. It was the only time she allowed herself to show some pride.'

'Ethan, who were these people?'

'Relatives,' he replies as if I should know this.

'OK, but it's weird how you know so much about them, like you've … researched them really well,' I finish, too cowardly to voice what I wanted to ask. I mean, he can't really believe he *lived* here. It's plausible to think he wanted to live here. His own home sounds terribly depressing. But this is not what Ethan means.

'I researched them all right. First-hand.'

This too is a strange thing to say. I decide to be brave. 'But the people that lived here –'

'Died well over a hundred years ago.'

'So … how do you …?'

'Know so much about where they lived?'

I nod, spooked and speechless.

'That's easy. You see, the woman who lived here – Rosalind Maclean – is a direct ancestor of mine. A great-great something-or-other on my mother's side.'

'Uh-huh.'

'And I lived here with Rosalind and her children – all six of them – for three whole months. Three great months, to tell the truth.'

Now I'm completely freaked out. Ethan is just too

peculiar. Matt was right after all with his distrust of this guy. He knew something, obviously. Well, I wish he'd told me earlier what it was. Here I am in one of the most isolated sections of the national park, alone with this weirdo, in the near dark.

I think I'm in trouble.

Chapter Eight

Ethan

I'm going too fast for her, but hey, I don't have a lot of time to play with. My main objective tonight is to make her believe, even if I have to shock her. Disbelief is the biggest hurdle to overcome. I have to open her mind to the concept that there is more to this mortal world than she's been raised to believe. That there is such a thing as the paranormal.

She plonks down cross-legged on the moist earthen floor, shaking her head and dropping it into her hands. Then she looks up at me with dark, suspiciously narrowed eyes. 'You're freaking me out. I think we should leave.'

'But I haven't explained —'

She sticks out her hand with one finger pointing straight up. 'That's right, you haven't. Now tell me how I healed my finger.'

I go and sit in front of her. 'You're a healer.'

'*What?*'

'I checked with Arkarian —'

'Why do you keep mumbling that strange name? Who is *Arkarian?*'

'He's my …' I try to find words she'll understand. 'My area supervisor.'

She squints at me. 'As in your employer?'

'Yeah, sort of. Well, yes, actually, but I don't get paid.'

She groans. 'You work for nothing? Somehow, Ethan, I can't see it.'

'Well, thanks. Whatever you think of me I'm not a mercenary. The rewards of this job far outweigh any monetary pleasures.'

'O-K,' she says slowly, humouring me, her head edging a little closer. 'What exactly is your job?'

Hmm, Arkarian told me to go slow. In other words, explain enough for Isabel to understand without blowing her mind and stuffing all chance of her believing what I say in future. 'I'm like a guard. Well, actually I *am* a guard. I was an Apprentice guard for a long time, but now I'm a Trainer.'

'So what do you guard, Ethan? Girls?'

'Very funny. And no, I don't guard girls, though that idea does have its good points. I guard *time*. More specifically, *history*. My job is to make sure it all happens the way it's supposed to, the way it already did.'

She greets this with a totally disbelieving lift of her eyebrows. 'Yeah, right.'

'I know it's a hard concept to understand, so don't worry too much about taking it all in just yet. What I want you to accept tonight is that there is this other world that works within our mortal one. Time in this other world isn't measured the same way it is here. There are all these different facets. Imagine a brilliant crystal that's mostly round.'

The only indication that she's listening is the narrowing of her eyes. But then she says, 'Are you trying

61

to tell me that in this other world time is round, like a sphere?'

'Sort of, but remember we're just talking about the measurement of time, which is, by the way, a very mortal concept.'

'Uh-huh?'

'Yeah, and, well, there's this place called the Citadel. It's huge. You have no idea – rooms and corridors you could walk through forever and not have seen it all. Well, anyway, time there isn't measured at all.'

'Really?'

'You see, way back in time –'

'Mortal time?' she asks with a mocking tone.

I try to ignore the tone, hoping my explanation will help unravel the mystery for her. 'Yeah, that's right. There was some trouble and, well ...' But the look on her face is too hard to ignore. She's not taking any of this in. I've got to keep this simple. 'Look, do you know your myths?'

'Which ones?'

'Greek. And Babylonian before that.'

'Hmm, are you talking about the creation myth, and how everything supposedly started from a mist called Chaos?'

I smile encouragingly, but go on to explain, 'It didn't exactly go like that. You see, Chaos is a woman, one very uptight immortal.'

Her eyebrows lift, just a little. 'You said that in the present tense.'

'Exactly.'

'What are you saying, Ethan? You're starting to freak me out again.'

'I'm trying to say that all our troubles began many

thousands of years ago when one very bored goddess decided to create a little chaos. She found a way to tamper with the past. At first it was just fun, but it gave her a sense of power above her compatriots.'

'The other gods?'

'Right. Well, this particular goddess began experimenting and soon discovered that by tampering with past lives, she changed the present. She realised that if she changed enough past events she could create a future that made her even more powerful. Her sole focus soon became total domination – of the world. The more she changed to suit herself, the more power she gained. Over the centuries she grew obsessed with the idea. She started recruiting her own army of followers and began a kind of order. We in the Guard have come to know it as the Order of Chaos. It's because of her and her Order that the Guard was formed. And it's sort of ironic that we refer to it as an 'order' 'cause her armies, and the result of their actions, create anything but order.'

Isabel doesn't say a word, just stares at me with those big brown eyes that seemingly grow darker every passing second. Then she sighs and shakes her head. 'That's ridiculous. And if it were true, why don't we see any physical proof in the world today?'

'There's plenty of proof, just look around. The result of this chaotic disorder is famine, plague, flood, war, hostility.'

She scoffs at me. 'Those things are either natural or man-made disasters.'

I think she's just being particularly stubborn. She's not even trying to allow the idea to take shape in her mind. 'OK, look, what if I tell you that you and I are part of a Proph— a plan.'

'What sort of plan?'

'A plan to preserve history and maintain a stable present, so that – and this is the important part – the future unfolds as it ...' I'm losing her again. 'Never mind.'

She groans dramatically. 'Why should I believe this fantasy story of yours? You know you sound completely off your head. Are you on something?'

'Were you on something when you healed your own finger this morning? Did you imagine the wound, or was it real?'

She glances down at her hand. I shine the torch on her fingers. She sighs and wriggles around. 'I don't know. It sure felt real.'

'It was real. You know it was. You healed yourself 'cause you willed it to happen. You're a *healer* and your time is approaching, so your skills are forming in a physical sense.'

For a second I think she's accepting, but then her natural human scepticism digs in and she shakes her head. 'This is too unreal. Everything you've said, it's not possible.'

An idea hits me. There's only one way to make her believe quickly. 'Hold on, don't move.' I get up, thinking I'll just have to use my other skill. Closing my eyes, I visualise exactly how the cabin was when I visited Rosalind in 1858, right down to the brick fireplace, the wood-burning stove and the window with the calico curtains.

'Oh, wow!'

Her soft exclamation as she staggers to her feet has me opening my eyes and looking at my handiwork.

The cabin is now fully restored, including the roughly made cedar table and chairs, stacks of bunks with their coarse blankets and lumpy mattresses, the family portrait over the top of the fireplace; and of course the cabin wouldn't have the right feel without burning kindling in the stone fireplace, and the warm scent of freshly baked damper wafting from the oven.

Isabel touches my arm with a trembling hand, her mouth gaping, eyes hugely round. 'Ethan, how?'

It's exactly the reaction I want. Complete awe. 'It's an illusion. It's one of my two skills. You saw me use the other skill in the classroom this morning. Remember the pen?'

She nods, still staring at the transformed room. 'You created this?'

'Only in your head. If you wanted to, you could look through it to the reality, but you're not trained to use that part of your psyche yet. I'll teach you though, if you let me. You see, you're one of the Named. And now you've been chosen to be my Apprentice.'

Her ingrained sense of adventure starts to kick in. It starts in her eyes. They lose their wild frightened look, switching to an interested, verging on eager, curiosity.

And I realise that for now at least, I have her hooked.

Chapter Nine

Isabel

Ethan is really weird, more than anyone else I've ever met or am ever likely to. But I can't deny what I see with my own eyes. The cabin, fully restored, smells and all, leaves me breathless. At least now I can rest assured I'm not going crazy and I really did heal myself this morning. Or maybe I *am* going crazy and this whole scene is part of my delusion.

I inhale a final whiff of home-baked bread before leaving the warm cabin for the chilling air outside. A few steps away I turn for a last look, but the cabin is gone. Without the proof before my eyes it's easy to think I imagined the whole thing. Instinctively I feel the top of my finger again. No wound. No tenderness. Nothing.

What on earth is happening to me?

Ethan tugs on my arm. 'C'mon, Isabel, we have to hurry. We can't risk upsetting your brother. We have to be careful not to alert anyone to what we're doing. There're these codes, you see, that must never be broken. The first is secrecy …'

By the time we get back to the house I sadly understand what's happening: I definitely am going crazy.

But we start training the very next day, straight after school, on the far side of the lake where hardly anyone goes. I've had all night to think about this strange other world within my mortal world, as Ethan puts it, and I have to admit it does sound a little exciting. Travelling backwards through time? Making sure the past evolves as it should? Wow.

But I'm no fool. It could still be some nasty elaborate hoax. A practical joke of the lowest degree. I wouldn't put it past Ethan, or Matt for that matter.

Once we get right around the other side of Angel Falls Lake, it takes another twenty minutes for Ethan to be satisfied there's no one in the area. He's really careful about this secrecy stuff. It's all part of their survival apparently. 'We should really be training indoors,' he explains. 'Arkarian has training rooms within the mountain but I find it stifling in there when we have all this.' He holds up his hands to the surrounding mountains and brilliant sky overhead. 'People rarely come here anyway.'

We find a small open glen surrounded by tall woodland on three sides and the lake on the fourth. Ethan puts his bag down and, as it's already growing chilly, decides to make a fire. Tediously he starts explaining where to get the tinder and how it must be laid first, with the smallest pieces of kindling placed gently on top in a pyramid, allowing enough space to start a flame. He goes to light the tinder, but the shredded bark he's using is moist. The fire doesn't start. I could have told him when he first collected the stuff not to get it from fallen timber lying on the ground, as it would have absorbed moisture, especially this high up

67

in the hills and close to winter. Standing dead timber is best. But as he simply assumes my survival skills are nonexistent, I let him continue, knowing the fire will take a long time to start.

A few minutes later, my patience runs out. 'Here.' I gather some tinder of my own, exchanging it with his stuff. 'Try this.'

In seconds a small flame is burning and soon the heavier kinding ignites. He stands back, staring into the flames. 'You've done this before.' It's a statement.

'Yes.'

'Well then, let's try something physical.' He quickly switches into lecture mode again, this time explaining a thing or two about the art of karate.

Now I know I really should tell him, but again he hasn't stopped to ask, assuming, I guess, that as I'm a girl, a small one at that, I wouldn't have any physical skills. So I let him explain the basic points on stance and breathing and how important it is to control the mind. He paces through a simple self-defensive movement I learned six years ago in my first lesson. Then I throw him. His back thumps down hard on the cold ground.

'Hey!'

'Yes?' I help him to his feet.

He stands back, crossing his arms over his chest. 'You've done this before too.'

I nod. 'I have a black belt.'

He's fast getting ticked off, ego thoroughly bruised. 'Anything else I should know?'

I do a quick mental check of the skills I've picked up over the years: rock climbing, abseiling, archery, fencing. I won competitions last year in both those last two sports. But I don't say anything to Ethan. I'm not sure he can handle the idea of a girl being able to do things like that.

He snorts and kind of hangs his head, then starts to laugh.

'What's so funny?'

'I think I'm starting to understand why Arkarian only gave me three weeks.'

I don't exactly follow, but somehow I sense it's a compliment.

Chapter Ten

Ethan

Training Isabel proves easier than I imagined. She can do just about everything physical. She's absolutely driven. It turns out she's a sports maniac. There's nothing she hasn't done. It has me wondering, though, why a girl (or a boy for that matter) would do all those sports. It's like she needs to prove something to herself, or someone else maybe. She's strong, no denying that! She threw me so many times in karate this past week I think maybe she should be teaching *me*; but her small stature holds her back in other ways. Though she has the skills to wield a medieval sword with accuracy, it has her arms aching after only a few minutes. So working with weights has become an integral part of her training. The other major aspect to her training is in the metaphysical world. Isabel's a healer, and though she managed accidentally to heal herself, doing it on call, forcing it to happen, isn't working. Even using her meditative karate skills is proving no help. Still, we practise every day. Until we break through this block, any other paranormal skills she has will probably elude us. In this area we have heaps of work to do.

We've met every day for the past ten days, mostly after school and nearly all weekend. Our time together hasn't gone unnoticed, even though I've tried avoiding Matt as much as possible, to the point of ditching the two classes we have together. But he's bearing down on me now as I aim to jump the back school fence.

'Hey, Roberts!'

I almost make it. But running would make me appear guilty of something, arousing his suspicions further, which could only make him hound Isabel for answers. If only he wasn't so protective of his sister, and so negative on me.

Turning around, I see his girlfriend is with him. Great! This is all I need.

'Hello, Ethan,' Rochelle says softly.

'Hello, Rochelle,' I say, and then it happens again. My breath catches somewhere in my throat, making me gulp for air.

And as usual when Rochelle is present in my company, Matt stiffens like a board. 'We have to talk.'

'About what?' As if I don't know where this conversation is heading.

'You know what. My sister.'

'Is she ill?'

'Don't be a jerk, Ethan.'

'What's your problem, Matt?'

Rochelle's eyes, as they always do, slide over me from head to foot. They come back up and she slowly smiles, sliding her hand through Matt's hooked elbow.

'I'll tell you what the problem is, you're spending too much time with Isabel. What the hell is going on between you two?'

For a second I don't reply. Firstly, I'm insulted.

What's wrong with Isabel spending time with me anyway? And why is he so upset? Does he think Isabel still has a crush on me? That was when we were kids. She's over that now. Today we're just friends. And this past week, training together, has proved just how good friends we can be, though it's just as well he doesn't know that.

So for Isabel's sake I'm not going to make this situation worse. 'I'm not doing anything with Isabel. We're studying, working on our history assignment together. That's all.'

'You're lying.'

'No, I'm not.' And I'm not, really. History is exactly what we're working at. 'Where do you get off calling me a liar, anyway?'

His jaw does that sideways shift again; this time I hear his teeth gnash together. 'That's easy, 'cause you are one. Remember, I know you from way back, and you haven't changed one bit.'

He's too much, but I'm not looking for a fight. If I had to I could flatten Matt with ease. No worries. But a punch-up is the last thing I want right now. I have more important things to do with my time and energy. 'Suit yourself,' I go to climb over the fence but he drags me down. 'Hey!'

Still holding on to my shirt, he says through gritted teeth, 'If you hurt my sister, I'll come after you.'

I shove him back hard enough to break his hold. 'What would be so wrong with me seeing Isabel anyway? She's a nice girl. I like her.'

He comes back quickly, pointing a finger roughly at my chest. 'You're *not* a nice guy.'

I can't help my eyes sliding to Rochelle, who until

this moment has been content to say nothing except with her expressive face and eyes. She knows there's no real history assignment. She takes history too. Whatever her reasons, she's keeping quiet. I don't want to think about why. Just looking at her now wearing that smug smile, what is she thinking? Probably remembering those conversations she initiated so long ago that forced a wedge between Matt and me. Obviously she doesn't care.

Matt catches the look I share with his girlfriend, misinterpreting it once again. He grabs my shirt front, letting loose with a fast left hook hard to the side of my head. His fist hits my cheek under my left eye, knocking me backwards. I get up, putting a finger to the rapidly swelling bruise. My fingertip comes away with a little blood. Hell!

Dillon suddenly appears at a run. 'Hey, what's going on?'

Matt turns slightly, an open hand held high. 'Stay out of this, Dillon.'

Dillon looks to me for an answer. 'He doesn't like me hanging around with his sister,' I say.

'Oh. Nothing to get into a fight about, is it?' asks Dillon.

The question is directed at Matt. His only response is the narrowing of his eyes. Then he steps right up to my face. 'If you hurt Isabel—'

This time I shove him back before he gets another chance to connect his fist with my face. 'Back off, Matt!'

Dillon grabs Matt's arm, keeping him from coming at me again.

'I swear –' Matt says, trying to break free of Dillon's hold.

I don't wait for him to elaborate. After all, his concern is for his sister, and this I can respect. 'I'd never hurt Isabel. You have my word.'

He stares at me with hard, dark eyes. 'Just how good is that, Ethan?'

He's remembering the many times I tried to tell him I wasn't after his girl. There was just some weird connection between Rochelle and me, an attraction that was hard to sever with a clean swipe no matter how I tried. But he wouldn't listen then, and there's too much time past now to try explaining all over again. So I say nothing. I just turn my back, jump the fence, and hurry into the woods.

Isabel will be waiting.

Chapter Eleven

Isabel

He's late, but at last I see him walking towards me, his hands dug deeply into his school trouser pockets, his head hanging low. Straight away I sense something is wrong. I start walking towards him, my heart doing a funny slow thump. Then I see his face. 'What happened?'

But I know already this is Matt's work. He's been giving me a hard time the whole past week, drilling me with questions about what I'm doing spending so much time with Ethan. The problem is Matt knows me so well, brushing his questions off is sure to make him only more suspicious. But what else can I do? Telling him the truth is of course out of the question. It would break the code, a vital rule. Anonymity is what ensures the Guard's protection. So I can't tell him why Ethan and I train up here every day, and I'm not going to give it up just 'cause Matt can't handle the thought that I'm spending time alone with Ethan. I just have to let Matt jump to his own conclusions. So far, Ethan hasn't done anything to make me believe one negative word Matt's said against him.

Ethan's finger runs over the egg-size swelling under his left eye. 'It's nothing,' he says. 'Sorry I'm late.'

'Here.' I take his hand and lead him to a fallen tree by the lake edge. 'Let me look at this.' It's a nasty bump, but the cut in the centre could only have been made by something sharp, probably Matt's silver ring, the one Rochelle gave him for his birthday last year. 'I'll get some water. It's so cold it should help reduce the swelling. My brother sure has one sharp fist.'

As I go to leave him, he grabs my elbow, stopping me. 'I didn't mean to upset him. Really. It wasn't a huge fight or anything. It just happened so fast.'

'So what does Matt look like now?'

He looks affronted, and I get it straight away – Ethan didn't hit Matt back. 'I'm sorry. I didn't mean to assume you'd pay back with your own fists. I'm not going to make excuses for my brother. I just wish he wasn't so obsessed with protecting me.'

He makes a scoffing sound, but softens his sarcasm with a small smile.

I go to the water's edge and dip the corner of my shirt into the icy water. Coming back I get on my knees in front of him and dab at the swollen cut with the wet shirt, washing away the few drops of surface blood. Being this close to Ethan starts having a strange effect on me. Suddenly my senses are heightened. My breathing comes short and fast, and my mouth goes dry, while my heart starts thumping so loud that I can hear its pounding rhythm between my ears.

'How does it look?' he asks.

Gently I run my finger over the swelling, wishing with all my heart to ease the pain, as part of me feels very responsible. If only Matt wasn't so protective. If only I could find a way to heal the rift between him and Ethan!

'That feels good.'

'Hmm?' I ask, unaware until now of the soothing effect my touch must be having.

Slowly I become conscious of Ethan's eyes focused on my face. Our eyes meet and my breathing stops altogether. My lips feel so dry I have to moisten them with my tongue and for a crazy, wild second I think Ethan's going to kiss me. But it's only his hand coming up to touch the side of his own face. Suddenly he jumps off the log and I nearly fall over with the force of his sudden move. 'What's wrong?'

'Wrong? Nothing's wrong. The lump is gone, that's what.'

He comes right up to my face, pointing to the spot below his left eye. 'Correct me if I'm wrong, but there's nothing there now, is there?'

I shake my head, unable to believe this.

'Even the pain has disappeared.'

Unconsciously I touch the area that was, only seconds ago, massive swollen tissue, rapidly bruising. Now there's nothing but smooth clear skin, not a scratch or mark anywhere. 'Did I really ...?'

He throws his hands in the air. 'Yes! You healed me. *You ... healed ... me!*'

'What does this mean, Ethan?'

'I think it could only mean one thing. It's time you met Arkarian.'

Chapter Twelve

Isabel

But I don't get to meet this famous wizard straight away. Apparently he's on some very important mission to ancient Athens, and will be away three days. Which is fine by me, as I'm not sure I want to meet Arkarian. It will be the final confirmation that this 'other world' stuff is real.

'He's not a wizard,' Ethan whispers.

We're three-quarters through our history lesson, sitting right in the back row in the far corner together. I catch Mr Carter casting a hostile look down our way, his eyes fixed on Ethan. He pauses, then goes on with his lesson, leaving us undisturbed. I write, '*What, then?*' on a slip of paper and quietly slide it to the edge of my desk. Ethan glances over, leans across and scrawls beneath my two words, '*TruthMaster*'.

'What?' Stupidly I hiss this word out loud. I had just never seen the term '*TruthMaster*' before, and it takes me by surprise.

In a flash Mr Carter is standing in front of us. Seeing the danger, both Ethan and I grab for the slip of paper with the unusual title scrawled on it. But Mr Carter is faster and snatches the paper up first, holding it at an angle high enough to read. As he does this his eyes widen, then narrow, then focus fiercely on Ethan. He doesn't need to say a word for either of us to know how angry he's suddenly become. His face has gone a dark shade, almost purple, his pupils dilating until his eyes look black, the paper in his hand scrunched to the size of a pea.

With the whole class watching, obviously dying to know what horrendous words could possibly be scrawled on the now crumpled up paper, Mr Carter calms himself, slots the paper into his trouser pocket and carefully takes his expression down a notch or two. 'Detention,' he says to Ethan in a deathly quiet tone. 'This afternoon. I'm supervising. It should prove an interesting hour.' He turns his attention to me. 'But I want to see you, Isabel, immediately after class.'

Ethan jumps straight out of his seat, flinging it backwards to hit the wall with a metallic scraping sound. 'What do you want with Isabel?' And in a belated attempt to soften his aggressive tone, he adds, 'I mean ... sir?'

Ethan's exaggerated defensive reaction has everybody sniggering and asking questions. I tug on his shirt sleeve. 'Sit down, you idiot!'

He glances around at all the attention he's gathering, his eyes in embarrassment shifting left and right. Finally he sits. Mr Carter shakes his head. 'You have so much to learn.' His words feel as if they have a double meaning. His hostility towards Ethan unnerves me, but so does his strange manner.

The buzzer indicating the end of the lesson sounds

and everyone starts gathering their stuff and leaving the room.

Ethan lags behind with me, but when the class is almost empty, Mr Carter orders him out. Reluctantly, and with a concerned lingering look, Ethan leaves.

When we're alone, Mr Carter asks me to sit down. I perch on top of one of the desks up front so that I'm closer to his eye level. 'Did I do something wrong, sir?' 'Other than your recent choice of seating arrangement, not at all.'

I ignore his sarcasm and remain silent. He says, 'I just want to give you a piece of friendly advice.'

It may be friendly but the tone of his voice makes me uncomfortable and nervous. My fingers clench tightly in my lap. He notices. 'I don't mean to frighten you, Isabel. I'm here to offer my hand in friendship.'

'What makes you think I need your friendship?'

'Hopefully you never will.'

I don't get it. This conversation is really weird. Teachers don't usually take such personal interest in their students. And here he is offering his friendship, yet to Ethan ... Suddenly I just have to ask. 'You're very hostile to Ethan. What do you have against him? He's one of your best students. Probably *the* best.'

'I'm not about to discuss my other students with you, Isabel. But it would be a good idea if you didn't hang around with him so much. He could have an adverse influence on you.'

'What makes you say that? He's a straight-A student, I'm a C. How can his influence be bad?'

'I've heard you've been hanging around a lot together after school.'

Finally I see what's going on, the whole point of this

conversation. 'Has my brother been talking to you?'

He nods slowly. 'Matt did approach me, asking about the content of the history project I set the class. He seemed to think there was too much in it. Told me how you and Ethan spend hours every afternoon and most of the weekend working together.'

Heat invades my body, niggling little electric pulses generating in my toes and working upwards, energising every cell. I try hard to stifle the insistent urge to skin my brother alive the second I see him. I take a slow, deep breath to try and calm down. 'What did you tell him?'

Mr Carter looks me straight in the eyes. 'I told him that if he had a complaint about my teaching techniques, perhaps he should take it up with the principal.'

My mouth drops open in a soft gasp. Mr Carter didn't tell Matt the truth, blowing our cover.

'As a teacher, Isabel, and as a friend,' he goes on, 'I can only advise. Ethan Roberts is a distracting influence. A C student can't afford distractions.'

I can't help my head shaking 'cause now I'm confused. One minute Mr Carter is coming down hard on Ethan, the next he's covering up for Ethan spending time with me.

He looks at me piercingly, and my spine prickles all the way down to my tailbone. 'Do you think I'm too hard on Ethan?' he asks.

'Well, yes.'

'Isabel, I'm not hard enough.'

'I'm a little confused,' I say.

'That's understandable. But one thing you must remember: trust *no one,* no one but yourself.'

Who is he warning me against? It sounds like Ethan, but Mr Carter's natural dislike for Ethan could cloud his judgement there. Just what is he trying to say? This conversation is too weird. I get down off the desk, eager to leave.

'Do you hear me, Isabel?'

I nod, backing towards the door.

'If you ever need someone to talk to, remember, you can count on me.'

At last I'm outside and take a deep cleansing breath. What was Mr Carter on about? Was he warning me against Ethan? And why would he tell me I can count on *him*, when he just finished telling me to trust no one, no one but myself?

Chapter Thirteen

Ethan

Arkarian meets us outside the entry to his chambers, welcoming Isabel with open arms and a warm embrace. 'It's so lovely to meet you at last, Isabel,' he says. 'Ah, all is unfolding exactly as it should.'

Isabel's face turns beetroot red. She swallows hard and licks her lips, eyes fixed on Arkarian's bright-blue hair. Today it hangs loose around his shoulders, enhancing its vivid colour. I laugh at her reaction. 'You'll get used to Arkarian's cryptic chattering, and his blue hair – eventually.'

'How you flatter me, Ethan,' he says drily while waving his hand towards the rock wall as if annoyed it hasn't read his mind and disappeared already. Obediently it opens to allow us entry into his domain. When I first walked into this dark hallway, softly lit with torches hanging from brackets on the polished rock walls, I was too young to take it all in. I can recall no feelings other than awe at the rock wall disappearing before my eyes. Isabel's eyes take in every detail of wall and ceiling as if memorising the position of each hair-line crack.

We get to the main chamber, which resembles a workstation you'd find at NASA headquarters a hundred years from now. The room, octagonal in shape, is lined from floor to ceiling with technical equipment that makes no sound except the occasional soft beep with a corresponding flash of light. The centrepiece is what naturally seizes Isabel's attention. She walks over and lifts a hand as if she can touch the palace that lies within the 3-D holographic sphere with the image of London at its centre.

Arkarian motions with his hand, and the whole 3-D sphere rotates so that now Isabel has a magnified image of the inside of the Palace of Westminster, specifically the Great Hall, where at least a hundred or more are gathered as dinner is bustled away by hardworking servants. A man dressed in bright clothing gathers the crowd's attention; sitting before them on a stool, he starts reciting a musical poem which soon has the audience in stitches.

'Geoffrey Chaucer,' Arkarian explains. 'On cue and on time. Good, good!' He rolls his hand again and this time the magnification is reversed considerably. Now we can neither see nor hear the goings-on inside the palace.

'Th—this history is happening now?' Isabel asks with a stammer.

Arkarian produces three hand-carved stools, and their sudden materialisation has Isabel softly gasping. I point to the stool in front of her with an open hand and she quietly sits, the three of us forming a triangle.

'This is the time period I'm monitoring at the moment. There's trouble brewing.'

'That's where we come into it,' I explain.

'Yes,' Arkarian says. 'And very soon too, Ethan. So how goes your training of Isabel?'

'Wonderful.' I explain how adept and skilled Isabel is in the physical arts, and how we've recently made progress in developing her healing skills.

'But I still can't heal anything on call.'

'Only when your passions are aroused,' Arkarian correctly observes. 'When you feel with your heart.' He forms a fist over the centre of his chest. 'That's how it is at first.'

Arkarian has Isabel completely enchanted. Her eyes gaze at him with a mixture of wonder and awe. I clear my throat to get her attention and to stop her staring so hard. Finally she flicks an embarrassed look towards me. 'Hmm? What were you saying?'

Her reaction amuses me, though I don't really get it. 'I wasn't saying anything. Arkarian was.'

She nods and swings her gaze back to Arkarian, her skin fast turning the colour of blood. That's twice she's blushed in the last ten minutes. What's going on with her? Now she's touching the hair around her face, tugging some behind her ears. 'Oh, yeah, that's right,' she says. 'Well the only times I've healed successfully was when I cut myself and unconsciously willed the wound to heal –'

'And when your brother hit me and you felt responsible,' I finish for her, glad to see her brain's functioning normally again.

'And what of your other skill?' Arkarian asks softly.

Isabel glances at me and I at her. What is Arkarian talking about? At our blank look he sighs.

'Don't pressure yourselves. It will evolve, with hard work and persistence.'

He doesn't say any more, but goes on to explain a little to Isabel about our positions as Guardians of Time. 'It has always been thus,' he begins. 'For longer than I can remember, and I've been alive for six hundred years.'

Isabel's eyes nearly fall out of her head when he reveals this about himself. 'How is that possible?'

'It's a skill. Like healing is yours. Mine is the ability to remain young, a kind of resistance to the aging process.'

'Wow.'

'Each of us that is Named has at least two skills, and sometimes, if we're fortunate enough, we have three. At your initiation ceremony the Lords of the various Houses will endow you with a special gift. Sometimes these take time to develop – you have to work on them. But your skills are different: you were born with them.'

He then goes on to explain about the purpose of those that are Named to be members of the Guard. And how the Order of Chaos devotes itself to changing certain aspects of history, attempting to create an altered present that will evolve into a future environment that suits their own requirements. 'Chaos, as we call this opposing Order, feeds and grows on evil – death, destruction, war, plague, malice. The more they create, the larger their armies grow, and the smaller ours become.' He leans forward in his seat. 'So you see, Isabel, we have our work cut out. And now you are to be one of us. But before you agree, you must understand there is always the possibility something can go wrong in any mission.'

Isabel's eyes drop to the ground, giving herself a

private moment to absorb Arkarian's words. Finally she lifts her head. 'I understand what you're saying, but I think I'm missing something.'

Arkarian shoots me a stare which shows just how impressed he is. Of course he knows Isabel's thoughts, but he is not going to reveal this to her at this early stage in her career. Most people become instantly uncomfortable with that knowledge. It's Arkarian's other skill, the one he didn't bring up earlier. 'Go on.'

'Well, why do we need these armies? Why do these people – this Order called Chaos – go to the trouble of stuffing up the past? What's the point?'

'The Goddess of Chaos wants the world at her feet. As head of her Order, she wants to rule.'

Isabel's eyes open wide. 'She wants to take over the world? You mean like a government?'

'The Order's ultimate aim is to destroy everything that we know is good, including human nature.'

I quietly watch Isabel for her reaction to this news. It's a lot to comprehend in one hit.

'They've already made two attempts to win control,' Arkarian explains. 'The third will be the final conflict.'

'Good will win, won't it?' Isabel asks for confirmation.

'The problem is that though the Guard is prophesied to win, Chaos works hard to change that.'

'That's why they tamper with history,' I add to the explanation. 'By changing certain past events, they can alter what we know as the present, creating havoc and destruction –'

'Which feeds their armies,' Isabel finishes.

Arkarian nods. 'They mean to create an environment that nurtures their growth and success, and they are growing now at an alarming rate.'

'So you're saying Chaos creates things like disease and war?' Isabel asks.

'Widespread diseases like plagues,' I explain, helping her to understand. 'Where there is disaster, it's usually at the hand of the Order of Chaos.'

'Unbelievable! But this conflict, it's not planned to happen for a long time, is it?' she asks hopefully. 'I mean, like way, way after we've been and gone, right?'

Arkarian avoids answering. Isabel isn't ready to hear this yet. It will just freak her out. Instead he moves us all back to the holographic sphere of London and the goings-on inside Westminster Palace, explaining my mission: to ensure that the young Prince Richard, son of the Black Prince, grandson of King Edward III, becomes King of England. His father has already died, about a year previously in France, and soon his grand-father will join him.

'There are plans to twist the minds of the council, but that's not your concern, Ethan. I believe an attempt on the future king's life will be made in the next twenty-four hours. It's going to be your duty to protect him and thwart this assassination attempt.'

'When do we leave?' I ask.

Arkarian straightens and looks at us both in turn. 'Tonight.'

'*Tonight?* But it hasn't even been *two* weeks! Isabel's not ready.'

Isabel has her own ideas. 'What are you talking about? After the things you just told me, of course I'm ready. I'm ready to do anything!'

Arkarian grins, looking pleased at her enthusiasm, and everyone's mood lightens. But I'm Isabel's Trainer, and enthusiasm is not enough. There are so many things I haven't explained yet, like the transition that occurs in the Citadel for starters.

Arkarian, knowing my inner thoughts, as I haven't bothered to shelter them, taps my shoulder. 'Remember, Isabel is to be an observer only tonight.'

'Sure, but there's still so much to learn. Physically, Isabel's ready for just about anything –'

'Thanks,' she says with a smile.

'But what of her other skill? We don't even know what that is.'

Arkarian waves my fears away. 'You're a talented guard, Ethan. Have some faith. Now go and instruct your Apprentice on how to prepare for her first journey. Her safe transportation is ultimately your responsibility.'

Chapter Fourteen

Ethan

As we walk down from the mountain, I try explaining what Isabel needs to know. 'Your journey into the past will happen while you sleep in your own bed.'

'Isn't that a bit risky? I mean, why can't the transfer take place –' she shrugs – 'in Arkarian's chambers?'

'I guess the transfer can take place anywhere, but it's essential that your body and mind are in a peaceful, relaxed state. This is something that's usually achieved when we sleep.'

'OK, so we have to be in an unconscious state?'

'Yeah, sort of. And while you're home and in your own bed, sleeping, it's unlikely anyone's going to notice anything unusual happening to you. You see, there's always the slight possibility of discovery, even if you're only away for a short time.'

'But if I'm home and appear to be sleeping normally in my own bed ...'

'And your mum walks in to check on you,' I continue her line of thought, 'she'll just think you're sleeping.'

'All right, I get that.'

'But if you're in Arkarian's chamber when you're transferred into the past, and have to be away for longer than expected, your mum, or anyone who's looking and can't find you, might start asking questions. When you're on a mission, I've learned, there's always the risk of the unexpected.'

She looks thoughtfully at the ground. 'OK, but I don't get how it works. The whole transfer bit.'

'It's like this,' I say, half turning towards her and using my hands to make sure she understands. 'Your soul can only be in one place at one time, but it can leave your body and occupy another, temporarily.'

'Then what happens to the owner of the body? Where's their soul?'

'I don't know. Maybe visiting another time. Don't worry about it.'

'OK, but are you sure I'll just look like I'm sleeping? It's not that Mum comes in to check on me a lot or anything. But she is a worrier.'

'Well, as long she doesn't try to wake you, everything will be fine.'

She frowns. 'And if she does try to wake me?'

'You'll look as if you've slipped into a coma with no ordinary vital signs.'

'What!'

I hold my hand up for her to wait a second while I explain. 'Don't worry so much! You won't be away for more than a few minutes, ten or twenty probably at the longest. Remember what I said about time and how it's only measured on a linear basis by us mortals?'

She tries to understand. 'Yeah, but—'

'Look, a minute in your sleep tonight will be approximately equal to a whole day in transit or in the past.

The most I was ever away was three months. And that is unusual, but I was needed badly and Arkarian watched over my mortal state for most of the ninety minutes or so.'

'OK, I think I get that part,' she says, but I get the feeling she's nodding and agreeing only on the surface.

'All the same, there are some precautions you should take.'

She tenses. 'Precautions? Like what? Don't leave a thing out, Ethan. There's so much—'

'Slow down! Remember you're only an observer tonight. You're not to do or touch anything, nor speak with anyone if possible – unless *not* speaking would appear suspicious. The idea is to fit in, watch and, hopefully, even enjoy yourself.'

'That's another thing: what do we do about language differences, accents and stuff?'

I curse Arkarian. Couldn't he have given me a bit longer to prepare her? 'There's this place called the Citadel, it's sort of a changing place,' I try to explain. 'It's where you go before your journey, and the last place you see before returning to your mortal body.'

'Why is it called the Citadel?'

'I don't know how it got its name, except that it suits. When you see it, you'll know what I mean. It's like a palace, and yet like a fortress or a whole village in one building. And there you'll be endowed with everything you need for the world you're about to inhabit.'

'You're talking about changing clothes and things?'

'More than that. Your appearance, language, under-standing of the appropriate cultures, basically every-thing you need to know.'

The more I explain, the more jittery Isabel becomes. She starts scratching invisible itches across her arms, tugging on her earlobes alternately, hugging herself and speaking rapidly. 'I think I get it ... I'm not sure, though ... I'm going to forget something ... Will you be there waiting?' She spins around, grabbing both my arms. 'You will be, won't you? Waiting in this ... this Citadel place, right, Ethan?'

We've stopped at the beginning of her quiet lane, the place where I usually leave her to walk on ahead alone. Tonight I decide to lead her right to her front door. I prise her fingers from my arms and, holding her hand firmly, start walking down the lane towards the distant light that marks her front porch. 'Isabel, you're going to be fine. And if there's anything I've learned about you these past two weeks, I know you're going to enjoy this journey. I swear you will. *Trust me.*'

She frowns when I say these last two words. 'Is something wrong?' I ask.

'No,' she replies quickly. 'Not really. It's just some-thing Mr Carter said.'

'Whatever it was, forget it. You know he's a jerk who's got it in for me.'

She nods but doesn't say anything more. And as we start down her footpath I try to remember if I've left anything out. 'Just go to bed as normal, not early or anything, but as you would on any average night. Got that?'

She exhales loudly. 'Right.'

We're nearly at her porch and I think this might be a good place to leave her, but just then the front door opens and Matt comes out. 'One more thing,' I say quickly, dropping her hand. The last thing I need tonight is a confrontation with an overprotective brother who hates me. 'Never say you're going to bed 'cause you're not feeling well or you have a headache or something like that. Sure as anything your mum will come in later and check on you. Or in your case, probably your mum and Matt.'

She scoffs a soft agreement and, seeing Matt make his way to the front porch stairs, runs off ahead of me, waving me away.

I decide to stand and wait exactly where I am to make sure she gets in without any hassle. As she goes to pass Matt I hear him ask, 'How's that history assignment going? Is it finished yet?'

Staring straight into his face, she replies, 'As a matter of fact, Ethan and I have just asked for an extension. We've just got so much to cover, we reckon it'll take at least another month.'

I can't help grinning. Matt's look of distress is worth waiting for. As Isabel runs inside, he turns to stare me out. I give a little wave and move back into the darkness. A few metres out of sight, I take off in a run. I have a lot to do in preparation for tonight's mission. It has to go well. It just has to. Before tonight I've always worked alone, but now I have Isabel to consider, to be responsible for as my Apprentice.

And I just can't shake this feeling that there's more to this mission than Arkarian is letting on. My instincts tell me it has to do with Isabel, or why else would the Tribunal be rushing through her training like this? I know I should trust them completely, but I can't help feeling uneasy.

Chapter Fifteen

Isabel

Mum's boyfriend Jimmy is here again. I try to bypass the two of them sitting closely on the settee watching television, but Jimmy calls out, 'Here she is, darl! Told you this little lady can look after herself. Isn't that right, sweetcakes?'

Inside I cringe, but I don't let it show. I sort of grunt a reply, the most I can manage. It's not that Jimmy's a bad person or anything, he's just irritating. He's small but built like a brick chimney, and his voice is like a young boy's that hasn't broken properly – that in-between stage where sometimes it squeaks and sometimes it reveals a hint of coming masculinity.

'When're we gonna meet this boyfriend of yours?' he asks.

I really don't feel like answering. Right now my stomach is rolling. I don't want to get into any sort of conversation while I feel as if I'm about to spew, not with mum, and especially not with Jimmy. He's been hanging around so much lately, staying overnight a couple of times a week. At least Mum's happy. I can't complain that he treats her bad or anything; he makes her laugh. And, well, Mum deserves happiness, and company for that matter. Matt and I are getting older, we're not going to be living with her for ever. It's just that Jimmy can be so annoying and he asks a lot of questions that are really none of his business.

'He's not my boyfriend.'

'Ah,' he says in a teasing tone. 'But I bet you wish he was.'

Oooh!

Luckily Matt comes in. He also tries to avoid Jimmy and starts heading straight upstairs. But Jimmy's too quick. 'Where's your little princess tonight, Matt?'

'She heard you were coming over.'

Well, isn't he in a good mood? Jimmy just laughs, an annoying whining sound. Suddenly I'm so tired I decide to go straight to bed – forget dinner, forget everything.

Mum, as always, picks up on my mood. 'Whatever you're doing with that boy, it's draining you. I haven't seen you this tired since that triathlon you competed in last month. You're not overdoing it, I hope?'

'No, Mum, I promise.'

'Good. Now have you had dinner yet? We saved you a plate. I could put it in the microwave if you like.'

Her offer is tempting, but I don't think my stomach could handle one morsel of food. 'It's OK, I think I'll just go to bed. I have a bit of a headache.' *Oh no, I can't believe I just said that!* 'Ah, I don't really. The headache, I mean ...' I touch the side of my face where a headache is now really starting to take hold.

Mum half climbs out of her seat. 'Are you all right, dear?'

'Yes. Fine. The headache's gone. Truly.'

I pass Matt, who looks at me weirdly. It's no surprise when he follows me right into my room. I try to close the door on him, but he gets through too quickly, plonking himself down on my green plastic blow-up chair. 'What's with you?'

'I'm sorry? I should be asking what's with you! What a hide you've got checking up on me with my history teacher!'

He simply shrugs like it's all part of the job – the job of suffocating me.

'Why can't you leave Ethan alone?'

'I don't like him.' He pretends a sudden interest in his fingernails.

'You used to be best friends.'

'That was a long time ago. Before ...'

I kick off my shoes and sit on the edge of my bed. Maybe, finally, Matt will tell me what happened to his friendship with Ethan. 'Before?' I coax as he seems to have come to a dead end.

'It's none of your business, Isabel.'

'Oh, come on. Don't you think it is now? I mean, you keep telling me not to spend so much time with Ethan 'cause he's "not a nice guy", but you don't give me anything substantial to go on.'

'Look, it has to do with Rochelle.'

'Well, that explains everything,' I say.

'What's that supposed to mean?'

'Where Rochelle's concerned, you're blind.'

He gets up, mad as hell. 'Has he twisted your mind?'

'We haven't spoken a word about Rochelle, actually. We've got better things to do with our time.'

One eyebrow lifts in a fine arch. 'And just what is that, by the way? You've been spending more time with

Ethan than at home lately.'

'Don't switch the subject,' I snap at him, hoping to distract him from asking any more probing questions.

We're both quiet for a minute and my weariness must show.

'Look, I'm sorry, Isabel. I don't mean to be so heavy with you. It's just the thought of Ethan and you together, it doesn't wash with me.'

'That's good.'

'What?'

'For starters, we're not "together", we're just friends working on a history project. That's all.' Unfortunately, that's the whole of it. Ethan doesn't appear interested in starting a relationship with me. Maybe he's just being careful 'cause Matt's so domineering. 'And anyway, it's not you who needs to like him. It's me. And I do, just for the record.'

'That's what worries me. You're spending so much time with him when I know how you've always felt about this guy. You've been in love with him since you were five years old.'

I could deny it but there's no point. And if this is the root of Matt's concern, if I can just manage to allay his fears, maybe he'll ease up a little. I lift my hands, trying to portray a genuine understanding. 'Matt, I promise you I have my feelings completely under control with Ethan. I'm not that scrawny little kid with the huge crush any more. I can deal with my emotions now. You have to believe me.'

He stares at me for a long minute, thinking hard. Maybe I've finally reached him, 'cause he turns away with a weary kind of nod. At the door he half-turns back. 'You're a bad liar, Isabel. But I understand what you're telling me. I'll back off for now, but if I find out he's ever hurt you, he'll be sorry he was born.'

The door closes behind him and finally I'm alone. I breathe a heavy sigh of relief and rub the side of my face where that headache is beginning to take hold. I'm tired all right, but too edgy to sit still long enough to fall asleep. Act normal, Ethan said. Easier said than done. He's been doing this time-shift stuff for years; but this is my first experience. I get off the bed and change into my red satin boxers and gym top. Is this what I'll be wearing when I arrive at the Citadel? I decide to throw my flannel pyjamas over the top. I get into bed and try to relax, I must be joking. That's impossible. Everywhere suddenly itches, even my scalp. I get out of bed and brush my hair, tying it back in a neat plait. I go back to bed but realise I have to use the bathroom. Quickly, I run down the hall and back again before I bump into Matt or Mum or worse, Jimmy, and get caught in meaningless, time-consuming conversation. This time I get into bed and try to slow down. My fingers are tingling and I'm slightly hyper-ventilating. *Slow!* I tell myself. *Breathe slow.*

I fall asleep and dream. Everyone is in it – Ethan, Matt, Mum, Jimmy, even Arkarian, whom I only met today. They're all gathered by the lake where Ethan and I go to train. I can see them all clearly, talking to each other as if they're just biding their time waiting for something. I must be in this dream too, it's starting to feel uncomfortably real, but I'm not part of their casual group.

Suddenly an eerie sensation hits my senses, as if something unidentifiable has entered the dream. It has an evil feel or aura. It's so obvious to me, yet the other five remain unconcerned, talking softly to each other, standing in a circle.

The sense of evil intensifies with the sound of a distant roar like a pride of hungry lions on a rampage. It goes on for a seemingly endless stretch of time, and I can swear in my dream that it's coming from the woods, yet somehow also from within my head. I wave at the group standing in a circle, trying to warn them to look into the woodlands to their right.

'There's something in there! Something evil! I feel it!' I scream at them.

But no one hears me, no one looks to where the evil is growing larger and more powerful, like a gathering electric storm. I need to warn them.

'Look!' I yell again, tears now coursing down my face, my arms outstretched, mouth open and strained in a loud scream.

And then I see it, a massive creature with a disfigured face with a single, wild-looking yellow eye, dressed in strange clothes and wielding a long sword.

It comes charging out of the woods like an enraged bear.

'Over there!' I scream one last time, for if they don't turn and run now they will all be massacred for sure by this hideous creature.

No one looks.

Chapter Sixteen

Ethan

I get home and Dad's waiting, which takes me completely by surprise. He usually goes about his day without noticing anything I do or say or whatever. Mum's different. Even while she suffers from severe bouts of depression, she still manages to maintain an interest in my life. I remember once, after a particularly long stint when she ended up in hospital for ten days, she told me that she would never really get over losing her daughter so suddenly, but sometimes her mind needs to take a holiday, and so it goes off on its own for a while.

'You missed dinner,' Dad says, leaning against the dining-table edge. 'That makes a perfect record – every night this week.'

His words have me frowning and wondering at the same time. I'm surprised that he noticed. Could he possibly be returning to the man Mum told me he once was? I decide not to get my hopes up, after all, it could just be that Mum's been nagging.

'Apparently you didn't tell your mother where you've been going or who you've been hanging around with.

You know how she worries.'

Ah, well, now that explains it. 'Sorry, Dad. My mistake. Tell Mum I was with Isabel.'

'Isabel Becket?'

'Yeah, why?'

'No reason. I just haven't heard the name in a long time. Isn't she Matt's sister? The one who used to jump out of trees all the time?'

A vision of Isabel climbing that old camphor laurel tree yesterday and hanging upside-down for thirty minutes, just to prove she could hold on longer than I could, flashes through my mind, making me smile. 'She doesn't do that any more.' Unless provoked, I add silently. Which doesn't take much.

'So you're saying you've been with Isabel every day for the past couple of weeks?'

'That's right.' What's got into him? 'Why the third degree, Dad?'

'It just seems odd, that's all.'

'Why?' A better question would be, *Why would you notice?*

His head does a shake that is more like a shiver. 'Where do you go, you and Isabel, all this time?'

His questions are heading somewhere. I just wish I could second-guess him, but I have no idea what he's on about. 'We just hang around by the lake, mostly. Why do you ask?'

'Where around the lake, Ethan? Not round near the falls?' His voice drops and tightens and I get a glimpse of where he's coming from now. But there's no way he'll come right out and say it. In fact, Sera's name has never been mentioned in all the years since she died. Sometimes I just want to scream it as loud as I can, right in Dad's face. Maybe it would jolt him out of his stupor, or whatever it is he slid into all those years ago.

'We do go round the other side, Dad, but nowhere near the falls, nowhere near the unusual flowers that grow around there.'

He hears the word 'flowers' and stiffens. Mum, who's been listening for the last few minutes from the doorway, comes in and gives me a hug. 'Hungry, Ethan?'

I hug her back. 'Not really, Mum. I think I'll go to bed.'

They let me pass without another word, which is a good thing, as the air in here has grown so thick that the act of breathing has become difficult.

In my room I flop down on the bed and stare at the ceiling. It's too early to sleep, but I'm dead tired. I decide to close my eyes for a couple of minutes, then take a shower and get ready for my mission. Instead I drop into another of my vivid nightmares. I feel it descend on me the second I close my eyes, but I'm helpless to stop it.

This time I'm swimming. In the lake, near the falls. I'm older than usual, about my own age now. There's no one about, just me and the lake, the water cold and dark, reflecting a deeply overcast sky. I wait with something akin to anticipation, knowing in my subconscious mind what's about to make an appearance: evil. There's no other term for it, no other way to describe the feelings, the sensations, the horror that evolves.

In my dream I start for the shore with long, fast strokes, that urgent feeling starting to kick into my stomach. It's out there, in the woods, watching, waiting. I hear it groan and every hair on my body shivers with trepidation. And then I spot her playing by the water's edge, her black curls bobbing around her head as she joyfully builds a castle made of stones.

'Sera!'

Too far off to hear me. I quicken my strokes. The creature is now bearing down on her at a run.

'Sera! Get up!'

She doesn't hear me and I stroke faster than ever before in my life. With every muscle aching, my lungs ready to burst, I swim even harder, faster. I have to reach her before the creature lays his hand atop her forehead. *'Sera!'*

Metres from the shore I hear the creature roar a victorious sound. He knows his prey is only seconds away from his touch. Then I see him emerge from the wooded edge, giving Sera mere seconds in which to move. *'Sera, run for your life!'*

She lifts her head and our eyes lock. I freeze half in, half out of the water. *Oh, God, no!*

It's not Sera any more. The face that stares back at me with wide and trusting eyes is Isabel's.

Chapter Seventeen

Isabel

I sit straight up in bed, totally disoriented, my body soaked in sweat, my heart racing and jerking, tears still moist across my face. It's dark but my eyes quickly adjust. I'm still in my bedroom. My clock reads 11.46 p.m.

I remember now the dream and the horror I felt caught within it. Where did that nightmare come from? Hell, obviously.

I lie back down just to get my breath and calm my racing heart. Slowly, I close my eyes, folding one trembling hand over the other across my chest. I'm so uptight I'll never get transported like this. And that nightmare, that can just go back to wherever it came from.

I hear footsteps coming up the stairs and unconsciously hold my breath. It's Mum. But she's not alone. I hear her give a little laugh. Another voice, only slightly deeper, laughs back. Mum shushes Jimmy with a giggle; their footsteps move on past my door.

Silence.

And then a rat-a-tat sound starts up in the ceiling.

That possum's back, probably, or a bird's got into the roof and can't find its way out. A creak sounds at the window, then a bang against my opposite bedroom wall. That's Matt's room. He's probably just rolled over and thumped the wall accidentally. Every sound tonight seems magnified; my senses are working overtime. If I keep this up I'll still be awake when dawn arrives. I forgot to ask Ethan what happens if I don't get to sleep, if I don't reach that relaxed state of body and mind. Surely my soul can't transfer while I'm still awake? This thought has my heart pounding again. I don't want to slip into a coma-like state while even partly conscious. I start thinking Ethan was right when he said I wasn't ready, psychologically at least.

As I think of Ethan my mind begins to slow. His face swims before my eyes, his voice calling to me softly, his hands outstretched towards mine. Slowly, I drift into that semi-conscious state of near sleep. A tingling starts up in my body. For a second I jerk awake, then quickly relax my breathing. It could be nothing, just hyperventilating slightly again. But then the sensation increases. Instinctively I want to fight it, but my mind has passed that state of consciousness now. I'm too far gone asleep. The last thought I have is of weightlessness, complete and utter freedom of movement and of mind.

Chapter Eighteen

Ethan

Somehow I pass from the dream and straight to the Citadel. That's never happened to me before. I think Arkarian has something to do with it, rescuing me from that nightmare that never ceases to plague my brain. Why can't I be rid of the thing? When I was little, my mother took me to counsellors. Each of them had a different idea on how to get me through the long scary nights. I've slept with lights on, puppies at my feet, soft music, meditative tapes, warm glasses of milk and honey, canaries and goldfish. Nothing worked. Every night the terrors recurred. Only after I started seeing Arkarian in the mountain did they ease off. He taught me mind control as well as all the physical skills of self-defence. Action seemed to help. I threw myself into the training so hard that sometimes I just fell asleep at night from pure exhaustion.

'Well, well, look who we have here!'

I spin around and find myself in the worst company ever – Carter's. It's a shock because I never usually meet anyone in the Citadel, except occasionally Arkarian for some last-minute instructions before a mission, especially if something's changed that I should know about.

The Citadel is a strange, wondrous place, laced with staircases and winding hallways, rooms decorated in exquisite and intricate detail. This room, though, is a little bizarre, mostly red panelling with a strangely hot feel to it, like a sauna without the steam.

'What are you doing here?'

This is a stupid question really. Carter's the coordinator, after all, and now that we're aware that we're both in the Guard, there's no need, I guess, for secrecy. This is probably what has him ticked off at me this time.

'You should know, Ethan. You did this, exposing my presence. The Citadel is about the only place now that we can have a conversation without fear of discovery. From here in we'll be awkward and wary of every action or word together. Are you proud of yourself?'

'Not if I have to bump into you every time I go on a mission.' I glance around, instinctively shielding my eyes from the red heat, which feels oddly hostile; and I have to wonder if Carter had a hand in selecting this room. It's no secret he hates me. It would be just like him to use his position to make me feel uncomfortable, or think he's teaching me a lesson.

'Well, of course you wouldn't have to if you weren't so foolish as to reveal yourself to me.'

'I learned my lesson.'

He stands back, crossing his ankles. 'I'm not so sure,' he says. 'But I will be sure to give appropriate evidence against you before the Tribunal.'

This surprises me. 'You're going to Athens?'

He smiles. 'To testify at your trial. I've been request-ed.' His hand reaches into his pocket, returning with a closed fist. His eyes take on a superior smugness as he unrolls his fingers. 'I'll be sure to add this incriminating piece of evidence while I'm there.'

It's the paper with Arkarian's title scrawled across it in my handwriting. Oh, hell! I'll never get my wings now!

'What did I ever do to you?' I can't help asking.

His head tilts slightly to one side. 'It's what you have yet to do, Ethan. And still you make so many mistakes.'

'I'm human. It's in our nature to make mistakes.'

'Stop thinking of yourself that way. You're a member of the Guard, and that means you can't afford to make mistakes. It jeopardises everything and everyone's lives.'

A crackling sound startles me and I turn round. It's not Isabel, but a fire hissing in the fireplace I didn't notice before. It takes a sudden leap in magnitude. No wonder it's so hot in here. I swing my attention back to Carter, glad it isn't Isabel yet. I wonder what could be keeping her. 'You're not perfect. Nobody is.'

'But *you* need to be.'

'What's that supposed to mean?'

'That you have a lot to learn.'

Suddenly I've had enough of this man. Isabel will be here any second and I have to try and get him moving on to wherever he's supposed to be going. 'Listen here, you might be able to get away with speaking to me in that derogatory way in the classroom, but you have no say over me in the Citadel, or anywhere else our paths might cross in history.'

He acknowledges this with an arrogant lift of his head. 'Perhaps.' He moves towards an open doorway;

at last he's leaving. One good step and I'll be free of him for a while. A prickly sensation grips me and I start scanning the sweltering room again for signs of Isabel. 'Who are you waiting for?' Carter asks with one leg out the door and already disappearing from sight.

'What makes you think I'm waiting for anyone?'

He scoffs, looking superior again. 'Your inexperience is showing as usual, Ethan. You're as nervous as a kitten with a ball of wool dangling in front of its nose.'

The man makes me want to swear and thump his head. Where does he get off being so arrogant? 'I have an Apprentice.' Instantly I realise what an idiot I am, playing right into his hands. When will I ever learn? Everything Carter's just said about me, I've gone and proven correct with my big mouth.

He steps back into the room, his right half reappearing. 'An Apprentice? They never gave me—' Shutting up suddenly, he just shakes his head and steps through the doorway.

The door closes behind him, all signs of it smoothly disappearing, and I realise this is not the room I'm supposed to be in. So what brought me here? That nightmare probably put me off course, sure, but I can't shake the feeling that Carter had a hand in my detour, though just how is unclear. But he does work in the Citadel. According to Arkarian, he's a coordinator here. Did he bring me to this room on purpose just so we could have this little chat? The man hates me, that much I know. And I'm getting the feeling his hatred is growing stronger every day. I will have to watch my back.

Then again, when have I ever been at ease in his company?

Chapter Nineteen

Isabel

I land with a thump and find myself rolling across a surprisingly springy floor. The light is strange in this room, kind of misty and not coming from a single point but more as if it is ... just there. The walls are bare and at first the whole room appears white. But then my eyes drift to each of the four tall, narrow pillars that soar for endless metres to a high domed roof of stained and intricately designed glass. It's as if the walls were drained of their colour so the ceiling could be viewed in all its brilliance.

I start to get up and suddenly Ethan's hand stretches out before me. 'You need to practise your landings.'

I take his hand and, getting quickly to my feet, notice that while I'm in pyjamas, he had the insight to wear a T-shirt and jeans to bed. 'Thanks for the warning.'

'Ah, yeah. I thought there was something I forgot.'

I tug at my pyjama top. 'Just as well I thought of wearing these. I don't usually sleep with so much on. Anything else I should know?'

He shakes his head, again pulling at his mouth.

'Sorry about that, but I can't think of anything right now. We have to hurry. It's hard to tell how long I've been here, but it feels like ages. What held you up?'

He takes my hand and leads me up a wide spiral staircase. Each step of it melts away behind us as we go. 'I couldn't get to sleep right away, and then I had this freaky dream.'

He goes completely still, the stairway half disappearing beneath our feet. It startles me. 'Ethan!'

We leap the last few steps to a narrow platform and run straight into another room. 'The stairwells are very impatient in this place. We're totally safe now. Tell me about your dream.'

But the room we've just entered has me forgetting the nightmare instantly. 'Tell you later.' I see rows and rows of medieval outfits, and all four surrounding walls are adorned with floor-to-ceiling mirrors. 'Do we get to pick?'

'Just walk past. What you need will select you.'

Unbelievably that's exactly what happens. I end up dressed in a long full gown of exquisite blue with a low neckline lined with a white cotton bodice, my feet in soft beige slippers. I take a look at my reflection and see that my hair has been changed to a deep russet brown, piled high at the back, most of it secured with clips and fancy crafted combs, the rest dropping to my shoulders in ringlets. Even my skin appears a different shade, much paler, while my nose and mouth have become definitely rounder. I spin around, holding my full skirt out wide. 'This is unreal! It's like I'm a completely different person!'

Ethan, who is now dressed in brown tights with a cream overshirt drawn in at the waist with a leather

112

belt, has also changed in other ways than simply his clothes. His hair is much darker than his usual brown, longer and thicker too. I take a close look at his face – unbelievable! His nose is fatter while that cute chin has grown markedly square. The look is not good. 'What happened to you?'

He shrugs and laughs at his newly acquired square look, then lifts a hand to the ringlets draping my shoulder. 'The Citadel gives us a new identity. Remember, your mortal body is still in your own bed in your own time. But who you are – your soul – is here.' He taps the area over his heart, then points to his eyes. 'And here too.'

'I think I get it. These bodies are kind of a temporary loan until we complete the mission.'

'Right, ensuring our true identities remain secure.'

I glance again in the mirror at the stranger staring back. But I don't feel any different. I still feel like myself, and of course my eyes haven't changed at all. I give a little shrug. 'It's like playing dress-ups, except this time we actually get to go on a real-life adventure. This kind of dress-up I could get used to.'

Ethan checks that his sword is securely in place, then takes my hand. 'Don't get too excited! We're not finished yet.'

He leads me to the middle of the room, where we stand close together directly under a high central point. We're supposed to have some sort of shower. But Ethan has an amused look on his new face so I'm not taking his meaning literally. After all, we're already dressed. He gives a barely perceptible nod and both of us are suddenly covered in a sprinkling of brilliantly coloured dust.

'What is it?' I ask.

Ethan gives a shake and helps me clear away the excess dust from my shoulders and hair. It disappears at our touch. 'It's everything you need to know so you don't look or sound like an idiot while in the past and give yourself away.'

'Thanks.'

'You're welcome. Now what's your name? And where are you from?'

'I'm Lady Madeline from Dartmouth, a coastal village sitting right on the English Channel.' I take a breath. 'Where did that come from?'

'It's your new identity. And I'm your cousin Hugo, Earl Monteblain's son. Now let's get out of here. We've wasted enough time.'

'Well, sorry, but you really could have told me all these things before now. You are supposed to be my Trainer.'

He gives me a sharp look of annoyance. 'They only gave me two weeks, remember.'

I don't reply. I was only kidding, and if he couldn't tell, then that's his problem. Guys can be so thick.

We take another stairway, which seems to disappear beneath our feet faster than we can possibly climb the narrow steps. At the top there's a small square platform. 'What took you so long getting here?' Ethan asks again, leading me into another room. This one is modest and quiet-looking, with simple furnishings that create an atmosphere of calm, the centre-piece a lounge suite that forms a square around a softly glowing fireplace.

'I couldn't get to sleep.'

We cross the room quickly and Ethan leads me to an

open doorway on the opposite side. Beyond its edges I see only darkness and a swirling mist.

'Was it the dream that kept you awake?'

I vaguely nod, trying to make out some form in the dark mist.

'We haven't the time now but you have to tell me about it later. OK? Now let's go.'

He means for me to step out into that vast nothingness at our feet. I tug him backwards a step to where I feel marginally safer. 'Wait a minute.'

He looks surprised, then his face softens. 'I didn't explain this part either, did I? Damn Arkarian! How can the Tribunal do this to me? Two weeks!'

The answer is obvious to me. 'Because they think you can.'

He scoffs. 'If anything, they're testing me.'

Glancing around the room, I see that the door we entered by has now disappeared. So there's only one way out – the doorway with nothing but mist beyond it. 'Where is this place exactly?'

'The Citadel?' He shrugs. 'It's neither here nor there. You can't see it in the mortal world, that's all I know.'

'Is it in space?'

'I don't think so. Arkarian says it kind of dwells in a place between worlds. But I'm assured it's the safest place in the universe. It can't be got to, even though both sides inhabit its interior in their transit stages. The problem is, we can't stay long 'cause time is immeasurable here, and it's easy to linger longer than you think with too much time passing in our mortal world.'

He leads me right to the edge of the open doorway again. 'Here, look,' he says, peering into the blank distance. 'Out there is our destination.'

'I can't see anything except darkness and fog, but I sense a vast drop below us.'

'It's only a small step – the same way all new adventures begin. I can't believe *you'd* let fear of the unknown stop you.'

I send him a death-stare before sucking in a deep breath. Finally, we do it together. I keep my eyes closed tight and it feels as if we've stepped down from a ceiling to a hard floor. I land and fall, hitting my left side on a cold stone wall. We're in a torch-lit brick hallway. I scramble up as two armoured soldiers make an appearance at one end of the hall. Ethan glances around and spots a door to our right. 'Quickly, in here! Let's work out where we are first, before having to explain our presence.'

The room is massive and draughty. A fire blazes within a brick fireplace. Brocade drapes hang across an open window and shadows from the fire flicker across the fabric, deepening its emerald green colour. There's not much furniture except a huge four poster bed with a trunk at its base, a solid wooden desk and chair, and a comfortable-looking armchair before the fire. The whole room smells of smoke and wood.

'Can you believe this, Ethan?'

'Hugo,' he reminds me in a whisper. 'Whenever we speak out loud we must maintain our identities. After a while it should come naturally.'

I understand, and can't help feeling foolish for having asked the question. Ethan, or Hugo for the time being, has been doing this sort of thing for years, but I can't hide the buzz I'm getting out of it. 'Look at this bed!' I jump into the centre of it and practically sink to the bottom.

'Feathers,' Ethan says. 'It's probably filled with goose feathers. But hey, you're supposed to be observing only. Don't touch anything, OK? You could get hurt. And I'm in enough trouble already, so don't go making more. Whatever you do is my responsibility.'

He starts to walk around the room, stopping with his back to the fire, fingers linked behind his back. 'It's definitely someone important's bedroom, but not the king's, nor the prince's I'd say. From what I can remember from the layout of this place –'

He doesn't get another word out as we both hear voices and heavy footsteps outside. They grow louder, then stop outside this bedroom's door. A few more shared words, and one set of footsteps moves on.

Ethan and I exchange a quick look. Suddenly, Ethan makes a flying leap to the bed, diving straight for its centre. He lands half on top of me, pinning me to the mattress. 'What the—?' Ethan suddenly kisses me. At first it's a shock, 'cause I'm not expecting this, but within seconds of his kiss everything changes. On some level I know a stranger has entered the room and stopped still at the sight of Ethan and me on the bed, kissing. But on another level there is nothing but Ethan and me. It doesn't register that we're in someone else's bed, even in someone else's time period. There's only Ethan kissing me. That's it.

But then Ethan jumps off me, pretending to be suddenly aware of our visitor. He staggers apologetically to his feet, dragging me with him. 'My lord,' he says, bowing at the waist to the tall man before us. 'My apologies. I had no idea, when I stumbled into this magnificent bedroom, that it was yours. If you'll give us but a moment, sir, we will vacate your room and

117

return to the hall where we belong.'

'And you will leave my bed as you found it, unoccupied?' the tall man asks, one bushy eyebrow raised in obvious amusement.

Ethan bows his head low. 'Yes, sir. Most definitely.'

The man looks me over. 'How unfortunate for you, lad. What is your name, and that of your ... companion?'

'My name, sir, is Hugo Monteblain, and this is my ...' He pauses momentarily, suddenly looking uncomfortable, but then his expression relaxes somewhat. Kissing cousins is not all that unusual in this period of time. He goes on to introduce me, 'My cousin, Lady Madeline.'

'Well, young Hugo, I would be pleased to oblige you and your lovely willing cousin here, but my time tonight is tight and I must prepare my speech to the council. There is a lot happening in the palace as we speak, and we must hope the result will be a new and rightful king.'

'How goes young Richard?'

The tall man's eyes widen slightly. 'Ah, an ally. The boy sleeps soundly in his bed.' He looks closely at Ethan. 'From which lands do you hail? I have many, and yet I don't recognise your name, though your face, looks familiar.'

'We come from Dartmouth, sir. On the English Channel.'

'Alas, I don't own those lands. Have we met before?'

'Nay, my lord. I have not had the honour.'

The man moves to his desk. 'That's unfortunate. You remind me of a man I knew once – something around the eyes – he helped me greatly once, a skilled young man who promised to return, but ...' He waves a hand in a gesture of annoyance. 'I haven't been given the opportunity to show my appreciation for what he did. It's as if he never existed.'

'I'm sorry, my lord. Had I made you such a promise, I would most certainly have fulfilled it.'

The man nods, his eyes shifting from Ethan to me.

I know I'm not supposed to say, do or touch anything, but I just can't resist this one opportunity. 'Perhaps the young man in question will yet return, my lord.'

Ethan's grip on my hand tightens. He doesn't want me attracting attention to myself. That's the idea of an observation-only journey, he had told me earlier.

'It's been many years, Lady Madeline,' the man replies sadly, sitting down heavily at his desk.

It's our cue to leave. Ethan bows again, asking whether the man requests anything from the kitchens. The man complains about his own manservant being lazy but doesn't take up Ethan's offer.

Outside the door I can't help squealing out loud. Ethan throws a hand over my mouth, grinning at me.

'Quiet! Do you want to get us both killed before this mission is half finished?'

'Who was that? Do you know? He carried such an aura of magnetism.'

He floors me when he says, 'John of Gaunt. Couldn't you tell?'

'I'm a C student, remember?'

He snorts loudly. 'Not for long!'

Chapter Twenty

Ethan

Isabel is completely enchanted. It doesn't take me long to realise she's born for this life. As soon as we return home we'll work hard at mastering her psychological skills. Healing we already know will be one of her main talents. But so far nothing else has revealed itself. There's still time, if we carry out this mission successfully. There's just this premonition I can't get rid of tonight – a prickling of my consciousness, a gut feeling something's wrong, or going to go wrong. Maybe I'm just nervous about having Isabel along, being responsible for her and all. I don't want her to get hurt, and I feel our training has been way too inadequate. But there's something else worrying me too. It's as if I've picked up some sort of stomach bug; an uneasy queasiness is kicking in and there's a strange lethargy starting to shoot through my limbs, making each step more difficult than the last.

I try to put these weird sensations aside while I figure out exactly which wing of the palace we're currently roaming. Recalling Arkarian's holographic sphere, and considering the location of John of Gaunt's bedroom, I finally get my bearings. Our destination is not far at all, but we're on the wrong floor.

As we head for the winding stairwell, I hear Isabel take in a sharp breath. I think it must be nerves kicking in, but then she says, 'Back there in John of Gaunt's bedroom … you know when—'

She stops suddenly and it hits me what she's trying to bring up – the kiss I stole from her on John of Gaunt's bed. I swallow hard as an uncomfortable feeling swamps me. I hope she didn't get the wrong idea. I mean, I really like Isabel, and the time we've spent together has been the best couple of weeks I can remember. Is there something wrong with having a girl for a best friend? That's how I feel about Isabel right now. I'm not sure if there could ever be more. Maybe one day, when I get over – I can't believe where my thoughts have taken me. I was about to say Rochelle. I'm over Rochelle, well and truly, so why the sudden stab of pain?

I take a deep breath and choose my words carefully. The last thing I want is to hurt Isabel's feelings. 'Um, that kiss, you mean?'

She nods.

'I'm really sorry about that. We needed an excuse to be found in that room. I didn't have time to discuss it with you first. I hope you didn't mind.'

She flicks her hand at me with a casualness I hope she really feels. 'No, of course. I knew that.'

We pass the room where the council is meeting. The faint sound of muffled voices can be heard through the thick double doors. Soon John of Gaunt will make an appearance, stating his reasons why his ten-year-old nephew should be the next King of England.

'Why does John of Gaunt not want the crown for himself?' Isabel asks, changing the subject.

'I doubt anyone would support him if he did. Nobody wants him to have more power than he already has. He's incredibly wealthy in his own right, with more lands and titles and earldoms than any other noble to date. And his sights are set on other titles yet to come.'

It's late, and if John of Gaunt is correct, the young prince will be fast asleep when we make an appearance. And as long as Arkarian is on cue, we'll arrive before the would-be assassin.

The entire length of the hallway is empty. Unchallenged we reach the door to the prince's bedroom. Where are his protectors? The palace guards? Cautiously I push open the door. No one appears to be about, which is strange considering this ten-year-old child will soon be king.

'It's so quiet,' Isabel comments, as we move further into the semi-dark bedroom.

An elderly woman, obviously a maid or nanny, spots us from where she sits huddled, stitching a tapestry by the fire. 'Who are you? What do you want?'

'Our names are not important. We're here to protect the prince. Where are the guards?'

'They were called away but a moment ago. They promised to return shortly.'

No sooner does the woman speak than a figure swathed in a long crimson cape enters the room from the adjoining dressing room. 'State your purpose for sneaking around the prince's bedroom!' he snaps at us.

His arrogance is off-putting. Who is he? My instinct says he's the assassin, pretending to be someone important. When we don't answer, he yells, 'Get out! I demand you leave the room now!'

'We're here to protect the prince,' I call out, fighting a growing nauseous feeling.

'By whose order?'

I hesitate only a second. 'John of Gaunt's.'

The old servant woman looks from the hooded man to me. 'Well, I don't recognise any of you, so how about you all get out of here and leave me to my peaceful stitching? Or will I have to call the king's soldiers?'

The second her words are out, the hooded man leaps across the room at her. His foot connects just once, but it's enough to send the old woman flying backwards.

Isabel runs to her side.

The sleeping boy's eyes flick open as the hooded man quickly grabs a pillow from the bed and throws it over the prince's face. The assassin is attempting to smother the prince right before our very eyes!

'Hugo, hurry!' Isabel calls out to me. At least she hasn't forgotten that as an observer she must not intervene. 'Why aren't you doing anything?'

But I'm having serious problems of my own. For some reason I feel suddenly numb and semi-paralysed, unable to run or even walk. My stomach is roiling while my head is heavy as rock. The room starts swimming before my eyes.

'Hugo? What's wrong? You look like a ghost.'

Doubling over now with pain shooting through my entire body, I realise what must be happening. 'Someone … I think someone is trying to wake me. I can't move.'

The old woman scowls at me as if I'm nothing but a piece of garbage left out for the palace cats. Getting to her feet, she runs into the hallway, screaming for help. Returning quickly, she throws herself at the assassin. He tosses the old woman fiercely backwards and she hits her head on the corner of a desk, sliding to the floor unconscious.

'Hugo, what do we do? I can't just stand and watch! You must let me help!'

The young prince, now fully awake, is struggling for all his worth beneath the strong hands of the caped man. I manage to get up, working through the pain and heavy-limbed sensations, and draw my sword.

The assassin turns to face me in combat but seeing how unsteady I am on my feet, decides not to draw his sword. He merely whacks me with an extended elbow, sending me reeling backwards to the floor. I try to get up again, but my stomach heaves and suddenly empties out with violent force. When I get a second's relief from the intense vomiting, I look up and see everyone staring at me, even the assassin and the prince.

'Oh, God, Hugo! Can I do something?' Isabel asks.

The most I can manage is to shake my head as drips slither from my mouth to the floor.

While the assassin is momentarily distracted, the young prince moves, scrambling across the huge bed. But the assassin dives for him, slamming him back against the mattress, and starts smothering him again.

Isabel, eyes wide and wild-looking, leans over me. 'Sorry, Hugo, but one of us has to act.' She reaches for my sword and, with two hands clasped tightly around the hilt, raises it in front of her. With a fierce war cry she charges at the assassin.

The assassin, forced to let go of the prince, groans and spins around, clearly annoyed at having to draw his own sword and the two of them fight while the boy looks on.

'Go on,' I say to him, nodding at the door, 'get out of here! Save yourself, Your Highness!'

The prince comes over to me, avoiding the mess around him with careful steps, and squats beside me without taking his eyes off the duelling pair. 'My coin's on her.'

Increasing pain shoots through my stomach and into my chest, my body lunges forward and the prince jumps back.

'Are you going to vomit again?' the prince asks while keeping his eyes riveted to the duelling pair.

I shake my head and try to have faith in Isabel, but I'm assuming the assassin is no novice, Isabel is. This mission was supposed to be observation only. But Isabel does well, holding her position and forcing the assassin back several paces until his back hits the wall. Then, with an amazing display of swordsmanship, Isabel maims the man, slashing his left arm. But it's probably only a flesh wound.

Beside me, the prince cheers. But I can hardly see him any more, the room is swimming and I feel as if I'm about to pass out. Something is terribly wrong.

Suddenly Isabel screams. For a second I think she's been hurt and I try to get up. It seems the assassin, frustrated and annoyed, has found a new strength. He disarms Isabel, whose sword flies off and lodges on the window ledge. She's in trouble now, and there's nothing I can do to help.

The assassin aims his sword with the intention to kill, but Isabel uses her karate skills, bringing the man to his knees and causing him to drop his sword. The prince cheers again and rushes for the weapon. It's heavy and he has trouble picking it up. In the meantime the assassin gets his bearings back and flips Isabel on to her back. From within his boot he flicks out a dagger and aims it at the prince.

'Look out!' I call.

As he throws, Isabel jumps on the caped man, knocking the dagger off its course. It lodges in the leg of a wooden desk.

At this moment the doors fling open. John of Gaunt and several soldiers come charging into the room, quickly sizing up the situation. The assassin, realising his work here tonight will remain incomplete, takes a flying run and leaps out of the window. It's a long way down, but I know he'll not leap to his death, but back to wherever and whenever he came from. The only consolation tonight is that even though I totally stuffed the mission, thanks to Isabel, the prince still lives.

John of Gaunt orders his men to pursue the assassin and bring him back alive, which of course they won't 'cause they won't find him, that's for sure. But off they go, running out the door, and John of Gaunt checks that the young prince is all right. Noticing the pool of vomit spread out over the floor he watches carefully where he puts his feet. He then helps Isabel into a standing position. 'My lady, His Highness and I are most grateful.'

He offers a hand to me, but I cannot move. The violent nausea and chest pain have increased so much in the last few minutes that I'm starting to think I may not make it back to my own bed alive. Breathing is too hard now as my lungs struggle to inflate.

'He's ill, my lord,' Isabel crouches beside me. 'What

do I do, Hugo? Tell me what to do.'

'Arkarian,' I mouth in a hoarse whisper against her ear. 'But not in front of ...'

She looks up at John of Gaunt. 'We need a room.'

Within seconds John of Gaunt has two of his men lift and carry me to a bed in a room down the hall. Isabel thanks them while shoving them out the door.

'*Arkarian!*' she screams, and in the same second the two of us are returned to the Citadel, where Arkarian is waiting, a deep frown carved into his forehead.

'Ethan, you must hurry.'

Isabel tries pushing Arkarian out of her way to get to me. 'What's wrong with him? Is it something I can heal?'

'Be patient, Isabel, he'll be well again soon.'

The pain eases and my lungs inflate again. 'I think I'm getting better already.' I try to sit up but fall back down.

'That's only because you're closer to your body. But you will be well again soon,' Arkarian explains. 'As soon as you return to your mortal state. But there's something I have to tell you first. It's about your—'

My stomach churns and I think I'm going to throw up again. I roll over as pain tightens like a rubber band around my head. Isabel jerks backwards and starts yelling, 'Hurry, Arkarian! Are you blind? He needs help!'

Arkarian nods and waves his hands over me with a strange impatient expression on his face. 'You'd better go then,' he commands, and before I have a chance to wonder what he was going to say, the room and every-one in it disappears.

Chapter Twenty-one

Ethan

I wake to see Dad gazing into my face, his hands on my shoulders shaking me. I have to think quickly: how long was I out? It couldn't have been much more than a couple of minutes, but the time spent in the Citadel is the unknown factor. We took so long to get going. Still, a few minutes at most, surely. All I have to do is act calm. He can't know anything. And he mustn't find out. It would be dangerous – for me, for those associated with me, and even for Dad. And there was my breach of one code already last week, and again with the handwritten note. My appearance before the Tribunal is coming up shortly. Hell, I have to be careful!

'Dad, stop shaking me! What's the matter?'

'Ethan? You were out cold.' He encloses me in a grip so hard his fingers dig into my shoulders. Then he stiffens and pulls back, eyes squinting and dark. 'What happened to you?'

'I was just sleeping, Dad.'

'No, you weren't.'

All I have to do is make him think he imagined my comatose state. He's talking through fear. It should be easy to allay those fears, now that I'm here and fine and talking to him. 'Dad, you had your hands on my shoulders the whole time. Look at me, I'm fine.' In fact a heavy lethargy has gripped my limbs. I just hope he doesn't ask me to get up and prove anything.

'Something strange is going on.'

'Don't be ridiculous! What could possibly be going on?' I stare him straight in the face, forcing myself not to blink, not to falter in any way. It's now, as my thoughts start to settle into some sort of order, that I wonder what he's doing here, in my room, in the middle of the night. 'What's wrong? Is it Mum?'

'She's all right now.'

'What does that mean?'

He shifts his glance to the door as though watching for her to make an appearance. 'She had a bad dream again, that's all. You must have been in it. She made me get out of bed and check on you. But you were so deeply asleep, I couldn't even tell if you were breathing or not. And when I shook you, you didn't respond.'

'I'm a deep sleeper, Dad.'

He peers at me as though, on some level in his mind, he's not buying my explanation. Then his head drops, a defeated gesture. 'I ... I'm confused.'

'There's nothing to be confused about. I was just so tired I fell into a deep sleep. I was in dreamland.'

This reference to dreams has his eyes open wide again. He sits at the side of my bed. 'Were you having a nightmare too?'

Although I did have one earlier, I still don't feel up to talking about it. Right now I'm too drained. 'Nah, just sweet dreams tonight, Dad.'

He almost smiles. 'There must've been a girl involved.'

Isabel's trusting face as she looked up from making the stone castle at the lake foreshore flashes into my brain. The sensation of evil about to drop on her from the surrounding woods hits me at the same instant.

'Ethan? Are you all right?'

I push the horror to the back of my mind. 'Yeah, I'm fine. I'm just really tired, Dad.'

He gets up and walks to the door, but doesn't leave straight away. 'If there's anything you want to tell me … Anything …' He turns his face slightly. It catches the light from the moon, and I see a glimpse of tenderness and concern. This look, this rare show of emotion, almost has me confessing my soul to him. Fighting this urge hard, I turn away, rolling on to my side, letting him know our conversation is over. Telling Dad, or anyone else for that matter, about the Guard would be a major violation of the code. But worse than that, Dad just wouldn't be able to handle it.

Chapter Twenty-two

Isabel

A week passes and Ethan fully recovers. What happened to him scared me and I don't want that happening to me. Tonight we go to Athens to the year 200 BC, a thousand years after the Tribunal was first established. Now it's the Guard's headquarters, where the Lords of the various Houses live unaffected by the mortal measurement of time. I'm going to be initiated as an Apprentice before the Tribunal. We'll be staying overnight, as Ethan's trial is on the second day; Arkarian is allowing me to stay for it but probably not to watch. It couldn't happen at a better time, because Mum is away with Jimmy for a weekend in the high country trying to catch some early snow. I just have to make sure I don't do anything stupid to make Matt want to check on me during the night, which is highly unlikely anyway. With Mum away I'm sure he'll make the most of the house this weekend with Rochelle.

I'm kind of looking forward to meeting the Tribunal, which is made up of the nine Lords of the Houses, even while I'm nervous about it too. There are apparently four women, four men, and an immortal who is neither. I have so many questions, but doubt I'll get to ask even half of them. Arkarian says that to even look upon their faces takes courage, let alone to stare into their eyes to ask a question.

'Are they ugly?' We're seated in Arkarian's main chamber, on his favourite stools. Mine feels as if it's going to collapse beneath me.

Ethan laughs. 'About as ugly as Arkarian.'

Arkarian gives Ethan a barely tolerant look.

'Do they have strange-coloured eyes?'

'Like mine?' Arkarian asks, looking straight at me with those deep violet eyes that are completely breathtaking this close up.

Ethan answers for me, which is good as I seem to have lost my ability to speak. 'Mostly, but it's how they look at you, or I should say through you.'

'I don't understand.'

'They're all Truthseers.'

I stare at Ethan, then at Arkarian.

'They can read your thoughts. Every one,' Ethan says with a grin. 'Even the thoughts you don't consciously think. Like the silly ones that just pop into your head.'

'Oh, no!'

'The first time I met the Tribunal I could hardly stop staring at Penbarin. You'll know exactly who I'm talking about when you see him. He's massive, in every direction. I didn't say anything out loud, of course. And I did stop myself from staring, but I couldn't stop myself from thinking, *Wow, isn't he a fat pig?* That was my first thought, then, *I wonder what he ate for breakfast, a side of cow?*

I can't help laughing, but Arkarian's voice is dry.

'Personally, I don't think about what people eat for

breakfast. I have better things to do with my thoughts.'

So now I have to watch not just what I say, but what my thoughts say as well.

Arkarian touches my shoulder gently; a comforting warmth spreads right down my arm. 'Pay no attention to him, Isabel. He's matured somewhat since that first meeting.'

Something clicks. 'How old were you exactly when you had these runaway thoughts?'

Ethan smiles. 'Five, I think.'

It's a relief, but only slightly. I know my own mind, and it hardly ever follows its own orders. I recall the first time I met Arkarian and how blown away I was by that blue hair. And then I saw his eyes – purple! Just looking into them had made me self-conscious and tingly all over. The thoughts I had were just plain sinful. But eventually I pulled myself together and started noticing other things, like his skin, pale and silky smooth. And as for his physique, well, I couldn't help noticing the strength in his upper body, like – wow!

I stop when I realise they're sharing a look that at first I don't understand. And then I get it. It's embarrassment – on my behalf. 'What is it?'

Ethan breaks it to me. 'You know when I told you Arkarian's title is that of TruthMaster.'

An uneasy feeling kicks into my stomach. 'Uh-huh.'

'Well, the fact is, the "Truth" half stands for Truthseer.'

'Arkarian's a Truthseer too?' I ask just to check.

Arkarian's eyebrows lift, while Ethan grins at me.

'How wonderful,' I whisper mostly to myself, recalling in a flash the multitude of embarrassing thoughts I've had about Arkarian while in his presence. I try

133

hard to resist putting both hands over my face in an attempt to hide. 'I mean, isn't this just great? Thank you for telling me, Ethan. Some Trainer you turned out to be. And your speciality is embarrassing your Apprentices, correct?'

They both laugh, then Arkarian gets serious. 'You two had better get going. We leave in only a few hours.'

As Ethan and I walk out of the mountain and down the long track home, I can't help drilling him with some of the thousand questions jumping around inside my head. He tries to answer them, but sometimes I sense he's purposely leaving stuff out. I wish I was a Truthseer so I could read his mind right now, but really I'm not so sure that's a good idea. Imagine what silly thoughts he would have.

But there is one question that I know he'll love to talk about. It's about getting what the Guard call his 'wings'. It's an honour, one of the highest possible. And Ethan is close. He's mentioned it several times while training. Apparently he's expecting to be awarded this power on his next birthday in a ceremony in Athens. 'What happens when you earn your wings?'

His eyes light up, I see the blue in them shimmer even in the semi-dark of early dusk. 'They're not physical wings or anything,' he says, 'not like a bird or an angel. You don't actually grow them either. It's a power you have to earn. They don't give it to everyone. Only those they can fully trust not to misuse it.'

'What can you do with this power?'

'It's the ability to dematerialise your own body and rematerialise it at will somewhere else.'

'Wow, that's incredible!'

'Yeah, why do you think I can't wait? It's the ultimate.'

Ethan is excited and I can't blame him. The trip into the past last week is still buzzing in my head. An absolute adrenalin rush from start to finish. Imagine being able to take yourself from one spot to another in an instant! The ultimate in self-defence. 'How long does it take to earn these wings?'

'There are three levels: Apprentice, Trainer and Master. But you can earn your wings at any stage, it's up to the Tribunal. Some members don't ever earn them, but it doesn't mean they're unskilled, just that the Tribunal doesn't think they can handle that amount of power.'

'Ah, I think I understand. So what would Arkarian be?'

'He's a Master, and he's had his wings for about five hundred and ninety years, or so he boasts.'

Boasts? Now this I find difficult to believe. I haven't known him long, but he doesn't seem the type. Right from the start I felt he was genuine, not putting on an attitude like most people I know. 'He doesn't boast. And I know he has the skill that keeps him physically young, but six hundred years? That's really hard to comprehend 'cause he just doesn't look it.'

'His body will always be that of an eighteen-year-old.'

An interesting thought! 'Are you sure he's not immortal?'

Ethan shrugs. 'Nah, it's just his skill. Others have it too, but it's rare.'

A thought hits me. Arkarian must have a life other than the times we see him in his high-tech chambers,

135

monitoring history. Where does he go? Who does he see? 'Does he …? Um—'

'What?'

'I don't know, have a …?'

He looks at me as if I've just grown two heads. 'A *girlfriend*? Is that what you're trying to ask?'

'No, I'm not.' Well, I am, actually, but Ethan's amused reaction has me dropping the subject quickly. I can't help thinking a lot about Arkarian since meeting him. Maybe it's his mysterious lifestyle I find fascinating. I don't know. He just intrigues me.

Chapter Twenty-three

Isabel

I go to bed as usual, though Matt is nowhere around. He's probably with Rochelle. Whether he's with her or not makes no difference as far as I'm concerned. His love life is none of my business. The first time Matt started going out with Rochelle, and I could tell how serious he was about this girl, I thought perhaps the two of us could be friends. But it didn't work out, and even to this day, Rochelle always acts indifferent to me. Matt thinks I exaggerate, but in his eyes Rochelle can do nothing wrong. And I can't say anything bad about her or he bites my head off. Boy, has he got it bad! Well, hopefully I'll be back in my body by the time he gets home.

I drift off to sleep quickly, waking with a sudden drop in one of the many rooms in the Citadel. This one resembles a museum, with sculptures (mostly statues of naked little boys) spread around the room.

Ethan is waiting for me again. Together we go to one of the wardrobe rooms, this one completely different to the last. I end up dressed in a white tunic made of some soft yet subtly reflective material, sashed at the

137

waist with a light-blue corded belt, a matching white cape draped over my shoulders. My feet remain bare, my hair unchanged, except for being contained in a single thick plait. I move to the mirror to inspect my new face and see my familiar reflection staring back.

'Your identity can't be concealed from the leaders of the royal Houses, nor from the immortal.'

'Oh.'

Ethan smiles at me. 'I should congratulate you,' he says, attempting to maintain a happy look, I suspect solely for my benefit. 'You've been elevated already. The white tunic represents your novice status and so should your belt, but you're wearing the first shade of blue, which stands for suitably honoured Apprentice.'

Inwardly beaming, I stand back as Ethan begins his walk. Moments later he spins around to face me, dressed in a similar floor-length tunic and cape, except his are all black, including the sash. 'What does your black tunic stand for?' I ask, but hardly need to. His crestfallen face tells me heaps.

'Dishonour,' he says softly. 'At least I haven't been stripped back to Apprentice status.'

I try to be sympathetic. Obviously the hierarchy of the Guard means a lot to him. 'They won't do that to you. The black looks good anyway.'

He grins bitterly. 'I'm ready? Remember time isn't measured in this place.'

'Right, let's go.'

From a room on a higher level we leap into a waiting yellow mist, and almost instantly drop to a rock-solid surface. As soon as they hit, my feet fall out from under me. Blue sky, the sound of birds nearby and the strong scent of flowers let me know even before I fully open my eyes that we're definitely somewhere outside.

Getting to my feet, I take a good look around and see several enormous trees covered in brilliant red, mauve and orange flowers. The ground is paved with golden bricks, and there are stone pillars shimmering in the heat of the sun. We're in a courtyard, bricked on three sides with long columned verandas, the fourth a large stone wall. There are benches placed strategically amongst brightly coloured and perfectly manicured flower beds. The whole scene is one of serenity, a place for rest and reflection.

'Ah, at last you arrive! I was starting to think I needed to organise a search party.'

It's Arkarian, waiting for us with a welcoming smile and an outstretched hand. Ethan grunts and grabs Arkarian's hand in a firm shake. I'd like to do the same, but seeing Arkarian outfitted in his shimmering silver cape over a matching floor-length tunic, his blue hair flowing freely behind him, takes my breath away. He looks amazing.

He nods with a small smile at me. 'Welcome to Athens, Isabel!' He waves his hand in a wide arc. 'Isn't it a beautiful morning?'

I swallow and give a little cough, feeling as if I'm about to choke, a normal voice nowhere in sight. It's Arkarian, his natural presence overwhelming me for an instant. It also doesn't help that the heat is so intense out here. What will it be like in a few hours?

He takes my elbow. 'Don't be nervous. Let's go inside where it's much cooler.'

Ethan pulls at his black tunic top.

'It's a formality, Ethan.' Arkarian tries to put his mind at rest. 'All your good work won't go unnoticed,

139

believe me. I'll make certain they understand.'

'Thanks, Arkarian.'

Arkarian leads us into a room of white walls and shiny marble floors. Here he sits with us on a low bench beside a table laden with hot dishes of cooked fish with peas and figs and bread. There's a crumbly-looking cheese that Arkarian explains is made from goat's milk.

Smelling the food suddenly makes me hungry. We eat, an unusual breakfast, although Ethan only toys with his food; and then Arkarian shows us to our rooms. 'Rest a while,' he tells me, 'you'll be called soon enough.' And to Ethan he says, 'We need to talk and go over your statement for tomorrow.'

Together they leave. Once alone, I walk around the large room with a certain nervous anticipation, marvelling at my new surroundings. The floor for one, oddly warm for stone as if it's heated from beneath, yet the room feels wonderfully cool. There's a four-poster bed with an elaborate net around it in the centre of the room. Along one wall a carved chaise longue stands beside a marble desk with matching stool. On the opposite side is an open window, without glass which looks out over that intimate golden courtyard.

I sit on the wide stone ledge for a few minutes observing the birds buzzing among the trees. As I watch, a sense of peace starts to fill me. My relaxed mind-state, coupled with the morning heat, soon has my eyes drooping. But they snap wide open quickly when a loud bang, probably a door slamming shut, resonates in the distance. It has me searching the far corner of the yard. A figure of a man, dressed in a long brown tunic, belted at the waist with a yellow cord and matching wide-sweeping cape, soon emerges. I stretch up a little to get a better view and see the man briskly cross the courtyard.

For a second I can't believe my eyes, and quickly slide down the window ledge out of view, sucking in a few good breaths. It can't possibly be …? But I just have to take another look, and catch him disappearing into one of the buildings below. It's him all right – my history teacher, Mr Carter.

What's *he* doing here?

As I slide back down to the floor, a few things start to make sense. Mr Carter's relationship with Ethan, for one. OK, they don't like each other, and I sense there's real animosity between them, but there's also a definite connection. This Guard thing must be it. They know they're both members, and this knowledge puts a strain on everything when they're together. It also explains Mr Carter's strange conversation with me, warning me at the same time as offering friendship of sorts.

So, does this mean he knows about me? Knows that I'm becoming an official member of the Guard today?

I don't get any more time to think, because Ethan opens my door and frowns at me. 'What are you doing on the floor?' In his all-black tunic and cape he looks regal and absolutely stunning. He leans down towards me with his hand outstretched. 'They're ready for you out there,' he says, helping me up.

At his words my hands go stiff and cold. Once I get to my feet I give them a little shake, squeezing my fingers into fists, opening them and closing them again to get some feeling going.

Ethan gives me a reassuring smile. 'Stop worrying.

You're going to be sensational.'

'Thanks, but I don't believe you. I'm not sure what on earth I'm doing right now. And I have to tell you about someone I saw here a few minutes ago.'

His head lifts up slightly. 'Carter?'

'Yes!'

'I saw him too. He's here to give evidence to the Tribunal tomorrow.'

'At *your* trial?'

'Uh-huh.'

'Oh, no!'

'Exactly. He's going to make sure I get nailed. But don't worry, he won't be going to your initiation.'

A thought occurs to me. 'Can I give evidence at your trial tomorrow?'

He looks at me funny. 'Assuming you're allowed to witness the trial in the first place, what would you say?'

'Well, that I've known you for a long time, and that ... and that you're a good ...?'

'Trainer? I haven't even shown you how to land properly. You end up fulfilling a mission that I stuff completely, having physical contact with a member of the Order of Chaos while on a mission of observation only. Yeah, right. I'm sure they'll believe you.'

'Hey, don't be so hard on yourself! You're a good Trainer. I trust you, Ethan.'

We've started down the white hallway, but when I say these last four words, Ethan stops and looks at me. 'Thanks, Isabel, that means a lot to me. Now I want you to forget my problems 'cause this is your day. You're going to walk into that room with your head held high. Just as it should be, OK?'

142

I smile back at his seriousness. Just as I do, the doors up ahead silently open backwards into a circular room from which emanates an aura of power beyond anything I've ever felt before. Immediately my mouth goes dry, my hands go numb again. But then Arkarian appears, standing in the open doorway with a smile on his face.

'They can't wait to meet you,' he says, pulling the hood of my cape right up to cover my hair.

Somehow I doubt it.

I forget for a moment that Arkarian knows my thoughts. 'You're one of the Named, remember.'

His words are comforting, but only for a second. Then, as he steps back to make room for us to pass, the nerves hit all over again. My stomach feels as if the birds from the courtyard have taken up residence inside and are now trying to get out through my ribcage.

Ethan takes my elbow. As my Trainer, he is allowed to accompany me inside. This is great 'cause my knees are not functioning as knees right now, but are more like jelly.

He leads me to the centre of a circle formed by the members of the Tribunal, all sitting equidistant from each other in the shape of a nine-digit clock. A stool appears before me, a similar style to those Arkarian provides in his chambers. I glance up from within my hood and he appears in my direct line of vision. He's wearing his hood now too, his face shaded deeply within, but I can make out his intense violet eyes. They smile at me, calming my pounding heart.

Once I am seated, Ethan gives my arm an encouraging squeeze, then looks straight ahead to the one that is immortal. 'I present to you my Apprentice, Isabel Becket.' He bows and moves out of the circle to stand beside Arkarian. Now I'm on my own. I take a deep breath.

As I understand it, each of the nine members of the Tribunal will introduce themselves and endow me with a special gift, a gift that belongs to their respective House. Lady Devine is first to speak, immediately to the left of the immortal. She stands and comes towards me, a beautiful woman with blood-red hair that hangs like liquid silk around her face and all the way down to her calves. She's wearing a loose-fitting white gown drawn in at the waist with a gold-plaited cord. Her bare feet are small and pale. 'I welcome you to the Guard, Isabel, from the House of Divinity, and bestow upon you the ability to bear pain.'

Up close her aura of strength and power is hard to take without squirming. It's not exactly scary, just overwhelming, making me want to run and cower and hide beneath a blanket and whimper. Inside, I know she's not going to hurt me, but I also sense that if she wanted to, she could do so in an instant, without even lifting a finger. As much as I would like to, I can't make myself look into her eyes, though they're strongly compelling me to do so.

She returns to her seat and the man to her left rises and glides towards me, introducing himself as Meridian. His stature is slight and he gives the impression of floating, rather than walking on his bare feet. 'From the House of Kavanah, I welcome you, Isabel. I bestow you with the wisdom to distinguish good from evil and illusion from reality.'

Brystianne is next, introducing herself as queen of

144

the House of Averil. This woman definitely resembles my mental image of a queen. She looks regal in a full-skirted gown made of shimmering gold. Her feet are covered in gold slippers. Her hair, the colour of ripe wheat, is piled high atop her head. 'Welcome, Isabel,' she says with a smile. Holding her hand up over my head, her eyes twinkling, she showers me with a shimmering sprinkle of dust. 'My gift to you is the ability to heal your own heart.'

Sir Syford from his own House of Syford follows, a man so tall and broad of shoulders that I instinctively draw back. With conscious effort I stop myself. He comes right up to me, peering down with coal-black eyes deeply set but amazingly warm. He smiles. 'My gift is that of judgement. May you always be able to view the spirit through the body.'

Elenna of the House of Isle endows me with the gift of knowledge. Beside her, a Lord named Alexandon of the House of Criers lays upon my head the gift of courage, then adds with a touch of humour, 'Though from what we've already witnessed, little more is needed here.'

His words have all the members smiling or giving a little laugh. He moves back and Arabella from the House of Sky and Water glides off her seat. As she draws nearer, my eyes become riveted to her face, so pale and delicate that I can see the fine blue veins beneath her translucent skin, which itself has a blue tinge, as do her lips. But it's her eyelashes that are most startling, long, thick and encrusted with what appears to be a blue frost of ice. With pale and blue-tinged hands she weaves a pattern over my head and announces in a delighted voice that her gift is that of sight – 'in all and any light,' she adds with a bit of a giggle.

Then comes Penbarin, every bit as huge as Ethan described, and even taller than I imagined. A real giant. He stands before me, casting me in an eerie shadow. 'Welcome, Isabel, from the House of Samartyne. Our gift to you is that of forethought and insight.'

He ambles back and now I am facing the immortal, who is, I am told, of no fixed sex. In my thoughts I wonder how I should refer to him or her. 'It' sounds disrespectful. The caped figure comes to stand before me, and in a firm, yet gentle, voice enlightens me, 'You may refer to me as Lorian. My House is that of the Guard, and I welcome you with the gift of sixth sense.' Lorian pauses and I raise my eyes a little but can't bring them to meet the immortal's. 'And now that our gifts have been revealed to you, Isabel, I ask whether you are willing to accept them, and take up your position as Apprentice?'

Lorian must be looking straight at me, but it feels as if this immortal creature's gaze is going right through me instead. I'm thankful for the stool beneath me, the edges of which I find myself gripping with frozen fingers.

'Isabel,' Lorian continues. 'Do you swear your fealty to the Guard, promise to serve and defend on its behalf, adhering to its secret codes, in readiness for the final conflict with the Goddess of Chaos and her armies?'

I swallow hard and nod.

Friendly laughter erupts around the room. Lorian explains gently, 'Your vocal promise is required.'

'Oh, of course,' I stammer, feeling my face heat up. 'I

do. I swear!'

Lorian smiles. I don't see it, but I sense it; and in that moment I feel a compelling urge to look upon Lorian's face. If I had a second longer to think about it, I wouldn't do it. But I don't think, I just lift my head to meet the immortal's gaze full on.

What I see there shocks me, sending me reeling backwards in body and mind, sucking the breath right out of me. I fall off the stool and land on my rear on the warm, shiny floor.

Lorian moves back, motioning to Ethan, who comes rushing over and helps me stand. I quickly get back on the stool.

'It's OK,' Ethan assures me. 'Others who have looked on Lorian's face have dropped dead.'

He's obviously joking; everyone is laughing, Lorian the hardest of all. Ethan's words are calming, but it isn't fear or anything that has this strange effect on me, nor the transparency of Lorian's colourless yet brilliantly shimmering skin. It's the shape and colour of Lorian's eyes that has affected me so – oval, and deeply violet.

So much like Arkarian's.

Chapter Twenty-four

Ethan

Isabel's initiation goes well. Arkarian, especially, is beside himself. 'Those gifts are the best I've heard them endow on anyone in the past six hundred years!'

Isabel can't help being caught up in his excitement. I'm happy for her too. She is after all my Apprentice. So after the ceremony Arkarian decides we should celebrate. He takes us on horseback to see a famous Greek play – a tragedy written two hundred years earlier by a playwright called Sophocles. Arkarian explains each scene as it unfolds. Isabel is ecstatic, on a natural high. Even though the play is graphic, deeply moving and somewhat disturbing in its intensity, she still comes out smiling as she wipes at her tears.

On the way back to the palace Arkarian detours so that we can get a look at some of the buildings of this ancient city-state. The Parthenon, built about two centuries earlier, is by far the most spectacular that he shows us. Made entirely of marble, it stands like a monument to the gods on top of the Acropolis, its many columns reaching towards the sky.

On any other occasion I would be thrilled with the

afternoon's sightseeing and play watching, but my stomach is in hard knots, making it difficult to enjoy anything. My trial is set for dawn tomorrow, and there's a rumour that it will go on for hours. What the hell are the Tribunal expecting that should take so long? How much evidence and how many witnesses do they have against me?

As we dismount, a servant leads our horses away to be cared for, and Arkarian takes us inside the much cooler interior of the palace. Once in the spacious foyer he puts his arm across my shoulder. 'Settle down, Ethan. You forget how respected you are among the Tribunal. They love your work, they applaud you, they laugh with you.'

His words are comforting, and for the rest of the late afternoon, as Isabel and I pass our time in the peaceful palace courtyard, I try to do as Arkarian says. But it's just too hard. This is the life I was born to live. Being a Guard is in my blood. I know this with every breath of my body. What if they take it away from me?

After a light supper, Isabel goes to her room and I go straight to bed, thoroughly exhausted. But it feels as if I've only just closed my eyes when Arkarian starts shaking me. 'Get up, Ethan. It's nearly dawn. You can't be late, the Tribunal is already gathering.'

I dress quickly in the all-black outfit provided, putting the cape on last, with the deep hood right over my head. If nobody sees my face, so much the better. But Arkarian has other ideas. 'The hood must be down, Ethan. You know better than that.'

I grunt but do as I'm told and follow Arkarian down the long hallway to stand outside the double doors of the Tribunal chamber. My hands feel useless all of a sudden, as if they're not attached to my arms. I clasp them together to stop this irrational sensation.

'Relax, Ethan.' Arkarian tries to calm me. 'Stop expecting the worst.'

'I want my wings, Arkarian.'

'I know. And you will have them.'

I raise my eyebrows at him. 'Even now?'

'Your breach was small, Ethan. The Tribunal will judge you fairly. It was only your first offence.'

A side door swivels and Carter, dressed in brown and tan, makes his way towards us. 'What if there were a second breach, in as many weeks?' I ask Arkarian in a whisper.

Colour drains from his face and I don't need to be a Truthseer to be able to read his thoughts. I open my mind to him, recalling the incident in the classroom with Isabel, showing him the piece of paper with his scrawled title written in my hand. He grips my elbow in a form of silent support as Carter pauses before us. 'Arkarian, Ethan, we meet again, and under such interesting circumstances.'

Every muscle in my body tenses. How I would love to take my restless fists and lodge them dead centre of this man's face!

Arkarian clears his throat loudly to smother my thoughts. I take the hint before anyone beyond these walls picks up on them. Carter, I know, is not a Truthseer. He can't hear my thoughts. But all nine members of the Tribunal are. The doors open inwards and the three of us turn to enter. Just then Isabel comes running down the hall. 'Wait!'

Arkarian shakes his head. 'I've lined up a leisurely day of baths and remedial massages for you.'

She eyes Carter, giving him an uncomfortable nod. His eyebrows lift as if Isabel's presence here only confirms what he suspected all along. He bows to her slightly. 'Always remember my words, Isabel.'

Arkarian looks at me with a query. I give a slight shrug. 'I don't know what he's talking about.'

Carter smiles smugly, giving us a small salute before entering the Tribunal chamber. Arkarian's gaze lingers on the man, but he soon remembers Isabel, who is standing beside us, fidgeting.

'Arkarian, I don't want a leisurely bath or massage. I want to see what's going on. I want to be there. For Ethan,' she adds, looking down at her entwined and twisting fingers.

Arkarian releases a long sigh, then closes his eyes in concentration. I swear he's communicating with someone – Lorian, at a guess – seeking permission. His eyes flick open. 'You're allowed to watch on the condition that you don't utter a single sound. Do you understand? No matter what you hear or how it goes for Ethan. All right, Isabel?'

'I promise.'

'Good. Now, Ethan, let's get this ordeal under way. But if there is one piece of advice I can give you, it's to keep your thoughts at peace and your mind open. Remember your own gifts from the Tribunal. Seek them out, refresh your spirit.'

I try to absorb these words, but my heart is hammering so hard it sounds as if it's shifted position to somewhere between my ears. So all I can do in the end is follow Arkarian inside. He walks me to the centre of the ring, produces a stool for me to sit on, then walks outside the circle to a position behind a crystal stand

151

on a square marble platform. He lays his palms flat on the crystal surface as if drawing strength from it, then begins to recite the statement he has prepared. He starts by talking about my adventurous and courageous nature and how earnestly I have taken on my new role as Trainer. He makes a point of how this enthusiasm, combined with the expectation to succeed in the eyes of the Tribunal, in order to attain my wings, pressured me into the action for which I am presently on trial.

About halfway through his kind words I realise what he's doing – putting the onus of blame for my faults entirely on his own shoulders. He's trying to get the Tribunal to blame *him* for my errors.

Arkarian flicks me an impassioned keep-your-thoughts-to-yourself kind of look. But I can't do that. I can't stand here and let him take the blame for my mistakes. No way. So I try to override his vocal words with contrary thoughts of my own, explaining how it was my own foolishness, my own attempt at impressing Isabel, my own stupidity that led me to breach the Guard's secret code.

Arkarian is still talking in my defence, but he's exasperated now. When he finishes, Lorian thanks him and asks him to sit down. He does, but only after giving me a warning stare to shut the hell up.

Carter is called next. He doesn't have a speech prepared, which surprises me. I thought he'd be only too keen to voice his disapproval. Instead he waits for questions. The first concerns my breach of the code. He recounts more or less how it happened, from his viewpoint as the teacher in the class at the time.

'Did anybody else witness this act?' Penbarin asks

from his seat to the right of Lorian.

'Only one, a girl by the name of Rochelle Thallimar. She had a clear view and took serious notice.'

Oh, no, not Rochelle! Here I'd been hoping no one else saw. This affair is going to turn out worse than expected, I feel it in my bones. Arkarian gives me a look that tells me not to give up hope.

'Do we have any instruction on this girl?'

Lady Devine answers Penbarin. 'Rochelle's mother died in a suspicious accident in the home when Rochelle was but five years old. Her father was, and still is, a violent man.'

This news has me riveted.

'Rochelle lived with her violent father for many years, following his restless footsteps around their country. He remarried twice, and Rochelle gets along well with her latest stepmother. Two years ago Rochelle saved the woman's life by physically stopping her father from bludgeoning her to death with a baseball bat. The woman was so severely beaten around the head that she fell into a coma from which she didn't arise for fifteen days.'

Gasps erupt around the circle. Isabel's mouth drops open, her eyes fill with disgust.

'Gerard Thallimar was charged and convicted and is now serving an eight-year prison sentence. Rochelle moved house once again, this time with her recovering stepmother to Veridian –' Here Lady Devine pauses, gathers her thoughts, then continues, 'I mean Angel Falls – in hopes of starting a new life.'

This is news to me. I want to hear it, and yet it feels like an invasion of Rochelle's privacy, and so part of me wants Lady Devine to stop.

But she doesn't. 'A ponderous chain of negativity surrounds her, which could be the result of her difficult childhood, or something more sinister.'

'What is your conclusion, Lady Devine?' Lorian asks.

'The girl has a strong mind …'

What are they doing, speculating like this? It just doesn't feel right.

'And I do believe the potential to create evil is strong within her. I feel—'

'*Stop!*' I can't help calling out. At the same time I wonder why I'm defending a girl I don't even like, the girl who purposely broke up one of my longest friendships; but whatever has happened to Rochelle is her business. My little trick in the classroom should not have resulted in her private life being assessed in such a judgemental manner.

Lorian looks to me. 'Do you have something to say, Ethan?'

I suck in a deep breath. 'Rochelle is not evil.'

'What makes you so sure?'

'I don't know exactly,' I reply honestly. 'Instinct, maybe. I can't really say. But I have met this girl.'

'Tell us what you know of her.'

Hell, where do I begin? Certainly I can't tell them about— I stop my thoughts quickly before I reveal more unsavoury qualities in Rochelle's nature. 'She's strong-willed and she does things that most people wouldn't, but I don't think it's because she's evil. I think she does these things simply to create mischief.'

'We would have no need for the Guard, Ethan, if it wasn't for the Goddess of Chaos all those thousands of years ago who sought to create mischief. It sounds as if Rochelle fits right in with the Goddess's ultimate plan.'

'No, Rochelle is not evil. I can't explain it, I just know.'

'You must give us more than that.'

'It's a gut feeling. I'm sorry, that's all I have.'

'Hmm.' Lorian lets the subject lie, then asks Carter if anyone else saw the breach.

'No,' he says, then clears his throat. 'But the *second* breach was witnessed by every member of the class.'

These words cause a hum of murmurs to erupt around the room. Lorian quietens everyone with one powerful look. Carter is asked to explain. He holds up the scrunched-up note with *TruthMaster* written in my handwriting, explaining how he came to find it sitting openly on a school desk for all to see.

A couple of Tribunal members start murmuring among themselves, and I feel others are murmuring to each other without speaking out loud. They're all jumping to the wrong conclusions. 'It wasn't like that!'

Arkarian warns me with a sharp look.

Isabel stands up as if to come into the circle, but Arkarian takes her by the waist and pulls her down beside him.

'Quiet!' Lorian brings the room to complete silence. 'Ethan, your version, please.'

I take a deep breath, attempting to regain my equilibrium. I need them all to believe me, to understand that I didn't intend to expose Arkarian's title in public. That it wasn't at all the way Carter describes. I also don't want to implicate Isabel in any way. Not that she would be blamed for any wrongdoing. She's my Apprentice; responsibility for her is all mine. 'The paper was not meant to be seen by anyone other than my Apprentice, and it wouldn't have attracted the slightest attention if

155

Croc-face—' I stop, seared to my seat. I don't dare look at anyone; the silence is enough to deafen me. I swallow hard and continue as if I hadn't blurted out those derogatory words. 'If Mr *Carter* hadn't drawn attention to it, that is. I was careful—'

'As careful as you were when Rochelle saw your stunt with the pen?' Lorian asks, already knowing the answer.

'I admit I made a mistake in that instance. But the title written on this paper was seen by no one else in that classroom.'

'Can you swear to that?'

Can I? Just how careful was I, really?

Lorian turns to Carter, who is forced into an admission of sorts. 'It's possible the word itself was not examined except by Ethan, Isabel and myself. Of course at the time I was unaware that Isabel was chosen for the Guard. I had my suspicions, but—'

Lorian holds up a hand and Carter shuts up.

After a short silence, where I suspect the Tribunal are sharing their thoughts without speech, Lorian shocks me by asking Carter for his direct personal opinion of my character, and whether he thinks I'm ready for the power of flight.

Arkarian jumps up. 'Why not ask me? I've known Ethan for many years, his thoughts and his deeds. I know what's in his heart.'

Lorian waves Arkarian away. 'That may be so, Arkarian, but Marcus has also known Ethan for many years, and spends much time with him in the classroom. Your opinion has already been given, by the way, with every burst of thought you've inadvertently shot our way. Loud and clear.'

Arkarian, suitably put down, sits without saying another word, and Lorian nods in Carter's direction. Carter's eyes shift to mine, narrowed in an assessing manner. 'Under my observation,' he begins, and I groan – thinking just get it over with. 'I do believe the boy has enormous potential.'

These words come as a complete surprise. My eyes search his, wondering where this compliment is coming from.

'I sense, as well as see to a certain extent, a strength of courage, determination and great skill.' Amazed I watch as Penbarin, Arabella and the others nod and murmur in agreement with each other. 'But I believe he still has a lot to learn, and that this will only happen with a maturity he has yet to develop. Therefore it is my opinion that Ethan Roberts is not ready for his wings.'

Among a general hum of murmurs Carter is dismissed with the thanks of the Tribunal. He leaves the room and a silence follows, where I know the members are all communicating with each other. Arkarian and Isabel share a worried but hopeful look in my direction. After what seems like an eternity, Lorian stands and motions to me to stand also. The immortal approaches me and raises both hands over the top of my head. In a flash, the room fills with blinding light. I try not to flinch. This is just a gift Lorian is bestowing on me. 'When you first received the gifts of the Houses you were but a child. With this light I refresh those gifts …'

Lorian steps back and the light contracts so that it now only covers my head and shoulders. My scalp tingles with the sensation of electric charges, which quickly make their way through my head to the rest of my body. A strong vision pierces my subconscious to illuminate the day when I was five and the Lords of the Houses bent over me, bestowing me with their gifts. I see them clearly again – Lady Devine, her floor-length red hair swaying and brushing across my trembling knees. 'Animation,' she whispers, and this time I understand. I have an affinity with all that is real and all that is unreal. That's why I can move objects and create illusions. The gift of animation enhances my inherited skills. Meridian ambles over next, endowing me with the gift of sanity, of which I was in sore need at the time. Brystianne follows with the gift of forgiveness, and Sir Syford brings enlightenment, so that I may one day be able to share my knowledge. Elenna offers physical skill and safety. Alexandon, from the House of Criers, gives me courage, just as he gave Isabel. Arabella, with her translucent icy skin, seemingly floats towards me, weaving her hands in a pattern over my small head, and offers me the talent of seeing reality through deception. Then Penbarin, the last of them, approaches slowly, aware that his enormous size would frighten this little boy. He smiles at me and caresses the side of my childish face. 'Insight and belief in thyself,' I recall him saying clearly now.

I shake my head as the light lifts off me and my boyish memories disappear. I look around and see everyone seated as they were, but the sensation lingers that each of the Lords has somehow touched my mind.

Lorian moves closer without my noticing. 'And now I renew my gift to you,' the immortal says, raising a hand again to hover slightly above my head. 'I offer the

158

light of maturity to fill you and strengthen your inner spirit.'

With these words my whole body jerks as if struck by a bolt of lightning. For a moment I feel as if I'm going to pass out. Lorian's head bows slightly. 'Ethan Roberts, it is the unanimous decision of this Tribunal that you shall not be stripped of your newly appointed Trainer status.'

Regaining my balance, I feel a flush of relief sweep through me. These words give me hope that all is not lost.

'Trainer is one of the most important positions of the Guard. Not all members are capable of carrying out this responsibility, to nurture the growth of our future armies.'

Yes! This is good news. Too good, it seems, as suddenly Lorian's voice takes on a serious edge. 'But the power of flight is something else entirely, and it is therefore with reluctance that this Tribunal must rule that you will *not* be issued your wings now nor on your next birthday.'

I can't stop myself from asking, 'Then when should I expect them?'

The immortal looks straight at me with eyes that make me want to run. I try hard to hold this powerful stare. My entire body trembles with the effort. Lorian says carefully, so that I hear and understand every word, 'The decision to withhold your wings, Ethan, is indefinite.'

It is the worst judgement ever.

Chapter Twenty-five

Isabel

From the moment the Tribunal passed down its judgement, Ethan vowed to win back their belief in him. For the last week he's been driven in preparing me for my first real mission, even though just where and when that will be, Arkarian refuses to give us one clue. So every day we train in our favourite grounds, a small clearing on the far side of the lake, surrounded by mountainous woodland and rising cliffs. There's enough privacy, especially now that winter is fast approaching and snow has fallen on higher ground.

I've started making good progress with the sword, and Ethan works diligently at enhancing my ability to draw out the gifts bestowed on me in initiation. The only one that has revealed itself so far is the ability to see clearly in any light, courtesy of Arabella from the House of Sky and Water. Reading by the moon, while sitting in my own bedroom in the evening, is a thrilling experience. But the other psychic power I'm supposed to have from birth still eludes us, and this drives Ethan crazy with frustration. At least my healing skills are improving, though too slowly for my own liking. It's the one and, so far, only power I have, so I would like it to be honed and ready, should it be needed.

'Here!' Ethan calls, dodging the tip of my blunted dagger again. 'Faster, Isabel! Not all your assailants will wait until *you* decide from which direction they're going to come at you.'

'You're so funny, Ethan. How about this?' While appearing as if I intend to strike high, I fake a downward thrust, ending up with the dagger pointing directly at Ethan's jugular.

He raises his hands and steps back from the dagger. 'Hmm, how well I've taught you!'

'If my fingers weren't so frozen I'd run this blunted dagger tip right through to your other side.'

He laughs, and goes and adds a couple of dry timber pieces to the fire. 'How about a hot chocolate?'

'Yes, please.' We've taken to bringing supplies with us for sustenance and warmth. Today, it's powdered chocolate drinks.

I squat beside Ethan as he prepares the drinks, warming my fingers by the fire. The sound of a twig crackling makes us both jerk to the side, startled. 'Did you hear that?'

Ethan nods silently as he stands and looks around, a frown buried deep between his brows. But then I spot the source of our fear. A small brown rabbit has ventured out of its warren, probably to warm itself by our fire, or perhaps it has caught the scent of our chocolate drinks.

'Look down, Ethan.' I point towards the edge of the clearing.

Ethan peers at the small brown rabbit, his frown

growing deeper.

'What's wrong?'

'I think it's hurt. Look how it leans slightly to one side. Is that blood on its hindquarter?'

I stand to get a better perspective, being careful not to startle the timid creature, but apparently my concern isn't necessary. The rabbit makes its way slowly towards me, not stopping until it reaches my feet. I stare at it with an open mouth, then at Ethan. 'Can you believe this?'

The rabbit sits up on its hindquarters, front paws dangling in the air, its small round eyes appealing to me in a way that is almost human.

Carefully I pick it up, as it is obviously injured.

'It wants you to heal it,' Ethan says. 'It senses you're a healer.'

'Of animals?'

'Why not? If you're gifted, who's to say it should be restricted to humans only?'

'Wow! So what's wrong with the rabbit?'

He gives a little laugh. 'You're the healer, Isabel. You find out.'

I lower myself to the ground cross-legged, holding the rabbit in my lap, careful not to move it unnecessarily. It doesn't squirm, just keeps looking up at me with those round, pleading eyes. Moving my hands over its limbs, I feel them gently, soon finding a broken bone and sensing the tissues and torn ligaments within. 'How could this happen, out here in the woods?'

'Hmm, good question.' Ethan squats down beside me, but his mind is on the surrounding woodland. He scours it for signs of something.

I go to work on the rabbit, soothing it with gentle

whispers, willing its injured tissues, ligaments and bones to mend. As I do this, I see it all in my mind, the bone reknitting, blood returning to their vessels, inflamed tissues healing without a scar. The rabbit gives a sudden jerk, then jumps off my lap, bounding and leaping with incredible speed in the direction from which it came.

'I'd say it's healed,' Ethan says, his voice a little in awe.

'That was incredible! I actually saw the healing taking place in my mind.'

'Maybe that's been your stumbling block. Visualising.' As he speaks, he stands up and walks around the outer edges of the clearing.

I go and stand beside him. 'What's wrong, Ethan?'

'I don't know, just a feeling.'

'Like you had at the trial?'

He gives me a pained look. Instantly I'm regretful. I didn't mean to remind him of the Tribunal and his sticking up for Rochelle. Those memories are still too raw for him to discuss. He hasn't said a word.

He turns away and starts putting out the fire. 'I think we should leave.'

'Is it the rabbit that's making you uneasy?'

'Yes and no. Why that rabbit came to you is not what's puzzling me; animals sense things sometimes better than humans. It's how it got the injury that has me worried.'

'There's no one up here, Ethan. Who would come? It's too cold.'

'We're here. And that rabbit didn't break its own leg.'

'Who would do such a thing to a gentle creature like that?'

'Maybe the question is not *who*, Isabel, but *what*?' In seconds he has the fire put out. 'Pack your things. Let's get out of here before some wild animal comes tearing out of the woods looking to break one of our legs.'

I can't tell whether he's joking or serious, only that he's feeling a sudden urgency. His instinct is prickling again. Quickly I locate where I put my jumper and the few other things I brought with me. We head down the mountain and make it almost halfway before I realise I left the most important thing of all – my backpack, which has all my school stuff in it. We headed up there today straight from school, in order to make use of the afternoon light. 'I have to go back.'

He doesn't stop walking. 'No way! It's too late.'

'I left my school bag.'

'What! How could you be so—?'

'Well, I did. You go on. It won't take me long if I run.'

He grabs my arm as I spin around. 'Forget it, Isabel.'

'I need my bag for school tomorrow.'

'We'll hike up there in the morning and get it.'

'But it's not waterproof. The frost and dew will get right in. All my books will be ruined, let alone if it snows overnight. It'll only take me ten or twenty minutes from here.'

My arguments don't make any difference. 'No, Isabel. We're not going back for it. You said you trusted me, now prove it.'

Silently we make it all the way down. When we get to my house I head straight inside. Peering through the front window, I wait until I can't see Ethan any more, then wait another full minute, making myself count every second. When I'm sure he's on his way home, I

164

take off out the front door at a fast run. There's nothing up that mountain; we train there practically every day. Ethan's just jumpy 'cause that rabbit's injury was unusual. But it could have injured itself. How are we to know? And Ethan's been so serious since the Tribunal hearing in Athens, adhering strictly to the codes and rules. He's blowing this incident right out of perspective.

I get to the top, panting hard after running uphill for most of the way. It's starting to darken now, but I can still see clearly, the dim light no hindrance any more. To my amazement, Arabella's gift of seeing by any light keeps strengthening. At this rate I'm going to have to learn how to control it so that I can turn it off when it becomes a hindrance more than a help.

I swing my gaze around the clearing, but my backpack is not in the place I left it. Did Ethan move it at some stage? I can't remember, but I doubt it, he was too busy keeping to his schedule. Then where is it? A prickling sensation runs down every fine hair on my back as a sense of evil slowly settles into my chest. Is this Lorian's gift of sixth sense I'm becoming aware of?

A rustling of leaves in the woodland to my right jerks my whole body, making my limbs go stiff. I'm fast freaking out and try to slow my racing thoughts. But another sound, the crunching of leaves underfoot, is way too real, and I know now for certain that something is out there, something that has a decidedly evil feel to it.

'Ethan?'

I'm not really calling him as I know he's probably soaking in a hot bath right now, warming his frozen limbs, as I should be, but I need to hear my voice and the sound of a familiar name. Perhaps this sense of evil is a figment of my imagination.

A shadow passes through the trees to my right. It's darkening quickly now as I stand here frozen to the spot, hardly breathing, my heart pounding at a staggering pace, but the descending darkness has no effect on my vision. The shadow moves quickly and stealthily, especially for its apparent size. As it draws nearer it takes on a more tangible shape. It's a man, a large man, tall and broad and wearing black leather boots with an animal-skin coat secured at the waist by a silver-studded belt. He breaks through the edge of the woodland and makes his way with heavy footsteps through the clearing to where I'm standing, frozen to the spot. My back pack is in his hand. Releasing his fingers it falls to the ground.

Move, girl. Move it now! If you turn and run you may have a chance of beating this man down the mountain. Somehow I get the feeling he wouldn't follow me, but my legs have stubbornly decided not to move. It occurs to me that this man is using some sort of power over me.

He draws closer, within arm's reach, and the sight of him now makes me light-headed and dizzy. 'I've seen you before.'

His voice is rough and guttural. 'We've met in your dreams.'

'What do you want?'

His head cocks to one side. 'To take you to a place where it is midnight every day.'

'What? I don't understand.'

His neck straightens and with one large gloved hand he pulls at the top of his head. He's wearing a mask, I

166

realise, and now he's taking it off. What I see beneath the mask makes me want to retch violently. My stomach contracts with cramps, making me double over. The man's face is hideous, one side badly scarred and missing parts.

He lifts my face with one massive finger to the underside of my chin. 'Now do you understand?'

'I … I only see an angry and bitter man.'

He roars, so loud I have to cover my ears so as not to damage the fine bones inside. It's the roar, I think, that shatters my frozen state. I don't need any sixth sense to know what's good for me now. Slowly I reach for my bag and start edging backwards, putting space between me and the deformed and hostile man before me.

He watches with a sly knowing look coming from his one yellow eye. 'You cannot run from me, Isabel.'

His knowing my name sends chills through all of my bones.

'I can find you anywhere, even in your sleep.' And then he adds teasingly, 'Ask the boy called Ethan. Tell him he can reach me through his illusions. Tell him I will come.'

Chapter Twenty-six

Ethan

If there's one thing I'm learning about my Apprentice, it's that she's as stubborn and headstrong as a mule. So when I walk away from her house I decide to go back and check. It's starting to darken earlier now that winter's almost here, but this won't stop Isabel going back up that mountain; her sight is incredible now, even in the dark.

Her mother Coral answers the door, wrapped in a dark-blue towelling robe, her hair wet as if she just stepped out of a shower. 'I heard the door bang a few minutes ago, Ethan. I'll just go see if she's in her room.'

A few minutes later she comes back shaking her head. 'It doesn't look as if she's been in there all afternoon. I could've sworn I heard the door.'

I thank her, my heart starting to thud. She picks up on my concern. 'Is something wrong? Matt should be home any second. He might know where she is. He keeps a close eye on her, you probably know that.'

'Yeah … I have noticed.'

'Should I be concerned, Ethan?'

'No, no. Not at all. I just wanted to tell her something. I'm sure she'll turn up soon. I'll give a call later.'

'All right, dear.'

Finally I get away, and take off at a sprint. With each pounding leap a sense of urgency increases inside, just why I'm not sure. I can't pinpoint where this danger is coming from. It's my gut instinct working overtime, I think, but the sense of something sinister in those woods tonight is too strong to ignore. Maybe I should have been sensing this danger all along during the days of Isabel's training, but only now, since Lorian's strengthening of my gifts, am I picking it up.

About two-thirds of the way up I hear the roar.

My heart practically stops. No way. It can't be! I've heard that roar before a million times, but only in my dreams.

I take off again, sprinting as hard as I can. I'm not far from the lake now, but it's almost completely dark, and I keep running into scrub and vines and logs and branches. Then I run straight into Isabel. We hit so hard we both fall to the side, rolling over and over each other downhill about twenty metres until our sides wedge solid against a fallen tree.

'Ethan!'

'Isabel, are you all right?'

'Yeah, I'm fine now. Sorry, I was looking over my shoulder and didn't see you.'

'What was that roar I heard?'

She gets up urgently, locates her bag, and starts dragging on my arm, yanking me over the top of the log. 'We have to get out of here.'

'What did you see up there?'

She's running now, still dragging on my arm. 'My worst nightmare.'

I stop at her words, but Isabel keeps going. 'Come on, Ethan. I'm not going back for you, that's for sure.'

I find her words ironic and run to catch up. 'You'll go back for a backpack, but not for me, huh?'

She sees no humour at all. 'Shut up, Ethan. Just keep running.'

We get to the bottom and I make her go inside to let her mother know she's home and will be sitting outside talking to me for a few minutes. She looks at me weird, but does it anyway. It takes her ages to come back out because Matt is home now and she had to make up some story about why she was late and why I want to see her.

She hands me a sports drink, sliding herself on to the top railing of the wooden fence I'm leaning against. She drinks half her bottle, then wipes her mouth with the back of her sleeve. 'I should have listened to you.'

I wait for her to go on. She stares into the darkness. I wonder what she can see; probably a host of night creatures that most people wouldn't even imagine are out there. 'I saw something, up there by the lake.'

'What was it?'

She shifts her head sideways to mine. 'A man.'

'*A man?*' I don't know what I expected, but my sense of danger, of evil, felt like more than just 'a man'.

'He was huge.'

Goosebumps break out on my skin in anticipation of what's to follow.

'He wore a mask, but then he took it off, and his face was …' Her hands cover her own face for a moment. 'Oh, Ethan, it was hideous.'

Words try to form in my dry mouth. 'What did this man's face look like?'

Her eyes open wide. 'It was only half a face, with train tracks zigzagging down the deformed side.'

'*What?*'

'Scars, Ethan.' She misinterprets my exclamation.

'No, I mean, how can that be?'

She shrugs. 'I don't know. Don't you believe me?'

'Of course I … It's just, you're describing someone that isn't real.'

She jumps off the railing and turns on me. 'Oh, yeah? You should have been there—'

'And you *shouldn't* have been there.'

'Oh, so because I didn't listen to you, you're not going to believe me?'

'That's not what I meant.'

'No, but I can see it in your face. It may be dark out here now, Ethan, but I can see your expression as if I were holding a torch under your chin.'

'Isabel …' I try to reassure her, but her description is way too real. Or, I should say, imaginary. It describes what is in my head, in my dreams, the nightmares that have plagued me ever since my sister died of that horrible brain aneurism when she was ten. How can Isabel see this man, this creature, when he only exists in my subconscious?

'Did he … did this creature …?'

'Hurt me or anything?'

I nod. She says, 'No. But I think he threatened me. And I think he was playing with me too.'

'What do you mean?'

'Well, he had my backpack, like somehow he knew that's what I'd come back for, and he said that he wanted to take me to a place where it was midnight every day.'

Her words could have come straight from one of my nightmares.

'Ethan? Are you all right? You look as if you're about to pass out.'

She makes me sit cross-legged on the cold hard ground. 'What is it, Ethan? Why do you look so stunned?'

I'm trying to figure this out through my suddenly numb brain. 'You must have been dreaming, and somehow we connected.'

'What! I wasn't dreaming up there, believe me. One second he was there, his massive hand under my chin, making sure I saw his hideous features—'

'He touched you?'

'Yeah, just for second. He spoke, then disappeared.' She snaps her fingers. 'Poof, just like that, he's gone.'

'What did he say?'

'Something about running from him, and how I can't. And that he could find me anywhere, even in my sleep. He called me by my name and he knew yours too. He said, "Ask the boy called Ethan. Tell him he can reach me through his illusions. Tell him I will come".'

'No way!'

'Who is this man?'

I stare at her. How can I explain when I don't really know myself? 'I don't know who it is. Up until a few minutes ago I thought this creature was a figment of my imagination, the lingering nightmare of a scared and traumatised child.'

She stares back at me hard, her hands on her hips. 'That man was real, Ethan. As real as you and me.'

It hits me where and from whom I can find the

answers. I start to take off at a run, but not in the direction of home.

'Hey,' Isabel calls. 'Where are you going?'

'To see the one person who can give me the answers I need.'

Chapter Twenty-seven

Ethan

Arkarian is waiting for me in his chambers. I don't give him a chance to explain. I'm too hyped up, my head brimming with questions. 'Did you see what happened?'

'No, I didn't, but the feel of him was all over this mountain. Is Isabel all right?'

'Yeah, she's fine. Who was that? And what was he doing outside my dreams?'

'Ethan, I think you'd better sit down. Are you sure Isabel's all right?'

'Yes!'

He produces a stool. I shove it out of my way. 'Tell me, Arkarian, who was that creature?'

He sits and draws in a calming breath, taking too long to answer.

'Come on!'

'His name is Marduke.'

'I know that name. Tell me from where.'

'He murdered your sister.'

His words hit hard. For a second I feel ill, I think I'm going to fall. Quickly Arkarian waves the stool back into position beneath me. 'Are you telling me my nightmares are grounded in reality?'

He takes too long to answer. 'Arkarian!'

'They have distorted slightly over the years. You were an eyewitness to your sister's murder, but nobody believed you. Of course your description was hard for the average adult, or even the average police officer, to imagine – tall as a tree, broad as a bear, one yellow eye, half a missing face, hands as large as watermelons, and a roar like a thousand lions in a cave. Is it any wonder they sent you to therapists?'

'But you knew I was telling the truth.'

'Yes, but it was decided that your young traumatised mind couldn't cope with the reality. You were losing your sanity, and at such a young age.'

'So you took me in and lied to me all this time.'

'We protected you only, Ethan. We never lied to you. We nurtured you through the hardest period of your life – losing your sister that way, it was tragic. Look what effect it's had on your parents, your father especially. He hasn't been the same man since.'

His words have me thinking. 'How do you know what type of man Dad was? Did you know him or something?'

He goes quiet and sort of still. 'You know my job is to observe. I've been around for a long time.'

I sense he's leaving something out, but Dad's not my concern right now, so I let the matter drop. 'Tell me why this creature, this monster named Marduke, is after Isabel.'

'I don't know.'

'That's not good enough. You know everything.'

'You flatter me, Ethan. What did he say to make you think he wants Isabel?'

'He threatened her.'

'What! How?'

I groan. 'I don't know – something about being able to get to her anywhere, even in her dreams. Mostly, I think she felt his threat inside. Will he harm her, Arkarian? Can you tell me this?'

He looks at me, clearly puzzled. 'I'll speak with Lorian. There are plans that may need altering now.'

'What plans?'

'I can't tell you.'

'More secrets? Are you lot playing with our lives? We're mortals, Arkarian. We die.'

'I'm mortal too, Ethan.'

'I don't believe you. You're six hundred years old.'

'Yes, but I've only lived that long because of my skill, you know that. It's this same skill that keeps me isolated from the rest of the world.' He holds out his hand producing a dagger in his palm, handle facing me. 'If you take this blade and put it through my heart, I will bleed red blood, profusely and quickly. And I will die.'

'Then tell me why your eyes are coloured violet? And don't feed me that line about how they change with time. I've seen no mortal with purple eyes. Only Lorian.'

He takes a calming breath even though it's me who needs one. 'I don't know why my eyes are this colour. I was born in France to a beautiful young girl who had no husband. My mother died in childbirth – mine, so I don't know what colour her eyes were, and I have no idea who my father was, though there were many rumours. I think my eyes were once blue. And they do change, Ethan. That's one of the many reasons I can't circulate in your mortal world any more.'

What he says makes sense and some of my initial

176

anger starts to dwindle. 'So this creature, Marduke, he's six hundred years old too?'

'Older.'

'Is he immortal?'

'The only immortal I've met is Lorian. I have yet to meet the Goddess. So don't worry, Marduke *can* die, and he will when the time is right.'

And then, finally, the pieces start to fit. 'He's the one in the Prophecy, the evil one, isn't he? How does it go?' I ask.

'*The traitor who will come and go.*'

'Yes. But doesn't it mention where he was a god of something?'

'Not that I know of.'

'But surely he must be descended from an immortal if he's older than, well, you for instance.'

'Not necessarily. He just has the skill of retaining youth.'

'Yeah, but you stopped aging at eighteen, Marduke didn't.'

Arkarian doesn't answer, and I wonder about his ability to stop aging. Could it be inherited, or a gift that can be awarded like wings. 'I wonder who you're descended from?'

'I'm sure we'll never know. I haven't discovered my ancestry and I'm hardly likely to after this great length of time.'

Whether he has any clues he's obviously not going to elaborate, nor even tell me what some of those rumours were about his biological father. I try thinking of the words of the Prophecy to help me figure this mystery out, but it's been so long since I heard them. That's when the idea hits me. 'I want to read the

Prophecy again. I was too young to take any of it in when you first showed it to me.'

He hesitates for a long moment and I think he's going to deny my request. 'Do you remember the way?'

'I think I could find it.'

'Promise me you'll stick to the rules. Follow them and no danger will harm you.'

'All right, but can Isabel come? She sure would come in handy, what with her being able to see in any kind of light these days.'

He laughs. 'Not a bad gift, I wish I had it.'

'So can she? She's an official Apprentice now. She should know it all – the truth, you know?'

Reluctantly, he agrees. 'All right. But check in here before you leave. If you take too long, I'll send a search party.'

'We won't get lost.'

'Perhaps, perhaps not, but you will get tired. And neither of you has wings.'

'We'll be careful.'

'You'll have to go soon, though. Isabel's first mission is coming up and she needs to improve her healing skills.'

I could tell him how much progress she's making in that area, but exhaustion is starting to kick in big time. I need to get home to a nice warm bed. Gripping his shoulders lightly, I say good-night. But as I start to leave, Arkarian comes out with the weirdest thing.

'Has your father ever asked you strange questions, or wondered where you go when you sleep?'

It takes me by surprise. But I'm too tired even to wonder why he's asking and just throw him a bemused look.

Chapter Twenty-eight

Isabel

Ethan is full of surprises. It appears we're going on some sort of adventure, way underground, to read an inscription off the remains of an ancient wall. It's early Saturday morning, the sun just starting to make an appearance on the distant horizon. Except for some early-rising wildlife, no one's awake. Why would they be? It's simply too cold.

I have to leave a note, letting Mum and Matt know I won't be home until late, as apparently this trip will take all day. It's just as well I'm leaving before either of them wakes, especially Matt. I've had enough of his questions and suspicions about my relationship with Ethan. But just what kind of relationship is it? Ever since that kiss in John of Gaunt's bedroom my head's been in a spin. Ethan hasn't made another move on me, and even though he explained how that kiss was nothing more than a diversion, the fact is, it did happen. And, well, I really liked it. Ethan is pretty clear that we're only just friends – he certainly hasn't tried anything since, not even when we get real close in training. We spend so much time together these days, and being with Ethan should be my dream come true, except the romance part is missing from his end. If I make a move to force a relationship between us, I'll just be making the biggest fool of myself, and ruin our new-found friendship as well, losing him completely.

It's too big a risk. I do like being his friend. We have a lot of fun together. I'll just have to wait until he gives me some kind of real sign. That's all.

As I close the door behind me, Ethan rubs his gloved hands together, blowing on his fingertips to warm them up, enveloping them in vapour. 'Did you leave a note?'

'Uh-huh.'

'Got the supplies I asked for?'

I point to the small backpack I use for my day hikes, ticking off the items one by one. 'Water flask, pocket knife, dried apricots, two apples, two ropes, notebook and pen, mini first-aid kit, and, oh yeah, this one I personally added 'cause it's the most important item, which you forgot.'

'What?'

I say this with a smile. 'Chocolate, of course.'

'It's good to see your priorities are in order.'

'I've been hiking before.'

'That I can believe. Well, save the chocolate for the way back. That's when we'll probably need it.'

We start moving off in the direction of Arkarian's chamber. 'So tell me, where are we going?' I point towards the mountain. 'Will we be seeing Arkarian?'

'He doesn't live in that mountain.'

'Oh? Then where does he live?'

He shrugs. 'He never said, and I never asked. Why do you want to know?'

Honestly, I'm not sure. It's just … I'd never tell Ethan this, but there's a strange craving inside me to know everything I can about Arkarian. 'He's interesting. Don't you think?'

'No.'

I wonder what's got him all bristly. 'Well, you've known him a long time. Weren't you his Apprentice? I'm yours, and I know where you live.'

'All I know is that he can't live in our physical world because he'd stand out too much now that his hair and eyes are so obviously different.'

What he's saying makes me suddenly sad.

'And of course,' he goes on, 'there's the fact that he doesn't age. Anyone he makes friends with would have to wonder why they're aging while he isn't, and as he can't very well explain the reason, he shuts himself off, I guess.'

'That's terrible!'

Ethan turns his head to look at me while we walk. 'Why? I'm sure there must be others like him. They probably all live together.' He shrugs. 'I don't know.'

The thought of Arkarian living with others like him irritates me somehow. We're quiet for the rest of the short trip. When we get to Arkarian's mountain, the rock disappears to allow us entry.

'Is he expecting us?'

'He knows, but he won't be here, so don't get your hopes up.'

As we step inside the torchlit hallway, my patience with Ethan's attitude finally snaps. 'What's got into you?'

He ignores me.

I follow him through the hallway into Arkarian's

181

octagonal headquarters, the light of the holographic sphere pulsing softly in the room. Beside it there's a message with instructions and a map. Ethan pockets them both, then writes a message back to say what time we left.

We go to another room which resembles an empty closet. Ethan runs his hand over the back wall, looking for something. I can't see what he does, but a soft click echoes in the small room and the back panel disappears. As we go through to another room, the panel immediately begins to re-form behind us, showering us in a layer of fine white dust; and before I have a chance to notice anything else about the cabin, it moves, dropping suddenly downwards. I realise we're in some sort of lift. Eventually it stops and a whoosh of cold air thrusts itself against my face, and then is gone. The air here smells of damp wood and earth, but the darkness is total.

I hear Ethan fumbling for something in his pack. 'Damn!'

'What's wrong?'

'I should have got my torch out first. Here, can you find it?'

I scoff at his suggestion. 'I can't see a thing.'

'Very funny. What about your gift of sight?'

'My gift is to see by any form of light,' I explain. 'Not *no* light at all.'

I put my hands out blindly, but he must have shifted around, so what I imagine are the flaps of his backpack are really the lapels of his jacket. Before I realise it, my hands are rummaging around inside his jacket front.

'Hey, what are you doing?'

'Sorry,' I mumble, glad it's dark so he can't see my face turning scarlet.

'Am I complaining?' he jokes as I fish my hands out and slide them around to his back, eventually latching on to his pack. My fingers close around something long and metallic. I pull it out, find the switch and turn it on. Now I can see clearly, way beyond the area the torchlight reveals.

'Wow, look at this place!' I exclaim, forgetting that Ethan can't see as I do.

'What is it?'

I shine the torch around the walls and down the narrow descending stairway, revealing the intricate carvings of the pillars, posts and stone walls.

'I remember this,' he says, taking hold of the torch.

We start moving, taking the stairs one at a time, being careful not to slip. It is so damp that drips can be seen forming down the walls in places, an occasional one dropping from the ceiling on to our heads.

'How old were you when Arkarian brought you here?'

'It was my fifth birthday, straight after my initiation.'

'And you remember the way?'

He gives a sort of mocking laugh and pats his jacket pocket. 'That's why Arkarian left the map.'

We walk down the stairs for ages; just as well I'm not claustrophobic. The air here has a tight, thin feel. After a while I get used to it and start relaxing. 'Look at this!' I stop beside a carved sculpture of Cyclops, a one-eyed giant of Greek mythology.

Ethan stops beside me. 'There's supposed to be three of them, called Lightning, Thunder and Thunderbolt. I wonder which one this is.'

His words make me suddenly nervous. I can't help peering around. 'Um, who cares, as long as we don't meet up with one while we're down here.'

He moves along a few steps, running the torch over a beaten bronze plaque. He scrubs a patch at the bottom with the back of his sleeve. 'Hydra,' he says.

'The many-headed monster slain by Hercules?' I go down the few steps and take a look for myself.

'Heracles,' Ethan explains. 'It was the Romans who called him Hercules. The name stuck.'

'I knew that.'

He gives me an amused look. 'After severing each head with his sword, Heracles seared the stumps with a torch of burning wood so they wouldn't grow back. But one head was immortal, and when Heracles cut it off, he stamped it into the earth.'

'Aren't you full of information.'

He shrugs and we keep walking. It's soon evident that this whole corridor is lined with images of mythological creatures. I wonder who collected the different artworks and put them here like a gateway to the past? The next carving is of Rhus, apparently god of the moon. Here he's depicted as half human, half horse. 'This place is unreal! Who knows about it?' I ask. 'Archaeologists would die to get their hands on these pieces.'

'Wouldn't they? But this city is too valuable to be excavated and exposed to the public. It's protected by the Guard.'

'There's a whole city?'

'Was. The city of Veridian, named in the Prophecy.'

'How can it be hidden?'

'Who's going to find it? First they'd have to get into

184

the mountain. On the outside it's a national park, so no big corporation's going to come in and mine it, or excavate or anything. It's not allowed. So at least for now it's safe.'

'What about the Order?'

'They know the city exists, but there's no evidence that they've managed to find their way in.'

'Do they know about the Prophecy?'

'Sure, from way back. Why do you think there are so many of us here in Angel Falls?'

Until he mentioned it, I hadn't thought. But now I start to figure it out. 'It's something about this ancient site. We're drawn here, aren't we? Both sides.'

'This is where the final conflict is predicted to occur.'

'Wow! So you're saying members of the Guard and the Order mostly live in our little town, drawn here by forces radiating from these ruins?'

'That's right. And apparently our mortal lives are connected.'

'So people that we interact with every day up there could be members of the Order and we wouldn't know it?'

'Yeah. And it has to stay that way for our own protection, although the Prophecy does say something about recognising the time drawing nearer as identities are revealed.'

'Oh, but, Ethan, that's happening already! We know about Mr Carter being a member of the Guard.'

He goes quiet for a minute. 'But I did that, by mistake.'

'Are you sure it was by mistake? Maybe you were just playing into the hands of the Prophecy?'

'Hell, you could be right. Hard to imagine Croc-face

being foretold, though.'

We keep moving, always downwards. I start pushing us along at a faster pace, trying not to get distracted by interesting objects along the way. Now I have an urge to read these prophetic words for myself.

But the path changes, the stairs becoming narrower the lower we descend, and partly eroded by landslides. We arrive at a point where the path disappears altogether. The last step is broken in half, with an open chasm a good ten metres across gaping out before us. Glancing down, I look as far as my eye takes me, and it's a dizzying sight. Straight walls on either side descend for what appears like a forever of nothingness. The path starts up again on the other side of this wide chasm, but that's no good to us. Crossing this will be impossible. Our trip is over.

'Well, that's that then.'

Ethan, torch in hand, examines the dark fathomless depths of the chasm spread out before us. 'What are you talking about? We've only just begun this journey.'

'We can't get across this, Ethan.'

He gets out his map and instructions, making me spin round so he can spread them out over my back. 'Here, it says this is the first bridge.'

I lift my eyes and skim a glance across to the other side. 'Listen, I can see for about fifty metres down that chasm and I can guarantee you there's no bridge.'

He folds up the map and points to a marked spot on Arkarian's instruction sheet. Nervousness shortens my tolerance radically. 'What am I looking at?' I ask in a deeply sarcastic voice.

He taps the spot with his finger twice. 'Read what it says right there.'

I look again. '"Cross the bridge using your imagination. Stick to the left side."'

'Exactly.' He folds up the sheet. 'Let's go.'

I yank on his arm so hard that he drops the two sheets. They start drifting down the chasm. I stare at them descending, lost forever. 'It's an omen.'

Ethan gives me a weird look and says, 'I didn't think you were superstitious.' Calmly, still looking in my direction, he puts out a hand and wills the sheets to his open palm.

I watch in awe as the papers, obeying his mental command, defy gravity and return to his fingers. Once they are safely back in his hand, he slots them into his jacket pocket.

I think about how he rescued those papers. 'Can you use your skill to rescue me like that, if I were to fall?'

'My skill doesn't work with living things – they have their own will.'

'Well, in that case, I'll stay right here.'

'Don't you want to read the Prophecy?'

'You know I do, but I can't cross a bridge that isn't there, Ethan!'

'What if the bridge was up here?' He points to his head.

'Oh no. I haven't got that good an imagination.'

An idea hits him and he nods to himself. 'All right, let me make this easier for you.'

He glances at the chasm, holding the torch directly in front of us, then he closes his eyes. A look of calm washes over him, and as he opens his eyes a bridge of sorts begins to form. By the time he's finished, the chasm itself can't be seen. In its place grows a magnificent garden with rose bushes and tulips in a mass display of brilliant colour. The scent of this garden hits my senses so vividly that I sneeze three times in quick succession.

'Sorry,' Ethan mutters. 'I didn't know you were superstitious *and* allergic.'

'Ha ha.' I swipe at my nose with the back of my hand, regaining some control. 'I'm not either, actually. It's just your garden is so full on.' I stare at the display in front of me, trying to come to terms with what I'm seeing. It's really beautiful. Directly through the centre of this garden runs a bridge of wooden planks, wide enough for two side by side. The railings are made of looped ropes.

No matter how stunning, I know what this is. Ethan's not fooling me for a second. It's an illusion. I recall how he restored his ancestor's old cabin, so while I'm impressed with this spectacular sight, I'm hardly reassured.

'It's not happening, Ethan. Forget it. This is nothing but an illusion. The chasm is still there.'

'Sure, but if it makes the crossing easier, why not use it? I did this for you.'

'You don't get it. I throw my hands in the air. There's nothing out there! There's no bridge! You can't fool me.'

He groans at my lack of faith. 'Isabel, if I cross, will you follow?'

I have to think about this. 'If you cross and live, I will follow. But that's not going to happen. You're not really going to cross, are you?'

He doesn't even hesitate. I reach out to stop him, adamant he's walking to his death, but unbelievably his feet don't drop through the first wooden plank, not one centimetre. He keeps walking until he gets to the other side, then turns and waves. 'Your turn!'

I gulp. What on earth have I agreed to? OK, I just saw Ethan do it, but he's got so much more faith than me. He's been in this Guard thing for twelve years. That's eleven years and eleven months longer than I have.

'Come on, or the illusion will fade and then where will you be?'

Still here on solid ground, the thought comes. 'All right,' I call back, but softly. 'Better an illusion of wood beneath my feet than nothing at all,' I grumble, close my eyes, and take my first step.

'The left!' Ethan yells. 'Keep to the left side!'

Quickly I move to the far left, gripping the loose rope railing and almost losing my balance. The bridge rocks. I try to steady myself, eventually easing my grip on the railing as I become aware of just how real the bridge is beginning to feel. But I don't dawdle. I have no idea how long Ethan's illusion is set to last. Hurrying the last few steps, I make it across, my knees as liquid as golden syrup.

I run straight into Ethan's open arms. He helps me straighten up. We burst out laughing. For me it's just relief, while he's probably laughing at what he believes is my ungrounded lack of faith.

I glance over my shoulder just in time to see the bridge gradually break up and disappear without a sound.

We move on, the terrain now subtly changing. The path is less clear, completely obliterated in places by mounds of dirt, gravel and puddles which form little trickling streams in low-lying areas.

All this water makes me wonder. 'Where exactly is this ancient city?'

'Under the lake.'

'Really? That's a scary thought. All that water over-head.'

'I know. But we're safe. Don't worry.'

Far from convinced, I follow Ethan as he clambers over a pile of boulders, wondering whether there's a fast exit somewhere, should it be needed. The possibility of having to get out in a hurry starts niggling at my brain. We've been descending now for a couple of hours. 'This path we're sort of following, is it the only way in? Or out?'

'There's another entrance at the bottom of the lake, I'm told. But the path directly linked to Arkarian's chamber is the easiest.'

My chest tightens but I try to ignore it, reminding myself that so far there hasn't been a problem with air. *Don't go inventing one!* Ethan pulls a rope out from my pack, sufficiently distracting my anxious thoughts.

'Here, tie this around that pillar over there, will you?' He looks at me half-frowning, half laughing. 'Do I need to ask if you know how to tie a secure knot?'

I don't answer. Instead, I take the rope and do the job, double-checking the knot with a firm tug.

Ethan smiles and shakes his head. 'I didn't think so.'

I follow Ethan down the rope to a lower level. Here the path disappears beneath some sort of cave-in. It takes us a few minutes to clear the way. We keep moving, always downwards. The original brick path is almost nonexistent now, but the direction is still relatively clear. Ethan consults his map and instructions occasionally, and sometimes we stop just to catch our breath and have a drink or something to eat.

'We're nearly there,' Ethan says, glancing back at me while munching into an apple.

'Watch out!'

With his limited sight down here, and momentary distraction, he nearly walks straight into a brick wall.

'Is this what we're looking for?' I wonder.

'No. But hang on, I remember something about this wall.' He gets out his instruction sheet again and starts to read. '"No need for keys. Blue is safe. Red you freeze."'

'What?' I lean over his shoulder to have a look, reading the same line. 'I don't get it. What does it mean?'

Ethan runs his hand over the bricks. After a second I hear a soft click, and a doorway appears, the bricks simply vanishing. We step through and find ourselves in a long, narrow hallway. Ethan goes to take a step. I yank him back, running his torch from left to right, showing him what he couldn't see – a pattern of crossing lights, like laser beams, some blue, some red, blocking our path at different heights and angles.

'Right,' he says. 'Now I remember.'

'How did you and Arkarian get past them last time you were here?'

He peers down at the beams nearest the ground. 'Well, I crawled under them and Arkarian used his wings.' He looks me up and down. 'You could probably do it that way.'

The lowest beam, a red one, is about a hand span from the ground. 'You must have been a scrawny five-year old.'

'Hmm, well, we haven't come this far to turn back now.'

Pulling a pencil from his pocket he tests the first beam, which is blue. Nothing happens. The next beam is red. As the pencil touches it, it ices over, making a sharp cracking sound. It splits into two. Ethan looks back at me and gulps.

It takes us both ages to work through the beams. At times we have to bend our bodies into shapes I never dreamed possible. Finally, Ethan makes it through and collapses on the ground. By the time I get to the last red beam I'm feeling the strain. My calves ache from having to hold them up so high or at odd angles. But I get a second wind as there's only one red beam left. It crosses the path at about hip height and I decide to step over the top of it. I get one leg almost across when I realise I've misjudged my own height. I catch Ethan's eye and he jumps up, helping me over. I almost make it, except I lose my balance, my arm swinging wide, and the sleeve of my jumper catches the beam. It freezes the entire sleeve. Ice hits my arm, making it go numb. Ethan helps me get it off.

He throws it to the ground, where the sleeve shatters into a thousand little pieces. 'You didn't want that anyway, did you?'

I take a last look at my ruined jumper, an old favourite. At least it's not my arm lying there in pieces. 'Wasn't my colour.'

Ethan takes off and I follow him. A door appears of its own accord behind me, sealing in the coloured lasers. It has goose bumps breaking out on my skin that have nothing to do with the fact that I'm now not wearing a jumper. 'Um, these unmarked doors and invisible bridges will be there on our way back, won't they, Ethan?'

'Hmm?'

His distraction, as if he hasn't a care in the world, irritates me. I go to grab his arm when I see what he's come up against this time. It's a door, heavy-looking and made of a grey shiny metal like steel or chrome.

'It's silver.'

'Are you sure?'

'Pretty much, from what I can remember. It's the vault.'

'How do we get through this … this vault?'

'I think …' He consults Arkarian's instructions to be sure. 'Oh, yeah, that's right.'

'What? Let me see that.' I take the sheet from his hands, mumbling with annoyance, 'All these booby traps! I wish I could meet the person who set these stupid contraptions in the first place.'

Ethan's eyes open wide. 'Isabel, *no!*'

'What?' I ask quickly, but get no answer. Ethan is backing away as the vault door has started to open. 'What did I do?' I scream at his alarmed face.

'We only had to make a wish, that's all. We could have asked for the door to open, but you went and asked to meet its maker.'

I look in alarm at the opening door. Annoyed-sounding growls from within let us know that we're suddenly not alone any more. 'Oh, no!'

The door opens wider, and as the dust starts settling, the figure of a man appears, brushing dust off his checked flannelette jacket. For an instant, I can't believe my eyes and have to blink hard. The man takes a step towards us and I gasp out loud. '*Jimmy?*'

'Hello, Isabel,' he says, his voice like I've never heard it before – mature and, well, like a real man's voice.

Also his eyes, even though they're definitely Jimmy's eyes, appear more, hell, I don't know ... intelligent somehow.

'Jimmy?'

Ethan comes up beside me. 'Jimmy, as in your mother's boyfriend, right?'

I nod, stunned. 'Uh-huh.'

Ethan recovers first and takes the hand Jimmy has extended. 'Nice to meet you.'

'Well, I would say a pleasure, except pleasure was what I was doing before Isabel ordered me here.'

'I didn't know—'

'It's all right, Isabel. Some things are meant to happen, and somehow I think this may have been one of them.'

'The Prophecy?' I ask him, still confused about it all. 'Did you really ...? How did you ... come to make these traps?'

'There came a need to protect the city,' he says and thumps his chest. 'And I was asked to do it.' He points over his shoulder to where the path splits into three. 'Let me save you some time: take the middle path. The left will kill you.'

'And the right?' Ethan asks.

'Ah, that'll just bury you alive.'

'And there's a difference?' I can't help asking.

'Just remember the middle path.'

'Anything else we should know?' Ethan asks hopefully, after all, it appears Jimmy would know.

He shakes his head. 'Can't think of a thing, oh, except remember to reverse the rules on the way out – you know, right side of bridge, red beam is safe, that sort of thing. Now I've got to go, your mum's cooking me ravioli bolognaise. My favourite. And I was standing right behind her when you wished me here.'

I give a little laugh that comes out all high-pitched. It's my nerves I realise, still trying to re-gather my senses.

'I'll tell her you're going to be late, and that you're OK. She worries about you, Isabel.'

He puts his hand up to wave as he starts to disappear. I grab his arm quickly. 'Mum isn't—?'

He peels off my fingers. 'She knows nothing. It's got to stay that way, otherwise she could get hurt.'

I stare at the empty space Jimmy leaves behind until Ethan takes my elbow, giving me a tug. 'Come on, you heard Jimmy. It must be getting very late.'

We take the middle path, which is unlike all the other paths so far. It's paved in silver bricks and the walls are lined with silver. At the end of it we come to a clearing of sorts. Ethan starts to run around like an excited child. 'I remember this.'

I follow him around a circular brick wall. He finds an opening and after a few twists and turns I realise we've entered a maze. But luckily Ethan seems to know where he's going and before long, panting and excited and filled with raw energy, he leads me to a wall several metres high and several more across, engraved from top to bottom and side to side with pictures and figures and hieroglyphic writing.

'This is it!' Ethan exclaims.

I walk from one end to the other shaking my head. 'It's beautiful, but … I can't read any of it.'

'It's in code.'

'Oh great. I suppose you brought a code decipherer in your backpack?'

'Very funny. We have to do it ourselves.'

'Of course, what could I be thinking? You know we're already late for dinner. How long do you think this is going to take?'

He just smiles at me, which infuriates me more. I hate it when he's so smug. It's all right when *I* show *him* up. That's different. He deserves it when he assumes I'm incompetent at *guy stuff* like wrestling and archery and outdoor survival.

In minutes he explains the code. And like any code, once you know it, it's surprisingly simple. Every seventh letter is written in English, except the letter is turned on its side, back-to-front, or some other twisted version.

I pull out my notebook and pen, and together we start working on the code. It takes us ages 'cause the wall is huge, the Prophecy longer than I expected. Finally we have all the letters and sit down, our backs against the silver wall, physically exhausted but mentally psyched up.

I flip the pages back to the start, then offer the book to Ethan. 'You do it. You read the Prophecy.'

He gives me a funny look. 'Why me?'

'I don't know, this whole business just freaks me out I guess. And you've heard these words before, so there shouldn't be any shocks.'

'I can't remember much from when I was five, Isabel. But here, give me that.' He takes the notebook and starts to read.

I close my eyes and let the words flow over me.

Before the world can be free
A bloom of murdered innocence shall be seen

In the woods above the ancient city of Veridian
Where nine identities shall be revealed.

It will come to pass that a king shall rule
But not before a leader pure of heart awakens
And an ageless warrior with an ancient soul
Shall guide with grace and providence.

Beware, nine shall see a traitor come and go
From whence a long and bitter war will follow
And the Named shall join in unity
Yet suspicion will cause disharmony.

A jester shall protect, a doubter cast a shadow
And a brave young warrior will lose his heart to death
Yet none shall be victorious until a lost warrior returns
And the fearless one emerges from a journey led by light
    and strength.

Take heed, two last warriors shall cause grief as much
    as good
From the midst of suspicion one shall come forth
The other seeded of evil
Yet shall be victorious while the other victorious in death.

We sit in silence for a minute and try to absorb these words, try to make sense of them. It occurs to me that Ethan has heard this text twice now, so the Prophecy should be clearer to him. 'So what does it all mean?' I ask.

He looks at me blankly, giving a slight lift to his shoulders. 'Well, the ageless warrior with an ancient soul, I think that's—'

'I know that one. That's Arkarian.'

He goes silent, which makes me suspect he knows more about this Prophecy than he wants to reveal.

'Are you also described in this Prophecy?' I ask.

His mouth opens but no words come out.

'Ethan, tell me what you know. I'm involved now. I need to know. Isn't that why you brought me here today?'

'OK. I think you're mentioned in it.'

'What!'

'Yeah, look ...' He points to a line about midway down the second page. 'I reckon you're the one referred to as *the fearless*.'

I can't help scoff at this, while my eyes skim over the rest of that line. '*A journey led by light and strength*.' I don't get it and glance at Ethan. His right leg has suddenly been afflicted by the shakes. 'What about you?' I ask. 'You're in this Prophecy, aren't you?'

His eyes flick away. He's not going to tell me. But he knows, and this knowledge makes him uncomfortable and nervous, and maybe even a little scared. 'Which line refers to you, Ethan?'

He starts to get up, brushing dirt off his jeans in the process. I get up also, determined to make him tell me. 'Which line is it? I can tell you know.'

'I don't know. Really. I'm only guessing.'

'OK, so what's your guess?'

He hesitates, and I think he's never going to answer, but just keep staring off into the darkness beyond the part of the maze the torch-light reveals. 'All right, I think I'm the brave young warrior.'

I snatch the notebook from his hand, flicking back to that particular line. When I find it, my lungs force themselves to expand. 'Will *lose his heart to death*,' I whisper.

Silence follows, and the enormity of it here, in this giant decorated tomb of a city, makes me feel claustrophobic suddenly. A crushing feeling descends, smothering me. I gulp in another loud breath.

Ethan snatches back the notebook and shoves it deep into my backpack. 'It's late. Let's get out of here. We can worry about those words some other time when there's more air to breathe. Just be careful where you put the damn thing. OK?'

I nod and begin to follow him out of the maze, but my mind can't stop going over the lines that keep repeating themselves in my thoughts. To think one of those lines might actually refer to me – what exactly does it mean? OK, some of that Prophecy doesn't make sense to me, but some of it does; and it's those particular words and phrases that scare me half to death.

Chapter Twenty-nine

Ethan

Isabel gets her mission. She's going to need her healing skills, and the use of her sixth sense too. There's a girl in Massachusetts in the year 1759, about our age, who's plagued with ill health. Her name is Abigail and she should be leaving her childhood ailments mostly behind by now, but she's not getting better. On the contrary, she's drawing dangerously close to death. Many contagious diseases like diphtheria, measles and smallpox, killed children of this period. But Arkarian suspects foul play.

We're in Arkarian's main chamber, after school, while he explains our parts. 'Isabel, you're going in as a housemaid, happy to have found service to help your own poor family out. While there you will befriend the girl called Abigail Smith, figure out what her health problem is, and heal her if the illness isn't natural.'

'What if it is natural, must I just let her die?'

'In that case, we know from history that she will recover.'

But how will I be able to tell the difference between genuine illness and attempted murder?'

Arkarian frowns. 'You'll know. Use your skills.'

'So what are these people like?' I ask.

'They're a prominent New England family; Abigail's father is a minister from a farming community not far from Boston. It's a happy household with four children, not a lot of money, but they're comfortable. The parents, William and Elizabeth, are very concerned about Abigail. Elizabeth in particular is overprotective, which not only worries young Abigail, but irritates her too. She's had no formal education – girls of that time often didn't – but her grandmother is educating her at home and doing a fine job. Abigail has a great love of books, so you'll find her an avid reader, Isabel.'

He hasn't mentioned my role yet. Taking a hint from my thoughts, Arkarian turns his attention to me. 'Now, Ethan, this is basically Isabel's mission, but as she's relatively new at this, and in the light of recent disturbing events, it's been decided you should go along and make yourself useful.'

Isabel flicks me a brief annoyed look like she thinks there's a conspiracy going on about her inadequacies, or something. She can be so sensitive sometimes as if she has to prove herself all the time. 'Are you going just to be my bodyguard?' she snaps at me.

I look at Arkarian to define my role. 'Yes and no, Isabel. Every mission has an element of danger, and lately, well, there's been some unusual events surrounding you. It would be a good idea for Ethan to keep an eye out for trouble. Remember, your skills are still evolving. It would be irresponsible to send you out there without backup. You're still an Apprentice, and a new one at that.'

She nods and keeps quiet while Arkarian turns his

attention to me. 'Now you, Ethan, are basically there to watch over the situation. It would also be helpful, once Isabel works out what's wrong with Abigail, to find the source of the foul play I suspect and eliminate it.'

I get it. I'm to watch Isabel without being intrusive, discover the culprit and deal with him or her. 'When do we leave?'

'Tonight. Be ready.'

We leave Arkarian's chambers and walk towards Isabel's place. She's quiet, her large brown eyes larger than usual, her fingers digging deeply into her jeans pockets, her eyes focused on the path beneath our feet.

'Are you OK?' I ask.

Distractedly she glances at me. 'Hmm?'

'You're not nervous, are you?' I try to put her mind at ease. 'I mean, this is a pretty routine mission.'

'My healing skills are miserable at best, Ethan,' she explains her worry.

'Listen, Isabel, you're ready, or the Guard wouldn't send you. Trust in them.'

She tugs out her hands and starts blowing on them. 'What if I fail? Who is this girl? What happens if she dies? Will the world be cataclysmically different today because of it?'

'Maybe it will and maybe it won't. Thinking about that isn't our job. We're here to ensure that the present and ultimately the future turn out as they should. If history has it that this girl Abigail did not die back in 1759, then she mustn't die tonight – not in the few days that we're going to be visiting this time period.'

'Who is she, exactly? I mean, does she do something important when she's older?'

I tell her what I know. 'When she's nineteen she's

going to marry a brilliant young lawyer named John Adams.'

She has a think for a second. 'Not President John Adams?'

'Well, he's not president when she's nineteen, but yeah, that's the one. And of course you know, don't you, that one of Abigail's sons becomes the sixth president of the United States later on?'

'Oh, wow,' she sighs and frowns at her feet, then kicks a stone out of her path.

'What's wrong?' I ask at her worried expression.

'What if I fail, Ethan? The responsibility is enormous.'

'If you fail – and there's always the possibility – we hope like hell that Abigail's premature death doesn't have significant impact on the present, and ultimately the future.'

'Have you ever failed?'

It's the question I've been expecting, yet dreading at the same time. 'Yeah, of course.'

'Were there consequences?'

I think about that convict mission only last year. 'I was supposed to stop a woman called Elizabeth Howath from being murdered. I knew that her assassin had taken on the guise of a soldier. When I arrived at the scene, Elizabeth was strung to a pole in the centre of a courtyard being whipped by a cat-o'-nine tails. The soldier was hitting her so violently that I felt sure he was the killer. I stopped it by creating the illusion that she had passed out. The soldier walked away, leaving her body to rot in the hot midday sun and I cut her loose. Staggering to safety, she found freedom in nearby bushland. I thought that because I'd stopped the flogging and Elizabeth still breathed, my mission was complete. But she died anyway, from a raging fever a few nights later, alone in the bush.'

'Oh, no!'

'All I'd had to do was tend her wounds and find her a safe haven until she recovered. But I didn't think of that.'

'Couldn't you have gone back?'

'You can't go back to the exact same time twice.'

'Oh. So did anything happen?'

'You mean, did the present change?'

She nods as we keep walking.

'Thirteen people were recorded as officially missing that night in the present.'

She grabs my arm. 'What do you mean?'

'Because Elizabeth Howath's life was tampered with, and she died years before she was supposed to, certain descendants that once existed, suddenly didn't.'

'So all her descendants were, what? Suddenly wiped out?'

'Not all. Arkarian believes some of those people would have been born anyway, through other heritage lines.'

'That's terrible, Ethan!'

'We only get one chance at it. If someone dies, they die, Isabel. If the Order of Chaos can kill someone prematurely, and the Guard can't stop it, then that's it. There's no second chance with death.'

'Oh, hell.'

'You're right that it's a lot of responsibility, but for what it's worth, the Guard is pretty good at getting it right most of the time, and getting us in there before it's too late. That was my biggest stuff-up so far, other than the night you came along and saved the situation from being a total disaster.' I see her smile to herself. 'Anyway, I learned from that experience.'

We walk quietly the rest of the way. At her front gate she turns and says seriously, 'I won't get it wrong, Ethan. I promise.'

As she heads off inside with a brighter step, I acknowledge the truth in her statement: Isabel will do her best. And Isabel's best is more than the Guard can ask for. But I know there's an added element in tonight's mission, a danger element. Arkarian couldn't keep his concern from showing. He suspects that not only the frail girl called Abigail could be in trouble tonight.

He suspects Isabel could be too.

Chapter Thirty

Isabel

This time I have some dinner, more because it's expected than because of any hunger. My stomach's rolling
around as it is. Jimmy comes in and acts the fool as
usual. The only indication he gives that we met the
other night in the ancient city vault is a lingering look
before he goes out to watch television with Mum.

I wash up, take a shower, then go to bed. Tonight I'm
not worried about Mum coming in to check on me. I
get the feeling Jimmy will keep her occupied for some
time. Matt crosses my mind, but he's not home yet; he's
having a night out with friends.

It takes me a while to fall asleep. My body, though
weary, seems to have too much restless energy shifting
around inside. I grab my notebook with the Prophecy
written inside, as I do almost every night these days,
and try again to figure it out. But my eyes start to
close, and suddenly I feel myself shift as if my body is
free-falling. Then I drop and hit a mildly springy surface.

I wake inside one of the most beautiful rooms I have
ever seen. An artist with every colour of the spectrum

available to him couldn't create a masterpiece to match the brilliant display in this room. Every wall is painted with murals of electric colour, some abstract, others landscapes so real it would be easy to think I could walk right through into the scenery portrayed there. From my position stretched out on the Citadel floor, I gaze up at the ceiling, which is equally vividly painted.

'Not bad, eh?' Ethan is already in the room waiting.

My head shifts from side to side, still in awe. 'Where does this all come from? Who decorated these rooms?'

He shrugs. 'Arkarian once told me there is a reason a room chooses you, but he didn't elaborate.'

He reaches down and helps me up. I rub a sore patch on my thigh where a bruise must be forming from the impact with the floor, sparking my temper suddenly. 'There is a knack to these landings, isn't there, Ethan?'

'Yeah, why?' he replies, oblivious to my annoyance.

I give him a hard shove. 'Then why don't you show me?'

His mouth forms an open circle, then settles into an embarrassed grin. 'Sorry. It's not that hard. We'll practise soon, I promise.'

In a wardrobe room several flights up, I end up dressed in a long grey cotton skirt over an off-white petticoat, a white blouse with a high neck, and black shoes with holes in the toes. My hair is mousy brown, slicked straight to my scalp and pinned severely in a bun at the back. Beneath a triangular white cap is my complexion, pale, as if I hardly ever see the sun. Ethan emerges wearing dark-grey trousers that don't reach his ankles, a simple beige check shirt and bare feet. He has black curls cropped close to his scalp and appears smaller in stature. Our appearance is definitely simple, tidy, poor and youthful.

After being sprinkled with the dust that will give us the knowledge we need to fit in with our destination, we go to the edge of the departure door. I'm so astonished by what I suddenly see stretched out before me, I take a tottering step backwards.

Ethan turns to me. 'What's wrong?'

This must be because of Arabella's gift, I think. 'I … I see it.'

'See what?'

'Where we're going. The town, the actual street, the … the house, with its little red windows upstairs, and the matching red door. North Street or, or Norton Street. Something like that.'

'Excellent!' He reaches for my hand and tugs me to the door opening. 'Now all you have to do to land on your feet is flex the ankles, preparing them for a spring. Let's see how you go this time.'

'What? Aren't you coming with me?'

'In a little while. They're expecting you. I have to plead for some odd jobs so I can have an excuse to stick around.' He gives my hand a gentle squeeze. 'But don't worry, I won't be far behind.'

I turn and get my bearings, then leap. Now that I can see where I'm going I'd like to think I can land without falling over. What did Ethan say? Spring and flex. But I hit the hard paved footpath like a brick dropping on cement. I get up quickly, glancing around, feeling the side of my leg for grazes. At least no one's about. I straighten my skirt, stagger up and knock on the front door.

A woman answers, tall, elegant, her hair pulled tight at the back. 'Yes, child?'

208

I thought I was expected. Now what? 'Ah, I'm Judith Evans and, um …'

'You're a lot smaller than I envisaged.'

'Yes, ma'am, but I'm a hard worker.'

'So I've been assured, and as I'm not one to judge a book by its cover, you'd better come in, child. You can prove your worth instead. It's been hectic in here, what with Abby being so ill. She's my second eldest and has lately been forced to spend a lot of time in her room. You're to clean her room without disturbing her. Do you understand?'

'Yes, ma'am.'

She nods and steps back to allow me entrance. 'I'll show you where you're going to sleep first. There's a room in the attic. It's not much, but it's comfortable. Then I'll explain your chores and duties. You can get started straight away.'

To get into the attic I have to open a square in the ceiling with a hook and pull a ladder down. With this skirt it's a chore in itself. But the room is not so bad, fairly large, as the attic runs the length of most of the top level of the house. The ceilings are low with cross-beams zigzagging the length and breadth of the entire room, and the bed is small and hard, the room icy cold; but hopefully I won't be staying long.

I soon understand exactly what's expected of me, basically everything from making beds to dusting, beating the multitude of rugs, starching all manner of white fabric, including the household linen, and helping out in the kitchen.

Keen to get on with what I'm really here for, I work through my duties as quickly as possible, leaving Abigail's room for last. I want to spend more time with her than with my chores, without having Mrs Smith complaining that I should be working elsewhere. I have a plan; I hope I can pull it off.

Abigail is sleeping when I enter her room. Quickly, I go about my chores. I drop my broom with a loud bang to the polished wooden floor, and she doesn't stir. What if she's already dead? But then she moans softly and I relax a little.

Having finished my chores, I go and stand by her bed. There's a book on a seat nearby – a selection of poetry. I place the book on her side table and sit on the seat. Glancing at the door, I'm grateful no one's around. For a minute I do nothing except watch Abigail sleep. She's small, but has the look of someone who still has a lot of growing to do. Her hair is long and plaited in two braids. She lies unnaturally still. Her bed linen is neat and tidy for someone who spends a lot of time among the sheets. Perhaps she's just a deep sleeper, not troubled by bad dreams. Her skin is pale, but that figures, as she's been so ill. I take her hand, close my eyes and begin to visualise.

What I perceive shocks me. Her body is in the midst of inner torment, every cell fighting some sort of alien and very unwanted invasion. I search through blood, bone, organ and tissue, desperately trying to find the source of this intrusion. My head pulses with possibilities and visual images. I suddenly feel nauseous.

'What are you doing?'

Breaking my concentration, I turn towards the voice, gently laying Abigail's hand back down on the white, stiffly starched sheet. 'Pardon me, ma'am, but Miss Abigail called out in her sleep. I sought to comfort her.'

Miss Smith takes in Abigail's sleeping form and gives

a tight nod. 'In future, Evans, you come and find me.'

'Yes, ma'am.'

Abigail stirs with a soft moan and opens her eyes. I start thinking that at last I'll get to speak with her.

'If your chores are done, Evans, you may leave now.'

Great, I'm not even going to get a chance to introduce myself. Reluctantly, I get up and with a last longing look at Abigail – or Abby, as her mother calls her – I start to leave. Abby's eyes are wide open now and looking at me questioningly. I give her a wide smile as I slowly back out of the room. Mrs Smith's stern eyes follow me all the way out the door.

With a little spare time on my hands, I go outside for a look around. It's a farm and there are lots of activities going on. I head towards the sounds of men talking and animals grunting and snorting. There's a square fenced-off area adjacent to a large shed that is probably a barn. I get a few strange looks from the workers there, and as I can't see Ethan anywhere, I go back inside. In the kitchen I help a woman named Mary prepare a stew with corn on the cob, sweet peas, turnips and other vegetables. But it's the pecan pie that grabs my attention: the largest pie of any sort I've ever seen. I get it out of the wood-fired oven carefully with two hands. It must weigh a couple of pounds on its own.

As we work, I ply Mary with questions about Abigail, but either Mary is reluctant to discuss the girl's health and background, or she just doesn't know much. I think, considering Mary's been working here for years, she's probably keeping quiet out of family loyalty.

I work for two days and still don't get any closer to Abby nor to the reason for her illness. Mrs Smith is so protective, hovering over her daughter like a watchful hawk. I'm also worried because I haven't seen anything of Ethan yet. Where is he? He promised he would be nearby. Well if he is, he's sure doing a good job of remaining invisible.

By the third night I decide to hurry things along. Abby is obviously not getting any better, while Mary grows snappier with her matronly concern. I sense Mrs Smith may be off-loading some of her concerns for Abby onto her. So when the house finally falls asleep, I slide out of bed, braving the cold with every step down the ladder. Hurrying on bare feet down the long narrow hallway, and with a quick look around, I open the door to Abby's room.

I find Abby sitting up, leaning against a stack of pillows and reading by the light from a single candle by her bedside. When she sees me she gives a little startled squeal. 'Oh, sorry,' she says with a slight giggle. 'I wasn't expecting anyone. You must be Judith Evans. Mother says your work is sloppy and poor.'

Her insult makes me gasp, but I realise quickly that she's joking. Even though the light is dim and her face should be in deep shadow, I can see her as if the room were showered in brilliant sunlight. A mischievous smile is clear on her face.

'I must work harder then, even though my knees and elbows are red raw from scrubbing these polished floors for hours every day.'

Again she gives a little laugh, which turns into a gasping cough. Instinctively I place my hand across her back, visualising her ribs through her raw and damaged lungs. There's fluid there, too much, and phlegm as well. In slow circular motions I try to soothe

the aching tissues and will the fluid back and out through its proper channels.

She stops coughing and sighs, leaning back against her pillows. Her eyes are wet from the intense coughing. 'Whatever you did, thank you.'

'I didn't do anything.'

'Well, don't go away, you brought me good luck. I can actually take a full breath now that horrible rasp is gone.'

This surprises me, as I've been cleaning in here every day while Abby sleeps and I haven't noticed the rasp before. 'Do you only get it at night?'

She wipes her eyes. 'Yes, especially when it's cold.'

Sounds like asthma or bronchitis, both common medical disorders. But this is not what I sensed that first day I held her hand. That was a body in revolt. If only I could take her hand again without arousing her suspicions or appearing strange. She reaches out to the wooden chest at her side for the jug of water there.

I pour her a glass, handing it to her. 'Would you like me to read to you?' I ask, forming an idea.

'I'd love that. My eyes are sore from this miserable light.'

'I could light more candles for you.'

Her eyes grow wide. 'Oh, no! If Mother saw them she'd make me put them out and go to sleep.'

'Pardon my saying so, but couldn't you use the sleep? Staying awake at night is probably why you sleep so much during the day.'

Her voice grows hoarse. 'I sleep far too long as it is!'

Her conspiratorial tone makes me smile. I take the book she's reading out of her hands, sit down and start to read one of the poems aloud. She enjoys it and asks me to continue, until I think she's never going back to sleep. But at last her eyes droop and finally close. It's the chance I've been waiting for. I glance around and listen intently; thankfully no one's awake yet. It has to be close to dawn by now, which is when the household starts rising, so there is no time to lose. I take Abby's hand and close my eyes and concentrate.

As before, the battle raging within her frail body thunders through my brain. Layer by layer my thoughts fold through her blood vessels, organs and tissues, searching for the source of her problems. Finally I see it. Damaged cells fighting a toxin that is very strong, yet subtly disguised. I understand now why even Abby's doctors haven't been able to find the cause. It's poison, probably administered in minute quantities so as not to be apparent, but harmful enough to eventually kill her.

I attempt to start the healing process straight away. It will take some time to repair all her damaged cells, but that's not the problem I foresee. Whoever is doing this will obviously keep doing so unless Ethan or I can discover his identity. How hard is that going to be? With all those chores I have to do, I can't possibly watch every person that enters or leaves Abby's room. And who's to say the assassin even has to get that close? Her food is prepared in the kitchen on a separate tray. Anyone could have access to it. And if the assassin realises Abby is recovering, he may decide to up the dose, enough to finish her off in one hit.

'Ethan, where the heck are you?' I ask this without expecting an answer. At first I didn't want Ethan coming on this mission just to baby-sit me. I get enough baby-sitting from Matt. For most of my life I can remember having this urge to do things for myself, and to do them as well as the next person or maybe even a little better. But Ethan is more experienced, and I'm not so stupid as to turn his help away when it's needed. Like now.

The door clicks softly behind me and I nearly jump out of my skin. Ethan walks in, barefooted on tiptoes.

He comes over and squats beside me as if this helps make him invisible. 'It's Wilbur, remember?'

'Of course. So where were you?'

'They wouldn't hire me. Apparently they'd just taken on a maid at a friend's request.'

'How did you get in here? I didn't hear a thing.'

'There's a window in the basement with a broken lock. No one saw me.' He looks over at Abby sleeping. 'Do you know what's wrong with her yet?'

'Poison.'

'As Arkarian suspected. What can you do?'

'I think I can heal her, but we have to find the culprit, or there's not much point if he can get to her again.'

'Any suspects?'

I shrug, completely at a loss. 'Mary prepares the meals, but anyone around here could find a way into the kitchen.'

'So you think the poison is coming through her food?'

'Well, I'm not at all sure, but Mrs Smith watches over Abby very carefully.'

A rooster crows outside, offering us a warning that the day is about to start. Ethan gets up. 'I'd better make myself scarce.'

'Where are you staying?'

He stands. 'Don't worry, I've managed to get some very dignified work tending the animals in the barn. The job comes with accommodation.'

There's something in his tone that gives him away. 'This work doesn't involve a shovel, does it?'

He grins. 'I see your sixth sense is outstanding this morning.'

The sound of a nearby door opening with a soft creak, and closing again just as slowly, has him running out and down the hallway. I decide to do the same, but footsteps immediately outside Abby's door make me turn and look to the window for an exit. But the door opens before I get halfway towards it. Having only a second to find cover, I dive to the floor, silently rolling under Abby's bed.

A woman enters, but it's not Mary, nor Mrs Smith, nor even Abby's sister. And there's a scent about her that is strangely familiar, though I can't readily place it. Seeing her face would be great, but if this is the assassin, then her face, her whole body in fact, is probably altered enough to disguise her true identity. Only her eyes would remain the same. Suddenly she speaks, one word, very softly and close to Abby's ear. I don't catch it. But I do catch the gurgling sound as this woman pours liquid into Abby's water jug. My heart jerks; this has to be it. This woman is tampering with Abby's water. And of course no one else will drink from it in fear that they might catch whatever ails Abby.

The woman goes to leave. I can't reveal myself or risk arousing her suspicions that the Guard is on to her now. Still, I just have to see who it is, in case our paths should cross by day. As soon as the door clicks behind her, I run out and take a peek, careful not to make a sound. But all I see is the caped figure of a woman darting barefoot down the hallway to the stairs that ultimately lead outside.

Ethan appears from the other end of the hallway, startling me into making a squealing sound. He covers his own mouth in a gesture meant to remind me to speak softly.

'Did you see that woman?' I ask once safely back inside Abby's room.

'Yeah. I saw her yesterday too. She attracted the attention of a couple of the men in the barn. They call her the widow Wittman,' he whispers. 'Apparently her name is Margaret. She moved into the house down the road about two months ago. She has no children, lives alone and keeps mostly to herself. Though once or twice she's brought over some freshly laid eggs and butter beans. That's probably how she managed to get hold of a key to the back door and make herself a copy. And remember, if she's from the Order, she won't be in her mortal body either. It'll be hard to identify her.'

'Well, we know what she gets up to in her spare time.'

'Exactly. So how is she administering the poison?'

'She tampered with Abby's water.'

He goes over to the bedside table, withdraws a small container from his trouser pocket, and fills it with the water. Pocketing the small bottle, Ethan quickly leaves, as the house is now rising.

I get rid of the water in the jug, washing it out thoroughly in the kitchen, and replace it with fresh clean water from the outside pump before anyone notices.

The day passes slowly. I manage to finish my chores by mid afternoon, and I decide to go for a walk to see

217

just where this assassin is staying. I reach the house at the end of a narrow lane and the sight of it makes me shiver. The front windows are broken, the porch railing is missing bars, and there's paint flaking off the walls in sheets. It's an old tumble-down house, but this is not what's chilling my spine. It's an eerie sense that something evil has taken up residence within those walls, something much more evil than the woman in Abby's room this morning.

I turn and run back to the Smith farm, but not to the attic for a rest. I decide to keep busy, keep my mind off the creepy vibes emanating from that old house. When night finally descends my nerves are still jumping. But I have to try to heal Abby tonight, and hopefully Ethan will find a way to stop this woman who calls herself Margaret, so that we can both return home safely. I just can't stop thinking of that evil presence, knowing it doesn't fit.

I find Abby sitting up waiting for me. She looks better, and I think the small amount of healing from last night followed by a day without poison has helped already. Those circles around her eyes are nowhere as dark tonight, and her energy level seems stronger too. 'Will you read to me again?'

'Of course.' As I sit in the seat, I take the familiar poetry book from her hands.

She takes it back and lays it face down on the bed. 'But first we'll talk.'

Uh-oh. 'Sure. What do you want to talk about?'

She sighs blissfully. 'I haven't been outside these walls for so long, you must tell me everything that's going on.'

It's a big ask, especially considering I don't have any

idea. Sure, the Citadel endows me with the correct accents and understanding of the era's culture, but it doesn't give me memories or information on current events. Seeing my blank expression, Abby pats my hand. 'I'm going to call you my lucky charm.'

It's a wonderful compliment.

'I've never felt so good since you arrived. Promise me, Judith, you'll never go away as long as you live. And when I'm married and have my own family, you'll work for me, or I'll work for you, whichever of us marries the wealthiest man.'

Quite a plan, and the most a woman of this period could ask for, I guess. But it's not my idea of an ideal life, and I have to let her know I won't be around then. 'I won't be here for very long, Abby. I'm working because my family needs a little extra money to help us with our move.'

'Oh, no! Where are you going? Not west, I hope. So many people are moving west. You are all so brave.'

I shrug noncommittally and she takes my news well. 'Never mind, but we shall write. Oh, how I love to write! One day I will write to the lawmakers.'

Her enthusiasm has me intrigued. 'And what would you say?'

She peers at me closely and whispers, 'I shall ask these men to pass a law that will allow women the right to have our say.'

I lean right back in my seat, admiring this girl who may be very ill but is incredibly courageous. I pretend to have a drink in my hand that I'm holding up high. 'Hear, hear. I'll second that.'

We talk for ages, not noticing the time drifting past. She tells me about her grandmother who teaches her to read and write. Abby makes it clear how strongly she believes all girls should be educated, and proves herself incredibly conversant in so many areas. Her broad knowledge leaves me stunned.

'How do you know so much?' I feel compelled to ask.

'I read, of course.'

She reads all right, and not just poetry, but history, theology, drama and politics as well.

Ultimately, Abby grows tired, and as I read her the last poem for the night, she drifts off to sleep. As soon as she does, Ethan comes in, glancing around and over his shoulder, then crosses the room to look out the window, peering in all directions. 'I thought you were never going to stop her talking.'

Oh no, did we really talk that long? 'She has a wonderful spirit, way ahead of her time.'

He groans impatiently. 'Speaking of time, you know we don't have much. Have you started to heal her yet?'

'I was just about to when you walked in.'

He makes an impatient gesture with his hands. Something's gnawing at him. I've never seen him quite so … disturbed. 'You have to hurry.'

'What's wrong? What's the rush?'

'You want to know what's wrong? Marduke is here. Marduke!'

'I thought so.'

He looks at me with wide-open eyes. 'You've seen him?'

'No, but I felt his presence this afternoon. He's in that woman's house.'

'Margaret. He's protecting her. I tried to deal with her earlier today, but Marduke interfered. So he knows the Guard is here.'

'Great! Well, what can we do to get rid of the two of them?'

He moans as if he's being forced against his will. 'We have to forget Marduke for now. We'll just deal with the widow Wittman. That's our mission. And I have an idea.'

I realise what he's saying. 'You want to wait till she comes back here, like she does every morning with the poison?'

'Yes. Now hurry. For my plan to have a chance to work, Abby must be cured.'

'So we can make a fast exit back to the Citadel.'

'Exactly – before Marduke makes an appearance. It's not up to us to deal with whatever that creature is. Let the Tribunal worry about him.'

I start working on Abby while Ethan quietly paces from the door to the window and back again. Occasionally he whispers to me to hurry, but I'm going as fast as I can. There's a lot of scarring to work through before getting to the poison deep within her cells.

Just as dawn starts to make an impact on the horizon, I sit back in my chair thoroughly exhausted.

'Is she healed?'

I nod and groan softly, all my weary body can manage. I didn't realise healing could be so draining, but then I've never attempted anything that lasted more than a few minutes. This session took hours.

The rooster crows, signalling the start of the day.

'Well done! Now go and sit by the window, I'll do the rest.'

But getting up seems like an enormous task.

'What's wrong? Are you ill?' Ethan asks worriedly.

'Drained.'

'Oh, no!'

'Sorry. I didn't know it would have this effect.'

He half drags, half carries me across the room, sitting me down by the window. 'Don't worry. We'll be out of here in a few minutes.'

'I sure hope so. I could sleep for a thousand years.'

Standing in the centre of the room, he closes his eyes and works his magic. He creates an illusion, an interesting one at that. He has filled the room with a wide array of water pitchers, some made of glass, some glazed clay or china. They're everywhere, at different levels, all filled to the brim with sparkling clear water.

I lift one eyebrow, questioning.

'A momentary distraction. I want her off guard long enough to glimpse into her eyes. To do that I need her to stare long and hard. It's a long shot. I'm just hoping to find something distinctive to identify her.'

'And if you do recognise her as a member of the Order? What then?'

He partly exposes a dagger from his shirt.

I gulp at the sight, thankful that my skill is healing. I think about that other skill that hasn't revealed itself yet and my body shudders. What could it be? I hope it's useful, like healing, and not something that can be used for killing.

The sound of the door clicking open jerks me from my thoughts. It's the woman, Margaret. The assassin. She steps into the room, and halts at the sight of the hundreds of water pitchers. She must see me sitting by the ledge, and Ethan standing in the centre of the room, but it's as if the pitchers are hypnotising her. I realise that Ethan's illusion is more than it appears, for Margaret's eyes, in the shadow of her deeply hooded cloak, remain fixed to the water jugs, moving slowly from one to the other. She seems to have forgotten her purpose for being here.

She turns in slow motion and now Ethan is directly in front of her, attempting to get a good look deep into her eyes. It's the only way one of us can be identified while in the past. The woman is obviously in a daze and appears not even to see Ethan before her. His head cocks to one side, his eyes squinting as though he recognises the woman in front of him, but then his shoulders lift slightly. 'I think she's wearing some sort of concealment,' he whispers.

'Like an eye mask?'

'Yeah.' He shrugs, then sniffs. 'But she smells familiar.'

'I know. It's her perfume. A flowery, soapy smell. Yet how is that possible? Wouldn't her scent stay with her physical body in her bed?'

'Of course.'

'So what now?'

The woman spins round suddenly as if she has found a way to break through Ethan's spell. But before she gets a chance to act, or work out what's going on, Ethan grabs her from behind, pinning her back to his chest.

She grunts, pushing hard against his arms.

'Tell me,' Ethan hisses in her ear. 'What is Marduke doing in this time?'

The woman inhales deeply, air hissing through her nostrils. 'You may as well kill me now for I'll tell you nothing.'

Just as her last word is out she starts to disappear; and suddenly Ethan staggers forward with nothing but air in his arms.

I look around frantically in case she's only transported herself and not left this time period. 'What happened? Is she gone?'

Ethan finds his balance, spinning around. 'I don't know ...'

With these words Ethan's illusion starts to break up. One after another the pitchers explode, the sound of shattering glass and ceramics rends the air. My arm flies up to cover my eyes. 'Hey, what's happening?'

Ethan comes towards me with his head buried beneath a protective arm. Just as he reaches me, his illusion disappears completely amid a burst of flashing green light, and we look at each other for a moment, wondering what on earth is going on.

'Are you all right?' Ethan asks.

I nod, still getting my breath back from the suddenness and the violence of that illusion gone insane. 'We have to get out of here.'

'Exactly.' But just as he takes my hand and starts to call Arkarian, a large image starts generating before us. As it takes deeper form, a sense of evil fills the room with such intensity it grows suffocating. Even before his shape fully forms, I realise who our visitor is – Marduke.

He raises his hands in the air and all the light in the room starts to swirl and form a spiralling rainbow drawn to his palms. He flexes his fingers and this swirling light quickly disappears, emptying into his hands, every last ray and beam.

The room becomes completely dark except for Marduke's one glowing yellow eye.

Ethan looks stunned, hardly breathing. I start worrying about his health, realising with a deep sinking feeling in the pit of my stomach, that this is the first time he has come face to face with his worst nightmare. And while he won't see anything in this darkness, he can make out Marduke's form from his glowing eye. 'Ethan, are you OK?'

He gathers his senses quickly. 'I could do with some light.' Keeping his eyes on the huge man before us, he feels his way to stand directly in front off me.

Instinctively I lift my feet, hugging my knees, and try not to inhale too deeply. The smell now is nothing like the flowery scent Margaret left behind, but that of something rotting, something foul.

Marduke's hands begin to glow as he motions Ethan aside. 'It's not you I want. At least, not yet.'

'What is it with you? What do you want with Isabel?'

'She's the first pawn to set my plan in motion.'

'What plan?'

'What do you think? I tire of these games you play. It's time the score is finally settled.'

'What are you talking about? Neither Isabel nor I have ever harmed you. We don't know you, except in our dreams …'

Marduke becomes irritated with Ethan's questions. 'You,' he says, flexing his glowing fingers directly at Ethan, 'I will deal with later.' Blue streaks of lightning flash from Marduke's fingertips as he motions them first at Ethan, then at the opposite wall. Instantly, the room fills with brilliant electric colour; and Ethan is catapulted horizontally through the air, crashing against the far wall.

Marduke turns his head to look at me and smiles with half a mouth. 'And now –'

But Ethan interrupts him, staggering quickly to his

feet, and screaming. It's a cry meant to distract Marduke.

It works.

Marduke groans, annoyed. 'You are either stupidly courageous or simply impatient for death.'

'Impatient for death,' Ethan replies in a hoarse voice, and, with his right hand held out, wills his dagger to his palm. 'Yours.'

Marduke lifts his massive hands once again, but this time Ethan is faster. He screams for a second time, a cry of rage, then hurls the shining blade across the room.

The dagger slashes straight into Marduke's shoulder, wounding him. Blood wells up and spreads down his left arm.

Marduke roars. The sound ought to wake the entire house and surrounding neighbours, but Abigail doesn't stir, and neither does the house. It must be under some sort of enchantment.

Marduke yanks Ethan's dagger out of his flesh. Blood spurts, sending Marduke into a frightening rage. He rampages like a crazed animal around the room, grabbing Ethan and crushing him inside his massive arm. For a second I fear Marduke may have broken Ethan's back with the vicious jolt, but then Ethan jerks forward, trying to break free of this huge man's hold. But Marduke is filled with a rage-induced strength that quickly reduces Ethan's thrusts to mere pathetic twitches.

'Watch,' Marduke hisses, pointing the dagger straight at me, his glowing hands lighting a path like a torch. 'Watch her die by your own blade.'

The dagger shimmers in his hand a second before

slicing through the air as Marduke flicks it straight in my direction. I see it coming, but can't move to save myself. My exhaustion from the healing session is still affecting my limbs, and moreover I think Marduke has thrown a spell over me. My eyes remain fixed to the glistening, blood-soaked blade.

The last thing I hear before the dagger hits, slicing deeply into the centre of my chest, is Ethan's impassioned scream. *'Arkarian!'*

Chapter Thirty-one

Ethan

Arkarian delivers us straight into the healing room in the Citadel, a room made entirely of brilliant shimmering crystal. With trembling arms he lays Isabel on a narrow table. *'What happened?'*

She looks so pale, her hands clutched tightly around the dagger jutting out of her chest, blood soaking her white nightshirt from neck to waist. 'What does it look like?'

Arkarian loosens Isabel's fingers, takes the dagger between his two hands, firmly but gently pulling it out and covering the wound with the palms of his hands. 'Who did this?'

'Marduke, of course! Didn't you see?'

'The room was black. Arkarian's voice is flat.'

'You can heal her, can't you Arkarian? This is the healing room, isn't it?'

He turns to me, tears coursing down his face, a sight that chills my spine. 'Ethan,' he says slowly, 'Isabel has a blade in her heart. She is already dead.'

'Nooo! Bring her back!'

'If only I could!' 'He shakes his head, staring fixedly

at Isabel's ashen face, as if in a daze. But I'm not a healer, and even if I were, her soul is already gone.'

'But her body is … still back in her room. She's sleeping in her bed.'

'For now. But her soul is not within it.'

'Where is her soul?'

'Lost.'

'No! Where? Can I find it and bring it back?'

His violet eyes pierce me. 'Her soul would be wandering the middle world for as long as it takes for her to cross the bridge.'

'And when she crosses this bridge, what then?'

'Her mortal body will stop breathing, completing her death.'

'Then there's still a chance to save her. To find her in this place and bring her back before her mortal body stops breathing.'

'It isn't possible. Nobody's ever done it before.'

'I will do it. Just tell me how. Help me, Arkarian.'

His hands fly up, then down again in a movement filled with panic. He spins around as if searching for something, then spins back, realising he doesn't really know what it is. 'Isabel has an affinity with the light, it's part of her gift.' He's thinking fast. Lady Arabella recognised it, that's why she gave her the gift of sight by any kind of light. Isabel will be drawn to the light of this middle world.'

'So what are you saying?'

'This light will show her the way to the bridge. Where others may take countless years searching, not really understanding what they're looking for, or even why they are on this path, Isabel will be drawn straight to it.'

'How long will her journey take?'

'Hours perhaps at the most.'

To me the choice is easy. 'I will go.'

'Ethan, this land is inhabited by all the middle creatures. Lost souls, souls that don't belong or fit in our mortal world.'

'I'm not afraid.'

'There's one more thing. Isabel must hear your voice or she won't turn away from the light.'

'I'll call to her. I'll scream if I have to.'

'You don't understand.' His voice is tight with a hysterical note I've never heard coming from him before. 'She will only hear the voice of her *soul-mate*.'

'What?' Instantly it occurs to me, and I thump his chest with the palm of my hand. 'Well that's me, Arkarian!'

His eyes shift to mine slowly. 'How do you know?'

'Since we were little kids she's had this huge crush on me. She doesn't think I know. And, well, when we were in John of Gaunt's bedroom, we kissed.'

'I know. I saw.'

'So you see, I'm her soul-mate.'

'All that shows me is that Isabel is in love with you. But what about you? Do you feel the same way about her?'

I stop for a second, searching for the truth in my heart. How do I feel about Isabel? 'I … Sure, I … I care for her. I think she's great. We're best friends.'

'Do you *love* her?'

'I, I don't know exactly, but …' My eyes move to Isabel's still and colourless body draining of blood. If I'm her soul-mate, then I have a chance to save her life. So I just have to be. 'I'm her soul-mate, Arkarian. I know this. Let me go. I have to try.'

'All right, Ethan. But first there are some things that you must know.'

Chapter Thirty-two

Ethan

This middle world is grey and dull, like a black and white video. Arkarian deposits me in the middle of a forest. The trees are differing shades of white and grey, the vines silver, stretching out around me like cobwebs. I pull the vines down out of my way, noting their dry texture, nothing like the silky moistness of a mortal forest.

I see her immediately, way up ahead, a small white figure in the distance. I run in her direction, looking for the light that's guiding her, but I can't see anything in the low-hanging grey sky. I find my path blocked by a fallen tree so high and wide I can only just see over the top of it. I throw myself across, finding footholds where I can, scrambling to the top. Out of the corner of my eye I see a dark shadowy movement. Instinctively I cringe to the side, just in time, as a tarantula the size of a small dog scurries on eight hairy legs towards me, screeching in such a high-pitched tone that my ears begin to ache. It spots me and tilts its head to one side as if trying to figure out whether I'm friend or foe. Suddenly it lifts itself up on its hind legs and screeches again, preparing to jump. Adrenalin shoots through my bloodstream, giving me a strong burst of energy, and I take a flying leap to the other side.

Running now as fast as I can, I remember Arkarian's warning: *'Your fears will be exaggerated. If you succumb to them, the creatures of your nightmares will become reality. Keep your thoughts pure and you will not be harmed. There is good and evil in that place, but mostly wandering lost souls, creatures unaware that they are even dead. They will inhabit the shapes of your fears.'*

I try to keep my mind focused on the white figure of Isabel speeding off ahead. I keep running until I finally find myself out of the forest and in a vast clearing that leads directly into a beautiful but grey valley, with a seemingly endless snow-capped mountain range to the distant right. It hits me just how vast and never-ending this place is. A movement from the valley floor catches my eye. A family of grey wolves, mother, father and five large pups, play and frolic in a field of lush grey grass. My heart leaps and I freeze to the spot, unable to take my eyes off these larger-than-life creatures. Is nothing small in this place?

Reluctantly dragging my eyes off the family of wolves, I search for Isabel. Finally finding her slight figure darting away, heading directly into the valley below. The same valley the family of wolves have made their home. I've heard that wolves are very protective of their young. I stretch up on the rocky ridge-top and cup my hands around my mouth. 'Isabel!'

But she doesn't hear me, even though my voice echoes deep into the valley. She must still be too far in front. Instead the wolves, all seven of them, turn their heads at the sound of my cry, sniffing the air through widened nostrils. And I realise with a sickening sensation in my stomach what I've done. The largest wolf climbs up on a boulder, lifts his head and howls. His mate joins him and also gives a lonesome howl. The sound of these howls draws others out. My heart thunders wildly at the sight that stretches out before me as literally hundreds of wolves gather from every direction. They start to move towards my ridge, picking up speed quickly, their long and lithe limbs pounding the cold grey earth. But the worst of it is the sight of Isabel, running on light footsteps, about halfway between the ridge and the mass of snarling and hissing wolves.

'Isabel!'

It's no good, she keeps running, oblivious of the approaching wolves. How can I make her hear me? I run straight towards her, faster than I think possible, and then harder still; but now that I'm not standing on the ridge any more, I lose sight of her. All I can see is the pack of huge wolves.

Now they're upon me. Grey dust flings into my face as the wind from their rushing bodies sends me flying and I expect to feel teeth ripping into my throat. But no – 'keep your thoughts pure,' Arkarian had said. They're only playing. I try to tell myself. No harm ... I glance up to see a wolf leap straight over me, then another. A small break in the pack and I sprint towards the only cover within sight, a boulder in the middle of their path. I scrunch up beneath it, making myself as small as possible, as they continue over the top and around both sides of my temporary hiding place, seemingly oblivious of my presence.

And all I can think is that Isabel must surely be lying

somewhere nearby, her body either smashed into the grey dirt or mauled to shreds.

Eventually, the last of the wolf pack leaps over me, and the dust starts to settle. A last lonely wolf pup prances around my boulder playfully. It catches sight of me crouched in a tiny ball covered in dust, and looks at me as if it recognises something in my frightened eyes. With seeming reluctance it turns away, sniffs the air, then moves on after the rest of the pack.

I get up and take a deep settling breath, scouring the countryside for any sign of Isabel, my mouth completely dry, expecting the worst. I see her, a slight figure in white, clambering up a series of boulders that border a river.

Relief washes through me, making my legs feel like the liquid in that river, but then the thought hits me that Isabel is supposedly heading towards a bridge, and here we are now following a river. I scream at her once again. 'Isabel!'

But still she's too far away.

I start running again, ignoring the pain developing in my chest from trying to run while my lungs are still full of all that grey dust. 'Isabel!' I call again.

For a second she pauses and I think at last she's going to turn. Instead, she bends down and sniffs a grey flower. The image sparks a sharp memory.

Instantly, a gust of wind like a mini-tornado descends over me, pinning me to the ground. And in a flash the wind disappears and a dark figure forms. I know straight away who it is; no one else is half as tall or evil or hideously deformed.

This time I will not act unthinkingly. I urge myself to find an inner calm before facing this man. 'Marduke, I didn't know you were a lost soul.'

He laughs, an uneven guttural sound. 'You willed me here, you fool.'

My memory, I realise. Now how do I get rid of him?

He grins with half a mouth. 'You can't.'

Hmm, he hears my thoughts too. I take a deep breath and try to see around him to Isabel up ahead. She's started walking again, hugging the river's edge. And this time I see something in the distance beyond her, something startlingly white. My God, I think it's the bridge.

When he speaks, his voice is teasing. 'You won't reach her, and even if you did, your voice is not the one that will make her turn.'

'You're lying.' I remember Arkarian's warning on how to dispel what isn't real in this world. 'You're also not really here.'

'But I *am*, Ethan. You created me in your thoughts.'

'An image from my dreams, yes, I know. But now I call you what you really are at this moment – a figment of my imagination.' I wave my hand at him. 'Be gone!' I walk straight towards him, my hands raised up, palms outwards, as if to shove him aside, while mentally pushing all doubts firmly away.

I recall Arkarian's advice: *'If you believe with all your heart, the illusion created from your own mind will disappear.'*

Just as I'm about to crash into Marduke's thick torso, he breaks up, leaving only sprinkles of grey dust.

'Yes!' Now for Isabel. I glance up ahead and see her standing on the edge of a shimmering white bridge. 'God, no, Isabel!'

She doesn't turn but seems to hesitate. I run, jumping over boulders in my way, ignoring the small animals scurrying across my path. 'Isabel!'

She steps on to the bridge, but finally I'm so close that she must surely hear me. *'Isabel!'*

She takes another step. I reach the very edge where the bridge begins; Isabel is no more than a few paces away. But with her back to me she takes another step.

'Isabel! It's me, Ethan! Turn around and look at me!'

She doesn't turn and I realise that I have failed. Marduke was right when he said I'm not the one who will make her turn.

I'm not her soul-mate.

What do I do now? In three more steps she will reach the other side. *'Isabel!'* But it's useless. She takes two more steps. Two steps closer to death.

Defeat hangs heavily inside me. There's nothing left I can do.

But suddenly a voice calls out from behind, one word whipping past my shoulder, not in any way spoken loudly, but filled with a vibrancy and deep passion all the same. *'Isabel.'*

She stills, her right foot motionless in the air. I turn and see Arkarian. He comes up and stands beside me. 'Isabel, turn around and come home.'

She turns, and the three of us disappear, straight back to the healing room in the Citadel.

And now Isabel is breathing again. The blood on her shirt is a stark reminder of what we've just experienced, but her wound is completely sealed.

She opens her eyes. 'What ... what happened?'

My eyes meet Arkarian's across the top of her body. His expression warns me to stay quiet. He looks down at Isabel. 'What can you remember?'

She pulls herself to a sitting position and rubs the side of her head. 'Marduke appeared in Abby's room. He …' She touches her bloodstained chest. 'He threw a dagger and …' Her eyes snap up and lock with mine. A tentative smile forms. 'Did you save me, Ethan?'

I flick a look at Arkarian. 'He most certainly did, Isabel,' he says softly. 'He is a true hero.'

As she smiles at me, mistaken love shining clearly through her eyes, I try to catch Arkarian's look. He quickly glances down, but not before I glimpse the pain and anguish that fills him.

Chapter Thirty-three

Ethan

Isabel believes that she was only unconscious; her memories are sketchy and vague, the grey place of the middle lands registering only as a subconscious memory. After assuring himself that her wound is healed and her recollections hazy enough not to cause her undue worry, Arkarian delivers her home.

But not me. He knows my thoughts, I'm baring them plainly for him to read. This mission should not have had the added danger of Marduke. Arkarian was aware of the threat, and so was the Tribunal, and yet still they let Isabel do it. They've been rushing her right from the start, with only a few weeks' training, and this was the result: her near death. What the hell is going on?

As soon as she leaves, Arkarian takes me to a different room, this one resembling a bar with bottles and armchairs and stools, but empty of customers. He pours us both a drink and takes the bottle with him, we find seats by a window. It looks out on nothing but dark swirling mist. I taste my drink and at first think it's just a soft drink of cola, but one burning sip later I realise it's something much stronger.

I get straight to the point. 'Isabel must be released from the Guard and her memory erased so she can live a normal life again.'

Arkarian downs his entire drink in one gulp and pours another. 'This is the life she wants. She's tasted it, she wants more, she was born for it.'

'No, Arkarian. It's too dangerous.'

'She's a healer, Ethan. There's a purpose to her life other than her mortal one. If she didn't understand this, her healing skills would frighten and confuse her.'

He might be right, but being frightened and confused is better than being dead. 'Surely there is a way around that? A way of enlightenment.'

'Impossible—'

'You must stop her!'

He sighs deeply. 'I wish I could, Ethan.'

We remain quiet for a moment, both staring into the swirling mist.

'We nearly lost her today,' I remind him.

He lifts his eyes to mine in silence.

'Can you guarantee something like this won't happen again?'

'No.' He holds my gaze.

'Did you know you were her soul-mate?'

'If I did, I would have gone in the first place.'

'What does this mean?'

He pushes his blue hair back and lets it fall again, obscuring his eyes. 'Some people live their whole lives unaware of who their soul-mate is. It has to be this way with Isabel.'

'Why?'

'We can never be together.'

'But if you care for her …'

He glances across at me. 'Firstly, there's the matter of my youth retention. This skill separates us into two completely different worlds. I can't live in hers; she would never have a *normal* life in mine, and she deserves that. Second – and this is a good thing – she's in love with *you*.'

'It's a mistake. I see this now. I mean, we're the best of friends and that's what we were meant to be in the first place. All those years as kids when she trailed after me and Matt, she just wanted to do the same things we did because they were fun things to do. And if we had allowed her to join us, then Isabel and I would have been best friends from the start, as we should have been, as we are now at last.'

'I'm sorry you feel that way. If I could choose anybody for Isabel, I would choose you, Ethan. You would be good for her.'

'But it wouldn't be right, Arkarian.'

His shoulders droop as he stares into the remains of another drink, looking as if all is lost. As we sit in silence I think about this soul-mate business. What if I didn't know Arkarian was Isabel's real soul-mate, would it make a difference to how I feel about her? I doubt it. But I do know one thing. 'If I had a chance of knowing who *my* soul-mate was, I would definitely take it.'

Arkarian glances up at me. 'Would you? What if she were someone from the other side?'

His question challenges my thoughts. How would I react if that were true? I decide Arkarian is just being particularly morbid. But his words do remind me of just how I've felt lately about the Guard – like I'm only a pawn on a chessboard in a game Arkarian is playing.

'Not me, Ethan,' he says. 'I'm also a pawn.'

'Then who's running this show? The members of the Tribunal?'

'The Prophecy.'

'Which was written before time. Ever since reading it again with Isabel I add, 'I've been bothered by one particular line – one even more than the others.' He waits and I ask the question weighing heavily on my mind. 'Tell me, who is the lost warrior that must return?'

Arkarian peers at me with eyes that wonder just how much I've figured out. 'Who do you think it is?'

'Marduke?'

'He's the one called traitor.'

All this secrecy is driving me crazy. 'With all that's happened lately, haven't we come too far for more half-truths?'

'That we have, Ethan.'

But he doesn't elaborate. So I try to work it out. The Prophecy says a warrior must return, which means this person has to have left the Guard at some time. Why would anyone do that? They sure would need a good reason. Nothing short of death would make me … These thoughts of death get my mind churning on a different level. What if it wasn't your own death that separated you from the Guard? What if it was the death of someone so close to you that their loss forced you into making the most drastic decision of your life? Like the death of your own daughter?

And now I recall Arkarian asking whether my father ever asked me strange questions, whether he wondered where I go in my sleep.

Finally, something shifts in my brain like a gear stick. 'The returning warrior is my father, isn't it?'

Arkarian remains silent, just keeps looking at me while I put these particular pieces together to form the correct picture. I lean forward in my seat, working it out. 'My father was Marduke's partner.' And then the main piece slots into place. 'You mean … he was the one who maimed Marduke in a fight that turned him traitor?'

'Never doubt it, Ethan, Marduke turned himself into a traitor.'

'So why Sera?'

'Marduke killed your sister because he believes the disfigurement resulting from the duel is the reason his woman left him. The mother of their small child.'

This is hard to believe. 'Because of vanity, my sister is dead?'

'Vanity, pride, pain, bitterness, all things that feed the armies of the Order.'

'Let me get this straight: Marduke turned traitor, giving up the Guard, because after his fight with Dad that left him scarred, his woman left him?'

Arkarian nods. 'Taking their child with her, she disappeared, and Marduke believed it was because she didn't want their child to look upon his disfigured face and be repulsed.'

'Has anyone heard from her since?' He doesn't answer straight away and I get the message he doesn't intend to. 'OK, tell me this: what does Marduke want with Isabel?'

He sighs, running his fingers through his hair. 'It's complicated. His interest in Isabel remains unclear, but we do know that for him revenge has not yet been fully exacted.'

'He killed my sister! And look at Dad, he's a shell of himself! What more does he want?'

'Marduke will only be satisfied when he and your father duel to the death. He killed little Sera because she was beautiful and he wanted to take from your father that which was most beautiful to him. But he also wanted your father to suffer as he believes he has suffered.'

'And as Dad was not a vain man it wasn't his looks.'

'But your father withdrew from the Guard, swearing he would never return. In this way he believed he was protecting his family from further pain and bloodshed.'

'Does Dad know about me being in the Guard?'

'He's finally starting to suspect.'

'*Finally?*' Well, now I'm starting to understand. But with this understanding comes a burning inner rage. I fly up out of my seat, pointing my finger at Arkarian. 'You're using me to lure Dad back to the Guard, aren't you? So he can finish his duel with Marduke, who won't rest until it's settled. That's why you came to me when I was four years old. You've had my life planned all this time. By putting me in danger you think to draw my father out.'

'Sit down, Ethan.' Arkarian won't be provoked.

I sit, my feet tapping and jerking restlessly while waiting for his explanation.

'Get this straight: you were Named at birth. We don't "make" members of the Guard, you are already "made", so to speak. We're aware from the day you are born, sometimes even before. But a member is given as long as possible to live their normal life. Only when their skills become obvious and start causing concern do we start the initiating process.'

'That's what happened with Isabel – she started healing herself.'

'That's right. With you it was different. You had just
experienced the tragic death of your sister and were
not coping. And as we didn't want to lose a future
member of the Guard to insanity, it was decided to ini-
tiate you at an early age.'

'OK, I know that. So tell me why you want Dad to
suspect I'm a member of the Guard? What happened to
the secrecy code?'

'Let me explain. Before little Sera was murdered,
your father had started a three-part assignment, a very
important mission, which he didn't finish.'

More pieces fall into place as my memory flashes
back to John of Gaunt's bedroom. 'That's what John of
Gaunt was referring to when he talked of the young
man who helped him once but never returned. He
must've been talking about Dad. He even said something about our eyes, and how mine were like this
other man's.'

'What you and Isabel did that day was to fulfil the
second part of your father's mission – securing the
rightful succession to the throne of England. But the
third part of the mission remains incomplete, and now
the situation is growing urgent. We need Shaun to
finish the job, although it's too late for John of Gaunt
to see the result. He's dying in a prison, put there by
his nephew King Richard II.'

'Was Dad supposed to rescue him?'

'No; to die in that prison is John of Gaunt's fate. Your
father's part was to protect his son as an infant, secure
the crown for the child Richard, and ensure that the
older King Richard continued with his plan to journey

to Ireland. But now John of Gaunt will die thinking the pact he made to secure his son's protection was dishonoured. Yet it's not too late to ensure King Richard journeys to Ireland. Unfortunately, he has an adviser by his side who doesn't have the right to be anywhere near the king, nor in that period of time. He's one of the Order's warriors, using the name of Lord Whitby, and he's talking King Richard out of going.'

'Let me get this right – all Dad has to do is get King Richard to continue with his plans to go to Ireland, and all three parts of his mission will be complete?'

'You've got it.'

'But why is King Richard's journey to Ireland so important?'

'So John of Gaunt's son Henry, or Hal of Bolingbroke, as he is known, can come out of exile to mount his campaign against Richard, which he can't do while Richard is still in London.'

'So why can't I complete this mission in Dad's place?'

'It's a matter of honour, Ethan. Your father made a blood oath with John of Gaunt to protect his son. That can't be fulfilled if Hal of Bolingbroke is never allowed home and dies in exile.'

'But you can't draw Dad out now that Marduke is hungry for revenge! It can only end in Dad's death! There'll be a duel for sure between them, and Dad hasn't trained for many years. Marduke will slaughter him.'

'Don't underestimate your father, Ethan. He was our very best. And the conflict with Marduke must happen one day, be assured. Marduke will not rest, but will seek to harm others who your father loves.'

'Or who matter to me,' I suddenly realise.

Arkarian nods. 'Marduke has been watching you and Isabel training these past few weeks. He's seen how close the two of you have grown. A bond of friendship can be as strong as a bond of love.'

I groan, my face dropping into my open palms. Arkarian's hand comes down on my head; warmth and a sensation of calm sweeps through me. 'We don't know exactly why Marduke wants to kill Isabel,' he says softly. 'All we know is that he's getting desperate to force this confrontation. That's why we have to act.'

I glance up into his face and feel his concern reach out to me. 'Tell me, what happens if Dad doesn't finish this mission to make sure King Richard II goes to Ireland as he's supposed to?'

'Richard will remain king, and eventually his marriage to the young Isabella will result in heirs—'

'And history will change.'

'Cataclysmically, and the odds of our winning the final conflict will weigh deeply against us. That is, if we're lucky enough to exist any more.'

Reluctantly, I understand that athough we're only pawns in this game, we're quite important, for the game has evolved into a serious and dangerous reality. My father is part of it, and so am I. These are the facts.

I look straight at Arkarian. 'What do you want me to do?'

Chapter Thirty-four

Isabel

I shift from the Citadel to my bed with the strong sense that someone is watching my transition. I open my eyes and look straight into my brother's. He can't know anything, of course, but after the experience I just endured, my nerves are right on edge. The sight of Matt sitting up in my green plastic chair, his serious dark eyes intent on me, gives me such a fright that I give a little scream. Then I notice he's holding something in his hand, and to my mounting horror, realise it's the notebook with the Prophecy written in it. Oh hell! I decide the only way to save this situation is to feign hysteria and scream louder.

Mum and Jimmy come running into my room, the door banging hard against the wall in their rush.

'What's wrong?' Mum asks.

'Was that you, sweetcakes?' This from Jimmy.

These two people are the last thing on my mind right now. I must get Matt to give back the notebook and forget about it. Arkarian's face swims into view before my eyes. What on earth will he think of me when he finds out how careless I've been?

Acting as if Matt has woken me from a deep dream, I pull myself up into a sitting position with the intention of yelling, 'Matt leave me alone!' but the first word that comes out of my mouth is not Matt's name at all. 'Arkarian!' I scream at the top of my voice. *Oh, No! Did I just call out Arkarian's name?*

I try to collect my thoughts quickly. 'I mean ... Matt, what the hell are you doing here? You scared me half to death. What's the matter with you?' I try to distract him as everyone starts talking simultaneously.

Matt stands up with his hand in the air, the notebook swinging loosely from it, as he attempts to shut everybody up. Finally, Mum and Jimmy calm down and Matt turns to me. 'I came in here earlier to ask you something, but you were sleeping. I would have left then, except I noticed this notebook lying on the floor.'

'Which you couldn't help reading,' I add, guessing correctly.

'I thought I'd ask you about it, and tried to wake you.' He turns to Mum and Jimmy. 'Do you know how deep a sleeper Isabel is?' Without waiting for their reply, he swings back to me. 'It took me half an hour. I swear I thought you were dead. And what the hell is Arkari— What was that word you just called out? Has it got anything to do with these weird notes?' He indicates the notebook with a slight tilt of his head.

Retaliation, I decide, is the best action to get him off the track. 'I don't know what you're talking about.' If I called anything out it's because I was dreaming, of course. And what *are* you going on about? Obviously I'm not dead. Next time you take to snooping around my room at night, don't wake me, OK? I like my sleep.'

I get up on my knees and snatch the notebook from his hand. 'Give me that! It's just a stupid poem I wrote, which I don't appreciate you reading. I wouldn't go through *your* stuff, by the way.'

'I didn't go looking. You must've knocked it to the floor when you fell asleep.'

'Whatever. You had no right reading my private thoughts.'

He peers at me with a weird look and says softly, 'Your private thoughts are really strange, Isabel.'

'I don't care. At least they're mine. Now can everyone go back to bed?'

Jimmy quickly agrees. 'What a good idea!'

'Not till I get some answers,' Matt says stubbornly.

'I'm tired, Matt. Whatever you're so hyped up about can wait till the morning.'

Jimmy tries again. 'Everything looks different in the morning, Matt. Why don't you go to bed?'

Matt gives Jimmy a hard stare and yells at the top of his voice, 'I don't take orders from you!'

Everyone goes silent. Matt's resentment of Jimmy's position in our household has become more evident every day. I catch Jimmy's look and try to tell him with my eyes to back off, I can handle my brother, especially now that I have the notebook tucked under my pillow.

Mum gives Jimmy's hand a little yank. 'Let's go, honey.'

They leave. Matt turns his back on me and walks to the window. He pulls up the blind, revealing an almost full moon, and suddenly my room glows with brilliant light. In my exhausted state this light is too much. Instinctively, I raise my hand to cover my eyes. Matt notices. 'What's the matter with you?'

'Nothing, it's just the glare.'

He looks around the room, then out the window to the night sky. I suddenly realise how he must see the room – dark and mostly in shadows. He points to the sky. 'But it's only the moon.'

I lower my arm and try not to squint. 'I'm just tired, OK? Now what's eating you? Why did you come into my room in the first place?'

He plonks down in the green plastic chair, making an annoying squeaky sound. 'I want to know what's going on.'

'Nothing. I was just in a deep sleep, that's all.'

He looks at me with half-closed eyes and a puzzled frown. 'I meant what's with you and Ethan?'

'Oh.' I have to relax before I make him suspicious for no other reason than my own stupidity. 'Well, it's still the same answer – nothing. Nothing is going on.'

'You can't spend as much time with someone as you do with Ethan, almost every day, and it not mean anything.'

After what just happened, with Ethan saving my life – though I'm not real clear on the details 'cause my head's in a bit of a mess right now – I think our relationship is finally taking off. The time we spend training in the hills around the lake is incredible, the most fun I've had in a long time. As for our trips into the past, nothing can surpass those adventures. Even getting stabbed in the chest doesn't deter me. Instinctively, I run my hand over the place Ethan's dagger recently pierced. Matt misreads the action.

'When are you going to admit the truth, Isabel?'

I glance up at him and he says, 'Look at yourself.

251

You're worse than a love-sick puppy.'

Withdrawing my hand, I tug the quilt up around my knees and chest, and take the moment to form the words necessary to get Matt off my back. 'Look, Matt, Ethan and I are just friends working on a project together. That's the truth.' Well, part of it, that is. A project so huge that I hope we'll be working together for a long time. But that's not what Matt needs to hear. 'I'll be honest with you, Matt. I really like Ethan. He's fun and not at all the weird person you make him out to be.'

He starts to object. I hold my hand up and cut him off, crossing the fingers of my other hand beneath the quilt. 'But I realise now my obsession with Ethan was just a childhood crush.'

Matt nods, seemingly content I'm telling the truth. I sigh, finally relaxing, and decide to get Matt right off the subject before he drills me with more questions. 'I looked for you earlier. Were you with Rochelle tonight?'

'I was for a while, but she said she was tired and wanted to go to bed early, so I went over to Dillon's. I thought he might know something about you and Ethan.'

'Why would you ask Dillon about me and Ethan?'

'That's simple: you're not telling me anything. And oddly enough, Dillon has kept being friends with Ethan, and friends talk.'

'And what did Dillon tell you?'

He shrugs dejectedly. 'Nothing really.'

My head shakes. My brother is obsessed – with suffocating me. But I don't want to encourage this line of conversation. 'You're way too serious for someone your age, Matt. You gotta get a better life.'

252

'You could be right,' he sighs. Pulling himself out of the chair, he leans over me. 'I'm sorry I scared you earlier. I shouldn't have tried to wake you. It's just the words in that notebook kind of gave me a creepy feeling I couldn't shake.'

He sounds so melancholy, and to get his mind off the notebook, I wrap my arms around him for a reassuring hug. 'That's OK. It was waking to the sight of your face that scared me half to death.'

He hugs me back, a rare sibling moment we haven't shared in years. 'Well thanks. How nice of you to say.'

As he draws away, a familiar scent hits me, sending a chill through my entire body. 'What's that smell?'

As he straightens, he sniffs the air. 'What? Do you mean that flowery scent?'

I nod but don't speak; my tongue feels as if it's doubled in size. The whiff of that flowery aroma reminds me too much of the scent left behind by the assassin in Abigail Smith's bedroom. I work some moisture into my mouth and try to swallow. 'Yeah, that perfume. Why do you smell of it?'

He shrugs and moves to the door. 'It's not perfume. But if you like it, I'll try to get you some. It's Rochelle's eye drops, for her allergy. She swears by it, says it works like a miracle on tired eyes. It does too, I tried some myself today.'

I force myself to breathe. 'Oh, really?'

'Yeah, she has it specially made by some out-of-town herbalist.'

I watch, speechless, as his jaw slides right, then left, a nervous gesture he's perfected over the years. And then he says, 'It's made from some sort of unique flower. A giant iris, I think.'

Chapter Thirty-five

Ethan

This week I train Isabel harder than ever before. We even practise our landings.

'We're going back to see King Richard II.'

'I thought you said we can't go back to the same time twice?'

'The *exact* same time. But Richard is thirty-two now.'

'Oh.'

'Yeah, and ...' I have to tell her about Dad and how the Tribunal want him to come back and finish his mission – and deal with Marduke. I tell her most of what Arkarian explained and how Dad has to make sure Richard goes on his planned trip to Ireland.

'But we could do that, couldn't we? Why drag your father into this, when he obviously doesn't want to?'

'Apparently he made a blood oath with John of Gaunt to protect his son Henry. And then there's his unfinished business with Marduke. The Tribunal wants Dad to finish the duel. They say it's time Marduke was put in his place, before any other innocent lives are destroyed.'

She catches on quickly. 'Like mine. They're thinking of the threats he made, and his presence in Abigail's bedroom when he tried to kill me.' She shivers all over as if wild horses suddenly trample her grave. 'There's something really creepy about all this.'

I hope it's her sixth sense and not a flashback. Arkarian says it would be bad for Isabel to remember the grey world and how close she came to death, that it could kill her adventurous spirit.

'So when do we leave?' she asks.

'Tonight. But don't be surprised when you don't go straight to the Citadel. Arkarian is having us all meet together in his chambers first.'

'And your father, will he be coming too?'

'He doesn't know anything – yet. I'm supposed to be the bait to lure him to Arkarian.'

'And just how are you going to do that?'

I don't tell her, 'cause I'm not so sure myself. 'I have to come up with something to stun him into realising the truth about me, but in a way that will make him angry enough to either want to protect me or want to kill Arkarian. Either will suffice. All he has to do is call Arkarian's name to get into his chambers.'

'That's *all* he has to do?'

'Well, he has to do it with feeling. That way Arkarian will hear him.'

She frowns deeply, like she's recalling a troublesome thought. I'm about to ask what that look means, but she waves me away, lifting her sword with two hands, raising it into position. It's still difficult for her, but she's making heaps of progress since we've been working her upper arms with weights. 'I get the feeling I'm going to need this skill before long.'

'How do you mean?'

'When we fight Marduke.'

She stuns me into silence for a moment. 'But ... *you* won't be fighting him. The duel is between Marduke and my father. There are rules about this sort of thing, rules even Marduke must follow.'

She stares at me as if deciding whether to say anything or not. I get the prickly sensation she's keeping something from me. 'He may want to kill your father, Ethan, but he tried to kill me. I say that gives me grounds to enter the duelling arena.'

I grab her wrist while it's still in the air. 'You're not going anywhere near Marduke again!'

'If only that were true! I'm not that naive, Ethan, and neither should you be. Wake up. Marduke brought me into this duel when he tried to murder me. And because he did it to get at you, you're connected now too. It's like Marduke is trying to draw as many of the Guard out as he can. Perhaps his thinking is to eliminate us while we're vulnerable. Your guess is as good as mine.'

'Well, the Tribunal sure is in a desperate hurry to deal with Marduke.'

'Why do you think that is?' She goes on to answer herself. 'Because the situation is growing out of hand, that's why, and the Tribunal knows it. How many others has Marduke linked to this duel? Hmm? If he can weaken the Guards here, at the site of the ancient city, then he and the Goddess are way out in front. He's doing her a favour by pursuing his quest for revenge.'

She drops these thoughts on me like a bomb, but apparently there's more to what she's been thinking about. 'Tell me, how well do you know Rochelle?'

The question surprises me and I stare at her for a second. 'Why do you ask?'

'Don't go getting all defensive,' she says.

'I'm not. Why would I be?'

'Just forget it.'

I grab her arm, stopping her from lifting her sword again. 'What are you talking about? And why did you ask about Rochelle? You know I can't stand that girl.'

She stays quiet for a minute, looking at me like she's seeing through to my soul or something. Her face suddenly goes a subtle red colour like she's been out in the sun a little too long. 'I think she might be ... I think she could work for Marduke.'

The words penetrate, but I can't believe she said them. 'That's rubbish!'

She lunges for my arm as I turn away. 'Ethan, think about it. Remember the scent that lingered around Abigail Smith's assassin, and how we both recognised it, but couldn't place it?'

'You've got it wrong, Isabel. Perfume can't transfer with the soul.'

'I know that! But Rochelle uses some sort of eye drops.' She waves a hand in my face. Eye drops, Ethan, that are made from flowers.'

'What?'

'Matt told me.'

Something inside me starts to boil up like a pressure cooker with the lid on so tight no steam can escape. Why can't everybody leave Rochelle alone? First the Tribunal jumped to conclusions because of Rochelle's rough childhood, now Isabel is making huge leaps because of some stupid scent we picked up in the past.

'You don't know what you're talking about. Just leave the girl alone, OK?'

She stares at me, and for a second I swear her eyes begin to swell with glistening moisture. But before I can make any sense of this, she turns away and starts acting like we never had this conversation. She lifts her sword easily this time with her two small hands, mumbling at me, 'Let's get on with this training.'

And so we train the rest of the afternoon, but cloaked in a tension-filled silence. By the time we call it a night and head home, I'm weary with exhaustion, unable to stop thinking of Isabel's accusations about Rochelle and Marduke. And now I have to prepare myself to confront Dad.

The walk from Isabel's house to mine takes longer than usual tonight as my feet feel as if they're weighted with lead. I take the time rehearsing some ideas. The one thing I don't want is to cause Dad any further pain. I've seen what effect losing Sera had on his life. But when I finally arrive home and find Dad staring fixedly at the television, all the subtle plans I'd been forming fly out of my head.

This is his life now – no life at all.

Is that a way for a member of the Guard, or even an ordinary man, to spend his days, as if living in slow motion?

I always wanted a father I could look up to. Other boys had them. Apparently I did once. I've spent my whole life trying to be that man – the man my father was supposed to be. And as I stare at his motionless form, a shiver darts through me: could this be my life one day – stationary and gripped in fear? It's this image that makes me say the words, 'Sera was murdered by

Marduke, and now he plans to kill Isabel. Only you can stop him.'

His shoulders jerk. He slowly turns, looking like a corpse dead three days, his face drained completely of colour. 'What did you say?'

I take a deep breath. 'I know all about you, Dad, and your otherworldly life. The fact is, you have to finish your mission, then confront Marduke, and get this whole extraneous war with him over with before innocent lives are lost.'

He climbs half out of his easy chair, turning to get a better view of me. 'You don't know what you're saying.'

'Denial, Dad? I wish I could find that *un*believable. But you know, it's just so like who you've become. I thought fathers were supposed to set examples. It's not that I want you to fight, Dad, I just want you to be who you really are. Live to the fullest of your potential. You know what to do – the choice is yours.' I turn, go to my room, flop down on my bed, stare at the ceiling and wait. I wait to hear his footsteps come down the hallway to confront me, demand answers, or at least to admit the truth about himself and who he was – who he is, 'cause I realise now that being in the Guard is not a choice thing. It's what we *are*. What Dad's done is cop out.

I wait so long without hearing a sound that I inadvertently fall asleep.

I wake and land in Arkarian's octagonal central chamber. Arkarian is not alone. Carter is sitting on a stool examining his fingernails. He glances at me and gives a small acknowledging nod. Jimmy is here too, and takes my hand in a strong shake. A puff of shimmering dust ignites the air in front of me and Isabel lands, squarely on two feet, her hands extended for added balance. She straightens and gasps in delight.

Her successful landing gets a round of applause from Jimmy and Carter and a big grin from Arkarian. He points to each of us in turn, ticking off his fingertips. 'One, two, three, four, and me five … Yes, we're gathering.'

'How many are we supposed to be?' I ask, catching his excitement.

'Eventually nine.'

'That's right,' Isabel says. 'That number's mentioned in the Prophecy. So who else is yet to join us?'

I think about this, coming up with the first missing member. 'Well, there's my father – the warrior who must return. That would make six.'

'Don't forget the warrior who can't be trusted.' Carter also knows the Prophecy.

Arkarian throws him a troubled look. 'I don't think it quite goes that way.'

Carter simply shrugs.

Jimmy remembers another line. 'The other seeded of evil.'

'And a leader pure of heart,' Arkarian says with reverence.

Suddenly, Isabel doubles over, stumbling forward a step. Jimmy is quick to catch her around the waist. Arkarian runs to her side. 'What is it, Isabel?'

'I – I don't know. My head is weird, my stomach …' She groans, then heaves. 'Get back!' With this warning she starts to vomit.

Arkarian looks over her head to Jimmy, his eyes asking questions.

'Matt went out hours ago. He hadn't returned by the

time I went to bed. I thought it was safe.'

His words startle me. 'What do you mean, safe? Safe from Matt? Is he suspicious or something?'

'He's been watching Isabel sleep,' Jimmy says.

'No way! But he couldn't know.'

Isabel, clutching her stomach, whispers hoarsely, 'He read the Prophecy.' She glances up at Arkarian. 'I'm sorry. It was an accident.'

'I know,' he says softly. 'Jimmy told me.'

'*Ark-ar-ian!*'

The word, screamed with undeniable emotion, echoes through the chamber. I recognise the voice; it's Matt's. 'Oh no, he's mad! How much do you think he knows about us?'

Isabel straightens a little and takes a deep gagging breath, her face distorted as she stares in distaste at the puddle of vomit before her. 'Um, there's something you should know.' We all wait nervously. 'I inadvertently called Arkarian's name the other night, and Matt heard.' Her eyes lock with Arkarian's. Neither of them speaks. They could be the only two people in the entire universe. Jimmy shares with me a tolerant smile.

'*Ark-ar-ian! Whatever you are, why does my sister not respond?*'

Isabel groans again, almost passing out this time. 'He's shaking me.'

Carter gets off his seat. 'The Prophecy would make no sense to anyone who doesn't know about the Guard. Matt's just hit the jackpot with the name. I'll go and pay him a visit. I'm sure I can stall him long enough for you to get to King Richard and back.'

Arkarian grips his shoulder, then lifts his hand to the

261

front of Carter's face with a circular motion. 'Good man! Now go, and hurry.'

Instantly, Carter disappears, leaving behind only a fragment of shimmering dust drifting to the floor. And for the first time I actually find myself liking the man. But it seems to take forever for Carter to get over to Matt's house. 'Where does he live?' I call out as Isabel's pain worsens and she vomits again. 'Doesn't he have wings?'

Jimmy rubs my arm. 'No, he doesn't, and remember, he has to wake in his mortal body first, then drive over to Matt's house. But don't worry, Carter drives like a demon possessed with the speed of light.'

I try to laugh. I try to relax. But it's hard with Isabel doubled over in pain. I know what this feels like. Her breathing has already started to become laboured. Arkarian, though not a healer, has nurtured many qualities over the centuries, and among other things, he has learned the skill of bringing comfort to the bereaved and pained. He's with Isabel now, and his touch is helping to keep her calm.

We can tell when she suddenly relaxes that Matt must be distracted, probably to answer the door.

'We can't wait much longer,' Arkarian says, and everybody knows who he's talking about, who we're hanging around waiting for – my father. While Isabel gets her breath back, Arkarian and Jimmy start clearing away Isabel's mess.

'We're wasting our time, he won't show,' I tell them. The thought that my father has chosen to ignore the struggle and hide in his shell makes me so mad that my blood boils. 'He's a coward!'

The second I say these words, dust shimmers in the

air in front of me, and Dad lands flat on his feet, his eyes looking straight in my direction.

'Dad! I didn't mean—'

'You call me a coward because you have no idea just how much courage it took to withdraw from the Guard.' He doesn't wait for me to respond. 'I wanted only to stop the bloodshed. You were just a tiny child. He would have come after you too.'

'I'm sorry, Dad. It's just, all my life you've been ...'

'A coward? Because I chose peace instead of war?'

Arkarian lays a hand on Dad's shoulder. 'By withdrawing, not dealing with the situation, you have in fact created more bloodshed.'

He looks outraged. 'How so?'

Arkarian glances briefly at Isabel. 'Marduke almost killed Isabel, possibly to lure you out, as she is someone your son cares for. He has also turned one of our Named ones into a traitor.'

This latter part is terrible news. I wonder who he means and whether I know him.

'Marduke is restless. He won't wait for ever, Shaun. He'll come after your loved ones, and all those they care for, the circle ever widening.'

Dad looks at Arkarian with pleading eyes. 'I don't want my son in danger. I just want him to live a normal life.'

'Like yours, Dad? Is that what you're doing? 'Cause I don't want that. It's not living.'

Dad's eyes narrow and he seems to withdraw. 'Ethan, you're my son. I don't want you to be a part of this dangerous game.' And to Arkarian he says with bitterness in his voice, 'I thought you were my friend, but you tricked my son and used his innocence to further

263

your own quests.'

'He needed our help, Shaun. He was four and had witnessed a horrible death. He was floundering on the edge of insanity.'

'No! I would have—' Dad pauses suddenly, realising that he couldn't help me then, as he's still unable to now. He gives Arkarian a hostile stare. 'Whether I could help my son or not, you and the Tribunal had no right to steal his childhood and youth. You should all be ashamed!'

Arkarian sighs. 'It's difficult to be ashamed, Shaun, when we're so proud of what Ethan's become.'

Dad looks suspiciously at me. 'I'll not let him make the same mistakes I did, Arkarian, no matter how twisted you've made his thoughts against me.'

'You're judging me unfairly.'

'Am I? I don't think so.'

'I admit, we did at first have a plan, a simple plan. We thought if you knew Ethan was training, you would come back, want to be a part of that. You were meant to be his Trainer, after all.'

'Ethan is Named?'

'Yes. But as you had withdrawn, training was granted to me. I've been honoured. Ethan has developed higher than all our expectations.'

'Are you lying to me, Arkarian? I don't trust you.'

'Of course Ethan is Named. We couldn't reveal the secrets of the Guard to him otherwise.'

Dad's eyes grow wild for a second. Finally he calms. 'If what you say is true, then what are Ethan's skills?'

Arkarian glances at me, lifting one eyebrow. Quickly I think, what illusion could best make Dad realise how much he is needed now, more than ever before? I think of Sera, and of the way she looked at that moment, so close to death, when she told me to remember Marduke's name. She was making sure I could identify her murderer, so that I could tell Dad and her death could be avenged. I could show this scene to Dad, play it out just as it happened, but decide against it. That event is still too raw, even after all these years. Dad hasn't dealt with his grief; it would only make things worse. He might withdraw completely. Sharing my thoughts, Arkarian agrees with me with a barely noticeable shake of his head.

I have another quick think. There is of course nothing stopping me from reminding Dad of the source of our problems – Marduke. Didn't he tell Isabel on that mountain top that I could reach him through my illusions? That if I called him he would come? What better way to prove my skills to dad than to bring Marduke physically into this room, while remaining within the safety net of my illusion. So now I know exactly what to do. Closing my eyes, I concentrate for a few seconds. Moments before he appears within a green light, the scent of evil fills the octagonal room. Isabel sucks in an audible breath, lunging backwards until she hits machinery behind her. Jimmy plucks a knife from his boot. Arkarian waves Jimmy's hand away. The creature in our centre casts a look around the room with interest, stopping when he sees Dad. Then he straightens to his full enormous height, raises his arms and roars.

'Marduke,' Dad whispers hoarsely as if seeing a ghost.

Marduke lowers his arms, locking eyes with Dad. 'You have grown old.'

'And you are even uglier than I remember.'

Dad's spirit almost makes me laugh out loud, knowing full well how vain Marduke is. But, instead, tears well up in my eyes as I glimpse a fragment of the man Dad once was.

Marduke's yellow eye blazes as bright as a flame at the insult. 'Count your hours with your loved ones,' he says in his guttural voice. 'You have only a few left. Finally, we will settle this argument. And of course I will win.'

'Don't be so sure!'

Marduke scoffs and spittle flies through the air, some of it landing on Dad's face and chest and arms. But Dad doesn't flinch one bit.

'Name the place,' Dad volunteers.

Marduke laughs, but I don't get why, and by the puzzled look on Dad's face, he doesn't either. But then Marduke makes himself clear. 'We meet in the woods of the Ardennes forest. You know the place.'

'But that's …' Dad glances at Arkarian. 'The site of our last mission together. In France where we duelled.'

'This time we will finish it.'

Arkarian brings up a valid point. 'You can't go back to the exact time.'

Marduke lifts one heavy shoulder slightly. 'We will meet a year to the day later.'

Dad stays silent.

Marduke swings back to him, grinning. 'If you don't show up, I will go on a rampage the like of which you've never witnessed before.'

'That attitude is bound to get you into trouble,' Arkarian says. 'Even the Order has rules.'

Marduke laughs outright this time. 'I have my god-

266

dess's blessings in whatever I do. I am,' he adds slowly and with mocking humour, 'her favourite after all. She worships me.'

Dad snorts loudly. 'You always were the ladies' man.'

Dad's sarcastic words obviously hit a sore point. Marduke seems to grow larger before our eyes, his one eye swelling. 'Bring three with you,' he spits out; and with these words he disappears, leaving behind a lingering foul smell.

Arkarian looks to Dad. 'He plans to bring five of his best.'

Dad remains silent, and nobody says another word. They're giving him time to think, to work through whatever demons still pound through him. Finally, Dad looks to me. 'That was amazing, Ethan. You have the power to bring reality into an illusion. I've never seen anyone do that before.'

'Your son is incredibly gifted,' Arkarian adds. 'He has other talents too. You should get him to show you when we're not so busy. He makes us all proud.'

As I listen to Arkarian's words, I try not to think about how I disgraced my position by revealing a skill in public, and how the Tribunal refuses to award me the power of flight because of my immaturity.

'Tell us, Shaun, what is your decision? Will you rejoin us?'

Dad inhales sharply. 'There's only one thing for me to do.' He sighs heavily, his shoulders drooping. For a second I think this means Dad has decided to leave, but then he crosses his arms in front of him. 'As usual you've boxed me into a corner, Arkarian. I'd better fulfil this mission, then finish with Marduke, if only to reduce the number of dangerous and distasteful creatures that surround my son.'

Arkarian smiles in relief and shakes Dad's hand heartily. Jimmy thumps Dad on the back. 'Glad to have you back, Shaun!'

Dad turns to Arkarian. 'It's been a while, but how is my friend John of Gaunt?'

'Dead,' Arkarian replies drily. 'And his son Henry rots in exile.'

'Quickly, Arkarian, give me my instructions.'

As Arkarian explains, he proceeds with the ritual of reigniting Dad's skills.

Chapter Thirty-six

Isabel

As Ethan and I have already met King Richard II, but were never properly introduced, we're to use the familiar aliases of the cousins Hugo Monteblain and Lady Madeline of Dartmouth, although only the names remain the same. It's expected that the king will not be too unfriendly towards us, as our lord is known to be a strong supporter of the king, who is fast losing allies in a world quite hostile to his asserting his regal power in his own right. He has exiled many important earls and nobles recently, John of Gaunt's popular son Henry among them.

Ethan's father – Shaun, as he has asked me to call him – will assume the identity of a distant relative of the king's own grandfather, King Edward III, and has his job cut out in earning the king's trust in the short time he has with him. but claiming he has lived most of his life in France – a country Richard longs to control should help.

Jimmy is to be the fictitious Lord Hamersley's page William. They go on ahead of us, arriving a few days in advance. after they've left, Arkarian explains to Ethan and me that we're to let go of any former impulse to aid King Richard II. 'Your mission to protect him is over,' he emphasises. 'Any lingering feelings must be put firmly to the side. Remember, your mission tonight is *not* to protect the king, but to make sure history runs its true course.'

'Then what are we to do?' Ethan asks.

'Your father and Jimmy may need you, just as Isabel needed you on your last mission. Marduke may add a surprise element. Be careful, watch your father's back, and Jimmy's too. Remember, Marduke is roaming where he shouldn't – in the past. It's bad enough that the Order of Chaos interferes with history, but Marduke's appearance is completely unwarranted.'

I understand what Arkarian is saying. 'He's using the Order to satisfy his own desire for revenge.'

'And apparently the Goddess is OK with this,' Ethan adds.

Arkarian runs a hand through his blue hair. 'So he says. She is apparently taken in by his charm.' The very thought sends shivers darting through me. 'Still,' Arkarian continues, 'you mustn't think about that now. You have your mission to complete. Upon your return, you will come back here for a strategic meeting. Then we'll face Marduke and his supporters.'

Arkarian pulls me aside for a moment, explaining in hushed tones how the Tribunal are thinking that if all goes well tonight, Ethan could be awarded his wings as a reward. I nearly scream out with excitement.

Ethan comes over. 'What are you two whispering about?'

'Can I tell him?'

'Later,' Arkarian says. Now the two of you go. And

270

be careful.'

With this final warning he bids us farewell, sending us on to the Citadel, where Ethan and I soon find ourselves clothed in elegant garments. My hair this time is transformed into a rich burgundy colour, most of which is piled high atop my head with a few ringlets dropping down. My skin has been made fair with an abundance of freckles, while Ethan's skin is deep olive, his hair black and thick to his shoulders.

We glance in the mirrors provided, impressed and slightly amused. I run my hand down over the full emerald-green skirt, luxuriating in the rich silky feel, then bunch the skirt between my fingers to check out my feet. They are encased in soft brown leather boots.

Ethan looks at me and gives a low whistle. 'Not bad!'

I whack his shoulder, but wonder silently whether there's anything behind the compliment. It seems all I do lately, especially since my last mission, is try to second-guess what Ethan really feels about me – beyond being my Trainer, beyond the fun we have together. After he saved my life I felt so close to him but so far he hasn't changed how he acts around me. He hasn't even once tried to kiss me for real. I'm starting to think we're destined to only ever be friends, and that maybe he still has feelings for Rochelle. Strangely the thought of only ever being friends has a comfortable feel about it, for I have come to value Ethan's friendship above anything else, and, well, when I close my eyes at night these days, it's not Ethan's face that swims into my dreams. But one whose eyes are a deep violet.

'Come on!' Ethan tugs me to the door, where the stairway meets us and leads us to a room on a higher level.

From this room we jump, side by side, and land in a corner of the Great Hall of Westminster Palace. There is a bustle of activity but no one is looking in our direction.

I land well, keeping my arms tucked neatly by my sides this time. Ethan grins at me. 'Well done!'

Excitement at achieving a proper landing at last, as well as the euphoria of being in the past again, has me slightly in a whirl. I can't help telling him what he has longed to hear, 'You know when Arkarian and I were whispering together earlier?'

'Yeah?'

'He was telling me that if this mission goes well, the Tribunal is thinking of giving you your wings as a reward.'

My words take him completely by surprise. He grabs my shoulders, holding me out from him, and stares for a second, his mouth gaping open. 'I can't believe this,' he calls out. 'I might get my wings after all! Yes, yes, yes!' He picks me up and whirls me around.

I thump his shoulder repeatedly, realising that my timing was slightly off. A private moment would have been far more sensible. 'Put me down! Everyone's looking at us.'

He lowers me to the floor, still grinning his head off, then realises what I'm on about as he notices that we have aroused the attention of everyone around us. He nudges me with his elbow and nods towards the front of the hall. I gasp in awe as King Richard II himself, whose attention we must also have inadvertently attracted, starts walking towards us. The crowd parts to allow him passage.

'Now look what you've done!' I whisper.

'*I've* done! If you hadn't told me that fantastic news about my wings …'

'How should I know you were going to pick me up and—'

The king stops directly in front of us. Ethan bows wide and low. I drop a deep curtsy at his side.

The king waves us up. And after staring at us for a few long moments, his head tilts to one side. 'I know you pair. We've met before.'

Ethan and I exchange brief worried glances. How on earth could the King recognise us? Only our eyes have remained the same.

'I don't believe so, Your Majesty,' Ethan says. 'Let me introduce myself—'

But he doesn't get a chance, King Richard shuts him up with his raised hand. 'Don't bother. I do hope you're feeling better today. It took the servants a whole day to clean the mess you left behind in my bedroom the last time you visited.'

Ethan and I exchange stricken looks.

'I knew we'd meet again,' King Richard says with a slight nod of his royal head.

The king turns his back on us, leaving us to stand there staring at his velvet garments. But then he gives a slight wave with a raised hand, indicating that we should follow.

We walk through the crowd that parts to make way for us. Shaun and Jimmy must be among them, but we can't look too searchingly. We are invited to sit at the main table on a raised platform on either side of the king and his very young wife – a mere child of nine – who shares my name, but, as I recall, spells it slightly differently.

I soon learn Queen Isabella doesn't speak anything but French. She hardly eats her meal at all, and barely sips her wine. As I'm sitting next to the young queen I try to make conversation with her, but my mind is on the king and Ethan, at how well they're getting along, mostly laughing together and drinking lots of wine.

The meal passes smoothly. Between courses, jesters come to entertain the party. But something doesn't feel right. I sense that someone is keeping their eye on the king and Ethan. As the evening wears on, this feeling grows so strong that I can't stop looking around to see if I can spot who it is, glancing into the shadows behind me and around the hall.

A man comes up beside me, speaks briefly to the young queen in her native tongue, making her giggle, then whispers to me, 'There are two of them here, one who acts as a servant.' Startled, I look into his eyes. This must be Shaun. He returns my smile but continues his warning. 'She has already passed you twice. Once she tipped poison from her ring into your wine goblet.'

'What? Did I drink it?'

'William replaced it while you were talking to the queen.'

'Oh. Remind me to thank him. And the other one? You said there were two?'

'The other one is a man. This would be his mission, I suspect, the woman his assistant. William informs me that he's also Marduke's right arm. He's disguised as the king's chief adviser, Lord Whitby. He just left the hall to arrange a meeting with the king and his council. He's the one with the heavy growth of facial hair.'

'I take it this Lord Whitby will be giving his advice to the king this evening?'

'Certainly. He's wormed his way into the king's favour; not an easy task these days. The king trusts few. I've been lucky so far; he believes my ties to his grandfather.'

'What should Hugo and I do tonight while you're in this meeting?'

Shaun glances wryly across at where the king and Ethan are chatting amicably together and raises his eyebrows. 'Watching, I think. When did you two become such close friends with the king?'

'When Richard was ten and we saved him from attempted murder.'

'He saw and remembered you?'

'The mission didn't turn out as planned. *You* were trying to wake Ethan at the time.'

'Oh, I see.'

The king sees Shaun and waves him over, introducing him to Ethan. They talk for a few minutes until King Richard announces to the crowd that he's withdrawing to a meeting with his advisers. As he steps back, he asks Ethan to join him, then speaks with his young wife in French. She looks relieved that she's not needed any more tonight. But before she runs off, he suggests she play the hostess a little longer, taking me for a walk around the palace, showing me the gardens and yards.

Personally, I love the idea of getting a first-hand tour of the grounds and rooms of Westminster Palace, but Ethan reaches out and takes my hand, pulling me to his side. 'If you don't mind, Sire, Lady Madeline has a remarkably astute mind, especially for a woman.'

I kick his shin from behind.

'Ouch! A-and she would …' Quickly he tries to regain his equilibrium as my kick was harder than I originally meant. '… dearly love to observe the meeting this evening, with your permission of course.'

King Richard peers at me closely. 'As I have witnessed her surprising talents once already, it would be a pleasure to have your company this evening, my lady. Please join us. There is ample room at the table.'

With this the three of us follow Richard up a winding stairwell and down a long hallway to a set of carved wooden doors. Inside, the room is warm but smoky, with a large oval table at its centre, twelve high-backed chairs surrounding it. In five of these chairs men of various ages sit having a discussion, until they notice the king and jump to their feet. The doors close behind us and the man with the big beard, standing just slightly away from the table, bows low to the king. King Richard introduces him as Lord Whitby, and makes Ethan and me known to the rest of his council. The men bow slightly, then all ten of us sit down, the sound of scraping chairs on polished floors loud in the high-ceiling room.

The conversation starts with the matter foremost on Richard's mind: is now an appropriate time to go to Ireland? Most of the lords at the table are in agreement with Lord Whitby: it really isn't a good time to leave England. The points they raise make a lot of sense. But then Shaun reminds the king why he wanted to go in the first place, and how important it has become that the king re-establish his English authority in Ireland.

Lord Whitby responds, reminding the king of his cousin Henry's ambitions. Shaun remains calm but

276

firm in his opposing arguments. The conversation becomes heated, and Lord Whitby grows visibly agitated. King Richard shakes his head and thumps his fist down hard on the table. 'Enough!' Then, surprising everyone, he looks straight at me. 'I want to hear from the lovely Lady Madeline, who has been sitting among this rabble quietly examining the situation. She saved my life once so I know she has only my best interests at heart.'

His words astonish me into speechlessness. Everyone's eyes bear down on me, most of them wide with surprise, as they would be, considering the king is asking for a lady's opinion. A lady they only just met a few minutes ago. And of course I realise what a responsibility has suddenly been thrust upon me. If Richard goes to Ireland at this time, John of Gaunt's son Henry will return to London from exile, something he can't do while Richard is still here. And what happens next is in the history books: Henry will gather support, and while Richard is in Ireland, he will have him deposed and thrown into jail, where Richard will be left to die of starvation.

And as much as I don't personally want to be the cause of Richard's death, I still have to do the right thing according to history. That's what I'm here for. Otherwise there'll be consequences.

Ethan peers at me with narrow eyes, as if he too is just working out what will happen to Richard if our mission is successful. And by the sudden look of horror on his face, it's only now dawning on him that this mission is meant to make sure Richard is deposed and murdered, so Henry IV can be crowned king.

Ethan looks as if he's about to stop me from speaking. I get a sudden image of what he's going to do just moments before his mouth opens. I throw my hand up, halting him before he utters one word, and quickly give the king my full attention. 'You honour me, Sire.' I bow my head, then look up and lock eyes with His Royal Highness. 'I do believe you should follow what's in your heart, trust in yourself and your original plan for a military expedition. Don't let these men of wisdom sway you from what you know is best. Do what you feel here.' I place a hand over the centre of my chest.

The king sits back and heaves a sigh that could only be regarded as intense relief. He nods. 'I most certainly will, Lady Madeline. My deepest thanks for making my decision so clear to me.'

Lord Whitby jumps out of his chair, his hands raised in anger. 'This is an outrage! Your Majesty, how can you take the word of a mere woman?'

King Richard takes offence on my behalf. 'I most certainly can. And as I am the king I'll ask you to leave the room, Lord Whitby, if you can't mind your manners and stop insulting my guest. I've had enough of your chattering and false claims these past weeks. I think you mean to sway me. Be careful or you'll find yourself in exile with Bolingbroke and Thomas Mowbray.'

Lord Whitby realises his mission is failing. He starts to panic. Surprising everyone around the table, he draws his sword. The others at the table, including Shaun, jump back and raise their swords in defence of the king.

But Lord Whitby, undeterred, points his sword in my direction. 'I know who you are,' he hisses, and for a moment wonder whether he really does. 'You're a trickster. You should be tried for witchcraft!' To the king he says, 'Your Majesty, I beg of you, do not be swayed by the temptations of a charming and beautiful woman.'

He doesn't realise it of course, but he's just given me an amazing compliment, as if *I* could tempt a king with my ... What did he say? I shake my head.

Lord Whitby tries again to sway the king. 'Your Majesty, have you heard nothing of my counsel? The charm of a woman will be your downfall. Is that how you want to be written up in history?'

'You insolent knave! King Richard exclaims. 'How dare you suggest—'

'It will mean your death!' Lord Whitby screams out.

King Richard raises his hand. 'Everyone, put away your swords. You especially, Lord Whitby. No one here means me harm.' He looks directly at Lord Whitby and says, 'I will go to Ireland with my armies as planned. It is what *I* desire.' He waves his hand at the rest of us. 'Now, all of you, leave me.'

The lords all stand and two of them urge Lord Whitby to put away his sword or they'll run him through with their own, reminding him how outnumbered he is.

Lord Whitby, utterly distressed now that his mission appears doomed to failure, returns his sword to its scabbard and storms from the room.

'Should we go after him?' I whisper to Ethan.

He swallows, seemingly in a daze. 'We just persuaded King Richard on a course destined to end in his death.'

'That is what we came for! Think of the alternative,' I coax him.

The room empties as the king calls for his manservants to help him prepare for his journey to Ireland, announcing that he plans to leave immediately. Shaun explains to Jimmy, who waits outside, how well the meeting went, and my part in it. Jimmy pats my shoulder. 'Well done, my lady! And now we must hurry and return to prepare ourselves for our meeting with Marduke.'

'What about Lord Whitby, or whoever he really was?' I ask. 'He sure was one unhappy little warrior when he stormed out of that room.'

'He's gone.'

'Are you sure?' Shaun asks Jimmy.

'Oh yes, I followed him. He summoned the maid and together they jumped out that window.' He points to the opening at the far end of the hallway. We go up to the window and look down at a three-storey drop. 'They disappeared before they were even halfway down.'

Shaun gathers us into an empty room. As no one is about, we're free to call Arkarian, who will return us to the Citadel in a second. But before Shaun opens his mouth to call his name, Ethan starts backing towards the door. 'You lot go ahead, I have something I want to check on.'

His action, his weird manner, has everyone's curiosity instantly aroused. 'What for exactly?' I ask, growing more worried by the second. Ethan's eyes are far too rounded for comfort, like he's in shock, or about to do something really stupid.

'I ... I just want to make sure the king leaves, that's

all. Then I'll follow. I'll try not to be too long.'

'But the man who was Lord Whitby, or his assistant, the poisoner, won't stop him now. Those two are gone,' I explain, then add, even though he knows this fact already, 'You know they can't come back to the same time. The king is leaving tonight, you can hear the armies gathering outside right now. There's nothing that can go wrong at this stage. And remember, we have an appointment with Marduke.'

'I know all this. Do you think Marduke's not on my mind?'

'He should be on your agenda.'

Shaun walks up to him. 'Haven't you been trained not to form attachments?'

Ethan scoffs at his father. 'I'm not attached to king Richard. I'm just doing my job, following it through. That's all.'

'Your job is over. Now we have to fight Marduke.'

'Yes,' Jimmy adds. 'Marduke and five of his warriors. No doubt Lord Whitby and the servant will be two of them, eager for revenge. Why else would they be in such a rush? We need you there to make up our numbers.'

Ethan nods. 'I'll be there. I promise.'

Backing away, he leaves without saying another word. I don't need my sixth sense to know that Ethan has something planned which is going to land him in a whole heap of trouble.

Chapter Thirty-seven

Ethan

I call Arkarian, who meets me in the Citadel in a room of bare walls painted black. 'You can't do this, Ethan.'

I drag my eyes away from the severity of the walls. 'I can and I must.'

He grabs my upper arms tightly and I feel his incredible strength. If I'm still in this body tomorrow, I'll have bruises for sure. 'It's an outright breach. You'll jeopardise everything you've worked for.'

He doesn't only mean my wings, but my position as well. I could be thrown out of the Guard, all memory of it erased. I don't want that to happen. But I can't allow a king to be demoralised and destroyed when I have the means to change things.

'Why, Ethan? Is he really worth the risk?'

I yank my arms from Arkarian's grasp and take a step back from him, giving my arms a shake to restore their circulation. 'I don't know, OK? I don't know why I'm doing this, but I have this inner compulsion to set things right for this king.'

'I've taught you not to get attached to your missions.'

'It's not that!'

282

'Then what?'

I look to the ceiling, also black, but there's nothing there to enlighten my mind. 'I can't explain it. I just know it's the right thing.'

He groans, shaking his head, and starts pacing the small unfurnished room. He gets to one end, turns on his heels and comes back, giving me a lengthy troubled look, then starts pacing again, his hands bunching into fists by his side. He turns once more, his hands now clasped so tightly that the skin has turned white at the knuckles. He comes right up to my face, his violet eyes piercing me, pleading, 'Ethan, this is one time you must think your actions right through to their possible – and probable – consequences.'

His obvious concern is touching, but not even his unusual show of emotions can sway me from this course.

He realises this and hisses through teeth tightly clenched, 'And you want me to help you?'

'I can't do it without you, Arkarian. You have to put me there, in the room where they're holding him, before he starves to death. I'll take full responsibility. I'll make sure you don't get repri—'

He holds his hands up in front of my face sharply. 'Stop! Do you really think I'm worried about that?'

'I'm sorry.'

He looks me in the eyes. 'Do you know what caused the dispute between your father and Marduke?'

While I know of the dispute, which saw my father slice off half of Marduke's face, I have no idea of the reason for it. 'Tell me.'

'They were a team with a difficult mission. A young woman by the name of Eleanor was to die during the

Black Death that hit France in the year 1348, but not before she saved the lives of her two younger brothers, soon to be orphaned. She was to make a journey with her siblings to family friends through the deep forest of Ardennes, into what is now Belgium. Once safely delivered, she was to return to her village to look after her remaining relatives – a dying father, an uncle and aunt and other loved ones. Eventually, she too would contract the disease and die.'

'So what happened?'

'Both your father and Marduke had a difficult time seeing where the danger came from. An assassin was attempting to infect Eleanor with the disease before she saved her brothers. Your father and Marduke spent sixteen days in her presence, carefully screening everyone and everything that came in contact with her, making sure she remained free of the illness until the time in history when she was to finally succumb.'

'I gather one of her brothers went on to accomplish something special?'

'Both did, actually, through their genes and various descendants. But that isn't even the point, Ethan.'

'I know. So what happened to cause my father and Marduke's quarrel?'

'Your father became attached to her.'

'No way!'

Arkarian looks at me intently. 'He wanted her to live, because, as he saw it, she deserved to. He was playing God, Ethan. And we can't do that. It's as bad as creating chaos. It makes us the same as them.'

'So what happened? Wouldn't Marduke let him?'

'It didn't go the way you're thinking.'

'What do you mean?'

'Marduke also formed an attachment to the girl. He fell in love with her, even while the woman he lived with sat at home with his child in her arms.'

'You're kidding!'

'He loved Eleanor with such passion that it blinded him. She was an exceptionally beautiful young woman and beauty impressed Marduke considerably. He too wanted to risk everything and rescue her from such an ugly and painful death. He couldn't stand the thought of what was going to happen to her beautiful skin and flesh once the disease took hold.'

I can understand this, as the thought itself is sickening, but still … 'What happened?'

'Your father came to his senses.'

'Oh.'

'But Marduke wouldn't listen to reason. He injected Eleanor with an antibiotic from his own time, one that was meant for him, should it be required.'

'So they fought.'

'In the deep forest of Ardennes. It was a hard and bitter duel, using weapons of the time – they're both superior swordfighters. Eventually, it was your father who took the first wound, a deep slash to his thigh, but before he passed out from loss of blood, he made one fierce final attack.'

'Slicing Marduke's face in half?'

Arkarian nods. I wonder what happened to the beautiful young woman who was the centre of their rift, and he reads my mind.

'She recovered from the plague, but the sight of so much ugly death scorched her soul and made her go insane. And the villagers who escaped the plague, and knew of her miraculous recovery, assumed she had been touched by the devil. They scorned her and called her a witch. She lived the rest of her life in a wooden shack buried deep in the Ardennes, alone.'

'That's terrible.'

Arkarian takes a deep breath. 'Now you must understand there are always consequences.'

'I understand what went wrong back then, and the point you're trying to make. But listen, I'm not saving King Richard because I've become emotionally involved. I don't want to play God. I wouldn't do that! My father and Marduke's past mistakes have nothing to do with me.'

Arkarian's whole face shows exasperation that a student of his could be so dense. He doesn't need to speak.

'Look, what I'm going to do will have no effect on the future, and won't send anyone insane.'

'How can you be so sure? No one knows what may happen once the unpredictable element is thrown in.'

I thump my chest with a closed fist. I believe in what I'm doing, even though I'm not really sure why. 'There's not going to be an unpredictable element, Arkarian, 'cause I'm not going to leave King Richard in the past as a free man. I have a plan, and a gut feeling I can't explain.'

'Ethan, you can never predict what might happen. And you must remember that our physical bodies can only be in one place at one time. It's your soul that can shift through time, housed temporarily in bodies that resemble your own. If you try to transport King Richard, he will only die – slowly and unpleasantly.'

His points are valid, especially the last about our souls and one body and such. Still, Arkarian's always telling me he doesn't know everything, and this time I realise he's right, 'cause something deep inside me feels sure that if I can get King Richard to Athens, and into the healing room in the palace quickly, this one time death will not result. Where King Richard is now, he's going to die anyway. Trying to save him will be worth the risk.

'I'll never ask anything of you again, Arkarian. Just this once, please help me get to King Richard before it's too late.'

Chapter Thirty-eight

Isabel

I want to go after Ethan, though I'm not sure where he's gone, or even why, only that it has to do with King Richard. But Marduke is preparing for battle and he's bringing five of his warriors with him, while we are five without Ethan. As we're already short on numbers, how can I run after Ethan without making our position against Marduke even more vulnerable?

We return to the Citadel, where we change and shift back into our sleeping bodies. I wake instantly, my heart skittering away as if waking from a dream where I'm racing towards a cliff edge with no way to stop in time. Finally, it dawns on me that I'm home and safe. I clamber out of bed, throwing on some fresh clothes, not even thinking what they are – jeans of some description, an old ratty jumper that dropped off its hanger a few days ago. The plan is to get to Arkarian's chamber as soon as we return to our bodies. There's heaps to do before meeting Marduke and his warriors.

Outside my bedroom door I bump straight into Jimmy, who shushes me with a sharp frown. 'Mum's sleeping, let's go.'

'Matt too?'

He shrugs. 'I don't know where he is. He's not in his room.'

We hurry down the hallway, but once we get near the front door, both of us stop in our tracks. The door is open, yanked off its hinges, smudges of blood on its slanted front. Furniture in the immediate area has been knocked around. Obviously there's been a scuffle where someone's been hurt. The last person I know that came to this door was Mr Carter. 'What happened, Jimmy? Do you think Mr Carter and Matt got into a fight?'

He shakes his head. 'I can't see that happening.'

'How well do you know Mr Carter? Sometimes he acts weird.'

'That's just him, Isabel. Don't jump to conclusions.' Jimmy pushes me towards the opening, then sets the door in place, repairing the hinges and fractured splinters with just the touch of his hand. Even the blood disappears. 'How does that look?'

'Great.' I'm surprised at his skill, but then remind myself that Jimmy is the one who set the traps in the ancient city, so the simple fixing of a door shouldn't really be too astonishing.

We take off with a run up the hill to Arkarian's chambers. We meet Shaun at the entrance and follow him in. Once inside the octagonal room, we realise straight away that something is terribly wrong. The first thing is that Arkarian isn't here, and neither is Mr Carter. Second the 3-D sphere in the centre of the room is black and motionless.

Jimmy looks particularly concerned, but tries to lighten the tension in the room. 'How can we form a strategy when our chief strategist has gone walk about?' He then tells Shaun about the break-in to my place. As Shaun listens, he walks around the room, touching things and looking under them as if Arkarian might somehow appear from beneath his fingers.

'What do you think happened?' I ask Shaun, with a heavy sense of foreboding.

'We're not likely to know until we track Arkarian down.' With these words he glances up and around at the ceiling. 'Arkarian? Answer if you can!'

Silence. And then Mr Carter bursts into the room. Even before he says a word, it's obvious that something catastrophic has happened. He doubles over, his chest heaving. Perspiration is pouring off his face, which is red from strong exertion.

'What happened, Marcus?' Jimmy asks, helping him to a seat.

'I've been running, mostly, after that madman Marduke.'

'He never was one for fair play,' Shaun says. 'Did he decide to start the tournament without us?'

'You could say that.' Mr Carter glances over at me, his eyes ready to impart bad news. 'And he's raised the stakes, considerably.'

I take a deep breath, thinking something must have happened to Ethan. But then he says, 'I'm sorry, Isabel, but Marduke's got Matt.'

His words hit me hard. 'Wh-what?' Even though I saw the destruction at my own front door, my mind won't register that this fight could have anything to do with Matt. He's not part of this other world. It can't be him!

'Tell us what happened,' Shaun urges, grabbing Mr

Carter's forearm in a solid grip. 'Hurry, man!'

'You know I went to distract Matt—'

Our nods and grunts urge him on. He sucks in a calming breath, and begins to explain. 'He'd let me in and we talked for a few minutes. Then suddenly there was a commotion at the front door.' Matt opened the door and there's this giant of a man grinning at him with half a mouth and only one eye. He wasn't wearing a mask or anything. Obviously he wanted to take Matt off guard.'

Jimmy puts his hand over mine. 'He's been watching you, and he's seen how close you and your brother are. This is how he works, getting to people through their loved ones.'

My eyes shut of their own accord. How can this be happening?

Mr Carter went on.

For a moment Matt just stared in disbelief. Then Marduke made as if to put his hand on Matt's head. I've heard about the power in that creature's hands so I called out to Matt to get out of the way. Matt's reflexes are swift. And sensing danger, he moved quickly to shut the door. Not that it would have stopped Marduke, but Matt didn't know this. Marduke put his foot in the door and, shoving it with his shoulder, knocked it clear off its hinges. His next move was like lightning, striking out at Matt's head with the back of his hand. The blow sent Matt flying against the door, knocking him unconscious.'

'Are you sure he still lives?' I ask with my heart clambering up my throat. Instinctively, my fingers fly to touch the area as though to calm it.

'Oh, yes.' Mr Carter looks up at me. 'Dead, he would

be no use to Marduke. The monster flung Matt over his shoulder and started running. I took off after them. He carried Matt up those godforsaken hills all the way to a clearing on the far side of the lake. I thought I would lose them, but then Marduke did something.' Mr Carter pauses and Jimmy hands him a glass of water. 'Marduke turned back and I realised he knew I was following him all the time. He raised his hand, creating a brilliant green light, then simply disappeared through it, taking Matt with him.'

'So what happened then?' Shaun asks with an impatient note in his voice.

'Unbelievable,' Mr Carter says, taking a sip from his glass. 'The green light remained for a few minutes. It was like a doorway. I could look through it.'

'What did you see?' I ask in a whisper, wanting, yet not wanting, to know what Marduke has done with my brother.

'I saw a dense forest where Matt is tied to a tree.'

Shaun sighs. 'I bet he's taken him to France – the Ardennes – to the year after our fight.'

It's Jimmy who realises the full horror of Marduke's act. 'He has taken Matt's *mortal body* to France.'

'What does this mean?' I practically screech.

The three men glance uneasily at each other. But then I start to figure it out for myself. Our mortal bodies cannot shift through time – only our souls. 'How much time does he have?'

Jimmy's shoulders lift in a shrug. 'It's hard to tell, but Matt is young and healthy. That will help.'

Silence follows, then Mr Carter goes on with his story. 'The other five warriors are already there, waiting for us with medieval swords.'

'Of course,' Shaun says. 'We'll have to fight with the weapons of that time. Marduke wants a re-enactment of our duel, but on his terms. A clever and cunning man.'

Right now I can't think of complimenting that hideous creature. 'What about Matt?' My voice cracks as I fight to hold back tears.

'He'll be all right,' Jimmy tells me, though he can't have any idea whether this is true or not. 'He's a strong lad.'

'He must be so confused.'

'The last I saw, he was unconscious,' Mr Carter says, 'and if we're lucky he'll stay that way until we can get him back.'

'How are we going to do that?' My voice turns shrill. 'There are six of them and we don't have Ethan or Arkarian.'

Jimmy rubs my arm, trying to comfort me.

Mr Carter gets up and walks a few paces, then stops and turns. 'There's something else I have to tell you.'

'About Matt?' I ask, almost screeching now. 'What more can there be?'

'They're using him ... Well, you see, as I left, I saw what they were planning.'

'Out with it, Marcus,' Jimmy urges.

'They were making a bed of dry wood around his feet.'

Everyone goes silent. I try to visualise what Mr Carter means. 'Wood? But why?' And then it hits me. 'They're going to *burn* him? While his mortal body is trapped in the past? Oh, my God!'

Jimmy puts his arm around my waist, drawing me to him, as panic starts to swell.

293

'Marduke means to use him as a threat. To bully us, you could say.'

For a few moments my strangled gasps are the only sound in the room as sobs begin to form deep in my throat. Then a whooshing sound draws my tear-stained face from Jimmy's shirt front. It's Arkarian, with his arms held out to me. I run into them and they fold gently but firmly around me. Instantly, I feel a calm centre through my entire body. I look up, and violet eyes, shimmering with moisture, lock on to mine; courage and strength fill me. 'Marduke has Matt,' I whisper. 'Trapped in the past.'

'I know. I've been briefed. But not for long, Isabel.'

'How can we beat this madman and his warriors? How, Arkarian?'

'With everything we have.'

'I'll die for Matt if I have to.'

'And I will die for you.'

He says the words so quickly, so plainly, that at first the intensity of them doesn't register. He draws away and the moment is lost. His presence gives everyone hope, sets them moving to form a plan. I stand to the side while Arkarian takes control, and Shaun, Jimmy and Mr Carter discuss strategy. Still. I can't believe we have a chance to beat Marduke unless we're at full force. 'Where is Ethan?'

They all stop for a moment and glance at me, and I see in their faces their own doubts. They know it too, we need Ethan and we need him quickly.

Arkarian sighs, which only fuels my own worry further. 'He'll come.'

'But does he know about Matt?'

'Don't think so.' Another intense violet gaze.

'But he *will* come, Isabel. Trust in him.'

'How long can we wait? How long before Marduke lights the fire beneath my brother's feet?'

'He won't light the fire unless he thinks he's losing.'

'*What!* So how do we win and not lose Matt in the process?'

'That's what we're trying to figure out right now, Isabel.' His voice is so firm that tears well up in my eyes again. Immediately his whole manner softens. 'Come and help us. Far better to have your mind focused on strategy than fear.'

'But I fear I'll fail. And I fear Ethan won't return in time. And I fear my heart is going to burst from beating so hard. And—'

Jimmy puts his arm around my shoulders and gathers me near. And as he speaks, his eyes rise up to glance across the top of my head to Shaun. 'It's always harder when it's someone you love that's in trouble.'

Chapter Thirty-nine

Ethan

Organising the release of King Richard takes longer than I expect, even though time is hard to assess when I'm out of my mortal body. Getting me into Pontefract Castle, where Richard is secretly being kept in isolation, is not the problem, thanks to Arkarian, but talking one of the Lords of the Houses into helping is something else. Again I must thank Arkarian. He pulls some strings and somehow arranges a meeting with Penbarin, the Lord of Samartyne. The Lord is grumpy at having been woken from a sleep with a beautiful woman. He warns me it had better be good. A few minutes into my explanation he's sitting on the edge of his seat, listening intently.

'Are you crazy, boy?'

'Probably, sir.' I pause for just a moment. 'But I'm going to do this whether you help me or not.'

Penbarin scoffs at my arrogance, briefly looking to Arkarian, who stands away to the side with both hands lifted in a gesture of puzzlement.

'He's been warned,' Arkarian says. 'He knows that the punishment for manipulating the past is likely to be his expulsion from the Guard.'

Penbarin looks back at me with eyes that seem to see through my brain. 'And still you intend to go through with this plan?'

'Yes,' I say plainly.

Penbarin's hands fly into the air. 'If I don't help you, your precious king will die a very slow and torturous death as every cell in his body struggles to survive outside his own time. The only way a mortal body can survive such a time shift is if he is placed in the sealed chambers here almost instantly.'

'I know, sir, that's why I'm standing here before you … pleading for you to help me make this happen.'

'Hmm, this is an intriguing situation,' Penbarin kind of hisses through this teeth. 'You'd risk your own future for this man?'

'Yes, sir. For this king.'

'And yet you can't tell me why you do it?'

'No, sir.'

Penbarin's eyes roll heavenward, indicating he's about to relent. I hold my breath until I hear the words themselves flow through his lips. 'I'll help you, Ethan, but only because I'll not stand by and watch a king die an agonising death because some young foolish Guard has a crazy notion to set things right.'

His words are a great relief.

'But remember this: I'll not support you at your trial before the Tribunal, which is sure to follow your breach of one of the Guard's strictest rules – never to alter the past with our own hands.'

As Arkarian and I leave Penbarin's rooms, I think about how I will probably be disbarred for ever, which saddens me immensely, and again I have to ask myself, what is driving me to do this? My feelings of friendship for this man, this hugely unpopular king, are not motive enough for such a gesture.

I honestly don't know.

Even though he clearly stated his conscientious disapproval, Penbarin will not back down now that he has given his word. So King Richard II will not die if I can get him out of that castle quickly.

And so Arkarian and I hurry.

I'm fully aware of just how little time I have to pull this off. And my guilt at leaving the others to battle Marduke without full numbers weighs my thoughts down so heavily, it's a wonder I can think straight at all. Leaving them short was never my intention. I just have to do this deed as quickly as possible. I've been away too long already, with my emergency trip to Athens, but without that detail organised there'd be no point to what I'm doing: it has to be all of Richard's body and soul that I shift through time. And I cannot just rescue him and set him free to roam around in his own time, for surely he'll gather support and try to take his crown back. And this is not the way history unfolds.

No way.

Arkarian leaves me in order to return to the others and prepare for battle. Meanwhile I shift through time to Pontefract Castle in Yorkshire – landing on a putrid stone floor full of dirty straw and rats' droppings.

King Richard looks up from his position slumped on the floor. His eyes are bleary, surrounded by dark circles, his face pale and gaunt. 'Hugo? Hugo Monteblain? How did you …?' He glances around the otherwise empty room. 'I'm hallucinating again.'

I squat down beside him. 'You're not hallucinating, Your Majesty.'

He waves a weak hand in front of my face. 'Haven't you heard the news? Hal of Bolingbroke now sits on the throne,' he says bitterly. 'I should never have gone to Ireland. They tricked and deceived me there, you know. I had no choice but to abdicate. And now I am to die here – I, a king, left to rot among foul garbage and vermin!'

I take his shoulders and give him a strong shake. 'You're not going to die here. I'll not allow it.'

His dark eyes lock with mine, but still his voice is piteous. 'And how are you going to get me past those guards, hmm?' He points over his shoulder to the thick wooden door with the small iron grille window.

'The same way I got in here. Now, can you stand up?'

A brief spark lights his eyes as he starts to believe. But a thump on the door has us both ducking to the ground. 'Who are you talking to in there?'

With a finger to my lips I give my head a quick negative shake. Richard replies, 'You leave me no choice but to converse with my own self to keep from going insane.'

The guard laughs, but not a friendly one. 'Wallow in your own medicine,' he says sarcastically and walks off.

'Quickly,' I whisper.

At the sound of retreating footsteps, Richard struggles to his feet with my arm for support. I take the silver cloak Penbarin gave me for the job, wrap it around the king, and call Arkarian.

But he doesn't appear.

The guard hears me call and comes back, thumping

299

again on the door. 'What's that strange name you call?'

'What?' King Richard snaps at the guard. 'I call no one. Dreaming is all I do. Who do you think would help me in this godforsaken hole?'

I see the guard peering through the bars and hold my breath, while hanging on to Richard and trying to conceal myself between the folds of the wide cloak. I need to call again, as nothing has happened as planned, but to call again will surely raise this guard's curiosity too high.

'What are you doing there?' the guard asks, seeing Richard standing in an unusual position with his back to the door and wearing a strange silver cloak. 'Something is going on.'

The sound of the key going into the lock has me deciding quickly to risk calling Arkarian again.

Nothing.

Oh, hell! I never meant to kill us both.

'Arkarian! For God's sake, where are you?'

'You do have someone in there.' The door now opens wide. 'You! Who are you? Where did you come from?'

'Arkarian!'

The guard draws his sword. I manage to hold Richard up with one arm and draw my sword with the other. Just then I feel the familiar sensations of imminent transportation taking hold. But I can't allow this guard to watch us disappear. Surprising him, I aim a sharp kick to the back of his head, and he falls to the ground out cold an instant before my body begins to shift.

At last, the king's prison cell fades from view.

Chapter Forty

Isabel

Marduke's tumultuous roar fills Arkarian's chamber, letting us know our wait is over. The unnerving sound causes chills to slice through my body, and the others feel the same, I sense. Our eyes shift to each other around the room, understanding that we can't wait any longer for Ethan to appear, and that we must go into this battle disadvantaged.

Arkarian hands us each a small bottle of blue-tinted liquid. 'It's time. You must all go back to your beds before any one of you is reported missing. Take the vials I've just given you; their contents will put you instantly to sleep. We'll meet in the Citadel and get outfitted with secure identities before shifting to meet Marduke in the Ardennes in the year 1349. Are we all clear?'

With Arkarian's instructions ringing in our heads, the four of us leave. I'm glad of Jimmy's company as we make our way down the chilly mountain to our respective beds. He keeps my mind occupied right up to my bedroom door, where he gives me a small encouraging smile. 'Everything will work out, Isabel.'

'How can you know that?'

'I trust in the Guard.'

'I don't know them like you do.'

'I understand, but you will.'

'What we're doing tonight, it's going to be dangerous, isn't it?'

He nods. 'You know it is.'

'If something happens to us ...' Suddenly a hard lump forms in my throat. 'I mean, if something happens to Matt, and to me, and to you too, who will Mum have left?'

He glances down at the small bottle held tightly between my fingers, then closes his hand over mine. 'Don't think such thoughts, Isabel. Take the drink, and let's go rescue Matt.'

When I get to my room I swallow the sleeping draught in one go. It starts working instantly. It feels as if I've only just laid my head on my pillow when a familiar weightless sensation sets in.

I wake suddenly in a room in the Citadel that simply takes my breath away with its overwhelming pink decor, so much like a page out of one of the many fairy-tale books Mum and Matt kept shoving at me when I was a little girl. Books that I would have nothing to do with. I wanted to read adventure stories with wild animals, danger and heroic rescues. These are the things that would have made him proud of me. This last thought takes me by surprise for I was *not* thinking of my father. No!

A feeling of intense sadness sweeps through me, making me want to fall to my knees and sob. Arkarian appears before me, his eyes full of compassion. It snaps me out of my sudden melancholy. 'Is everyone here yet?'

Unfolding a finger, Arkarian indicates a point beyond my shoulder. I spin around and see Jimmy, Shaun and Mr Carter already waiting.

'Let's go then.'

Arkarian leads us to one of the wardrobe rooms without saying a word, but I know from his lingering gentle expression that he knows my every thought, the inner turmoil I suddenly find myself in. Why am I thinking of a father who has never been a real part of my life? Why now?

We end up clothed in medieval armour, which protects our chests and backs mostly, our legs remaining free of the stiff metal, but still protected somewhat by soft chain leggings. I glance into one of the many surrounding mirrors and see a reflection of myself and the others. This time I have reddish hair and freckles. The four men have all reached for their swords, testing them for feel and weight. A shiver slithers down my spine: how many of us will return with our lives?

Arkarian catches my eye through the mirror and stares back at me with a concerned frown. He's obviously heard my negative thought vibrating – probably pounding – through the air. He shakes his head slightly and asks about the feel of my armour; I sense it is meant to distract me.

I shrug my shoulders, trying to accustom my small body to the bulk and heaviness. It takes a few minutes to adjust, and I realise it's moulding itself to my shape. 'It's OK,' I tell him. I feel for my sword but the scabbard hanging at my hip is empty.

Arkarian comes towards me with a sword in his hand. I reach for it, my fingers wrapping around the hilt with ease. It feels as if it were made for my hand. A

303

warmth penetrates into my palm.

'I'm not very good with a sword,' I say as I lift it into the air and feign a forward thrust.

He stands back and looks at me seriously. 'This sword belonged to Gawain, one of King Arthur's favourite knights. He was small, like you.'

'I've heard of him. History has it that he was very courageous.'

'Oh, yes. I had the pleasure of witnessing him in action a few times. He handed me this sword on his deathbed.'

I stare at the sword, wondering if Arkarian's words are going to be an omen. 'So was he killed fighting with this sword?'

Arkarian gives a small laugh at my misunderstanding. 'Hardly! He died aged eighty-two.'

'Oh.'

He looks down at the sword I hold with comfortable ease. 'The handle was carved by Merlin himself, dipped in gold at King Arthur's request.'

This information floors me. I turn the handle over in my hand, marvelling at how snugly it fits, and how light it feels, for the blade is as long as any other I've trained with.

Arkarian watches as I study the sword as if waiting for me to figure something out. 'It's enchanted to fit the hand of one who will do it proud.'

I almost drop it. 'Wow! That's a lot of pressure, Arkarian.'

'Do you think so? The sword obviously doesn't. It likes your hand, Isabel. Besides, it grew tired of its previous owner.' He grins and I realise the sword's previous owner was him. 'Almost six centuries is a long time for any relationship, even that of a man with his sword,' he laughs lightly.

Arkarian is so right, six hundred years is a very long time. He smiles at me and I remember again his ability to know what I'm thinking. I'll have to make sure Ethan teaches me how to mask my thoughts – if we survive.

'It's yours now,' Arkarian says softly.

I feel honoured and bow my head as tears suddenly fill my eyes. Why is Arkarian doing this – giving me his sword? An enchanted sword that he's had for so many hundreds of years, given to him by a great and respected knight on his deathbed? Arkarian lifts my face with his hand; our eyes connect and hold – brown with violet. The room spins for a moment, then seems to disappear as if there is nothing else in my vision except Arkarian's deeply violet eyes.

Slowly, we become aware that Shaun is standing beside us. 'Marduke grows restless.'

Arkarian nods, breaking our connection. 'Then we must hurry.'

Following the others, I too go and stand near the open doorway. One after another we leap into a thick, dark forest, five instead of six, to battle an embittered and traitorous warrior who has been living the past twelve years only for this event. And how prepared are we, I wonder? I ask this question of Arkarian the moment we land on firm ground. The plan they've been working on has for the most part been kept from me, whether intentionally or not.

'It's a solid plan, Isabel. You have your part in it.'

'But you've only told me the part that concerns me. "Draw the female warrior to the side and deal with

305

her." I can do more than that.'

'And you will, when you have dealt with the female warrior the way I told you—'

'Unmask her.'

'Yes. She's Marduke's central spy. Her eyes – her only identifiable feature – will somehow be concealed, I suspect, by a skin-tight facial mask that conceals the shape and perhaps even the colour of her eyes. Unmask her and she'll run; and we'll have one less to contend with. Her position is too valuable for Marduke to risk revealing her identity. Those will be her instructions, I'm sure of it. But it won't be easy. Her mask will be like skin, and probably stretch in a band from one ear to the other.'

'OK. But what about Marduke? How do we get to him while keeping Matt safe?'

He hesitates. 'The plan is not a secret from you, Isabel. We just want you focused on your part.'

'Why do you have such little faith in me?'

'It's not that.'

He's being vague on purpose. 'I wish I could read *your* thoughts, Arkarian. Don't I deserve to be in on this plan too? Matt's life is at risk. He could be dying right now, his body out of its normal time. He's an innocent in all of this. And I'll be fighting too, or else why did you give me the sword?'

He stops mid-stride, turns and looks at me. It's dark, but the moon, though half, lights the whole escarpment for me. 'As much as my first instinct is to protect you, Isabel, because you have limited experience, this is not the reason you haven't been told the plan.'

'Go on.'

He remains silent as if considering whether I can

handle the reality or not. It occurs to me that maybe they don't really have a plan – but no, I heard them organising one. They're up to something. Jimmy even disappeared for a while, running out on some urgent errand.

Finally, I think I guess the truth. It sucks the breath straight out of my lungs, leaving me gasping for air. 'The success of your plan depends on Ethan, doesn't it?'

He remains silent for a moment. His pause sends chills deep into my soul. 'Not entirely.'

I laugh a kind of hoarse cackle. 'You're relying on someone that may not even show. My brother is lost.'

Wordlessly, we continue walking through thick woodland, and I tell myself to be more positive. Ethan will turn up. He must! But I can't stop the negative thoughts from punching through my brain. 'Ethan doesn't know the plan, so how can he help even when he does get here?'

Arkarian sighs softly, 'Isabel, have faith. It won't take much on Ethan's part. He's very good at what he does.'

'So where did Jimmy go?'

'He had to locate someone – a girl – and plant a visual image of her in his brain, which ultimately he will pass to Ethan.'

'Who is she? What does she have to do with all this?'

He holds his hand up to silence me as we suddenly find ourselves at a small clearing. I hold on to my question. I have a feeling I will soon find out, if I live long enough to see this battle through. I can't easily forget Marduke's threats and torments. For whatever reasons, he wants me dead too.

I look up and groan, 'cause with the help of my gift

of sight, I can see Matt clearly ahead. He's standing on a makeshift platform, tied to a massive tree, his head hanging in unconsciousness or slumber, the side of his face swollen and streaked red with blood, his skin ashen with an eerie green tinge. Weirder still are the numerous patches of dark circles on his exposed skin, as if blood lies trapped beneath the surface. But worst of all, beneath the small platform, a bed of wood stacked haphazardly, almost a metre high, sits ready for lighting.

My body shivers at the sight, for beside him stand four of Marduke's warriors, two on either side, all with one hand resting on the hilt of their swords, knees slightly bent, eyes scouring the landscape. They can't see us yet, I realise. But there is one who can.

'Ah, at last! What took you so long?' Marduke appears before us, the masked female warrior at his side. 'Waiting for someone?' he teases in his rough, thick voice.

I ignore him, concentrating on the masked warrior, the one I'm supposed to single out. A sense of familiarity pulses through me as I stare at her, and I know in my heart that this is the woman who tried to murder Abigail Smith, and she is also the servant who tried to poison me at King Richard's table. Poison must be her specialty.

The harder I stare, the more she avoids making eye contact. I think this strange, considering she's wearing a mask meant to conceal her eyes. I get swamped with another strong sense: this woman is nervous, and possibly afraid. But of what? Does she think I'll recognise her by looking into her masked eyes? It's not her eyes that will give her away, but more her subtle flowery scent. I smell it already. But I can't jump to conclusions, for what if I were wrong? A mistake in judgement could cost a life tonight. But if my suspicions are correct, how can this woman stand here ready to defend her master when the one she purports to love stands ready to be executed?

Marduke suddenly roars, nearly shattering my eardrums; but all I can think is, good, maybe Ethan will hear you and come running. What could be taking him so long? With the roar comes movement from the trees. My eyes flick up and around. The trees have come alive with more warriors, a dozen at least. They jump to the ground, quickly surrounding us, while the four guarding Matt stay put.

I kick myself; why didn't I see this coming? With my gift of sight I could easily have spotted Marduke's army among the trees, if I had only thought to look. But I'd been so concerned for Matt, and so focused on Marduke's spy, that I allowed Marduke to trick us into walking straight into a trap.

Marduke grins with his half-mouth, yellow eye sparkling with mirth.

'You never did fight fair,' Shaun says in an offhand manner, and I have to wonder at his calm.

It's obvious that whatever plan we have is now doomed. The warriors draw their swords, forming a kind of Catherine wheel around us, ready for the assault. We don't stand a chance. We're all going to die here at the hands of this madman, who's certainly had time enough to plan – twelve whole years!

Well, if I'm going to die here, there's one thing I promise to do first: unmask this traitorous spy before me, even if it's with my last breath. With this thought fierce in my head, I also draw my sword. The spy swings around, sword in hand, and the fighting begins.

Marduke gives his spy a lingering look. She backs out of the circle, making sure she has a quick exit if required. We're now between the attacking warriors from the trees and the four guarding Matt. Out of the corner of my eye, I see he's starting to stir. 'No, don't wake,' I mumble to myself. It would be far better for Matt to die blissfully unaware than to witness the slaughter of his sister first. But he only groans, and I realise his pain is so intense he feels it even through unconsciousness. He can't stay out of his own time for much longer or he'll die anyway.

'What shall I call you, masked one?' I ask as I force the spy ever backwards.

Her thrusts are long and skilful, but her words, when she finally answers, are not what I expect. 'You're so naive, Isabel.'

She knows who I am. I try not to sound surprised; at least now I'm certain it's Rochelle. 'How do you know me?'

'I saw Ethan use his powers to impress you in the classroom. It didn't take much to work out your involvement, especially when you started hanging around him in a big way. I heard about it endlessly from Matt.'

'Then it wasn't Marduke who told you.'

Her eyes roll. 'Marduke says little. He keeps to himself most of the time. His sole focus is nothing but revenge – and pleasing the Goddess.'

'Why do you work for Marduke?'

'You make it sound like a job I applied for. Do you think I chose to be Marduke's spy?'

My fingers go momentarily lax, loosening my grip on the sword, but magically it stays glued to my palm. She thrusts again, forcing me backwards three steps. I sense she wants me to understand her reasons, or maybe it's just a technique to keep me from securing total concentration. One lapse and she could run that sword straight through me.

'He tempted me at first, made me think his way was the one I was born for.'

I try to maintain complete focus while keeping her talking. 'But you see now that it isn't?'

'I'm not a fool, Isabel. Look at Matt. D'you think I want this? He's in agony right now, dying before our eyes.'

The passion in her voice feels real. 'Then leave Marduke. Arkarian will protect you.'

She scoffs at this suggestion. 'Marduke will kill me.'

'Not if we kill him first.'

'There are others he answers to. I'd never be safe.'

'Arkarian would find a way.'

She peers narrowly at my face. 'Are you insane? You speak as if you can win this battle. You can't, Isabel. Marduke is cunning, his superiors even more so. The Goddess is besotted with him.'

'But he is so—'

'Ugly? What do you think she thrives on? Ugliness, disease, war, horror – they make her stronger, richer, more content. And soon there will be so few of the Guard left to defend the past. Everything will change. Evil in the form of pestilence, war and hatred will flood the world. The Order will reign supreme. What can one person do?' She goes on to answer herself. 'Nothing, Isabel. Nothing.'

But Rochelle has it wrong. Doesn't she see that every person makes a difference? That as long she works for the Order, they will be that much stronger?

'You're the one who's wrong, Isabel,' she says simply.

'What? I didn't speak out loud.'

'No, but I heard you all the same. I'm a Truthseer.'

'Oh, no! Whenever we've talked in the past, you've heard my inner thoughts?'

'Not only yours.'

It hits me who she's talking about. Ethan, of course. This must be how the trouble started between Matt and Ethan, which eventually broke up their friendship.

'Exactly,' she confirms. 'Ethan has feelings for me, although now they're nothing more than hatred and disgust. But back then, even while I was Matt's girl-friend, every time we met, I knew Ethan wanted me.'

'He would never have purposely hurt Matt.'

'He didn't. He kept his thoughts completely under control. But he couldn't stop me from picking them up. How I wanted to—' She shakes her head, breaking eye contact, which causes a momentary lack of concentration. It's an opening I can't allow to pass. I rally hard, forcing her deeper into the woods. Her back hits a tree and with a fierce rallying thrust I disarm her. Her sword flies into the air. I bring mine up to lie horizontal at her throat. 'It was the plan,' she hisses, looking scared for the first time.

'What plan?'

'Marduke's. To break up their friendship. To make Matt fall in love with me.'

'For your life, tell me why?'

'Marduke is into pain and suffering and just about

312

anything to hurt people, especially Ethan, his father, or anything to do with them. It's his revenge. It clouds his judgement.'

This much I understand, but how can I trust her when she herself admits to having become a traitor through her own weak spirit?

She heaves for breath as my sword tightens across her throat. 'Don't kill me! I can still be useful tonight.'

'Your use is done here. Don't push your luck.'

'Look, I was confused at the time Marduke first approached me. He showed me things, like how my father beat my mother to death. He told me that since half my genes were inherited from my father, I was born to be a part of the Order of Chaos, it was my destiny. At first, I didn't believe him. I didn't want to. I tried not to. But I was vulnerable, and power is food for the weak.'

I recall how tragic and disturbed Rochelle's childhood was, living with a violent father. But still, if I let her go, how do I know she won't simply turn around and try to kill me with a weapon concealed on her body?

'I can't prove that I won't harm you. You wouldn't believe me anyway. But if you can find it in yourself to trust me, somehow ... somehow I'll prove your faith was worthwhile.'

I think hard, my arms growing heavy holding the sword so long at this height. The blade presses into the skin at Rochelle's throat, causing a trickle of blood. She's asking me to release her, but how can I do that? For starters, if she's telling me the truth, Marduke will realise she's turned on *him* and will probably kill her immediately. But then it occurs to me how I can give her a way out. A way out that will leave her free to choose. It will be up to her then to decide what to do with her life. Everyone deserves a second chance. Don't they?

Suddenly, I recall how Rochelle tried to poison me that time in the past with King Richard II. She knew my identity then and still she—

'It was my job. If I didn't, I would have been reported. I wasn't alone on that mission. But there wasn't enough poison in that goblet to kill you, Isabel. Only to make you ill for a short time.'

Taking the risk that she's telling the truth, I slide the tip of my sword beneath her skin-tight mask, raising an edge near her left ear. It lifts, and with a flick of the sword, peels away, coloured lenses and all, revealing Rochelle's brilliant green eyes, looking slightly reddened and irritated from the mask.

With nothing to protect her identity now, Rochelle has Marduke's blessing to turn and run. She takes one step backwards and gives a barely perceptible nod before disappearing into the woods.

I don't get a second to analyse whether I've done the right or wrong thing. Arkarian's voice sings out, 'Hurry, you're needed here!'

I run back into the clearing. What I see there leaves me gasping and breathless. Many warriors are now lying dead or maimed on the clearing floor. Marduke himself stands beside Matt with a flaming torch in his hand, poised ready to light the timber at Matt's feet. The guards on either side of Matt are now fighting Arkarian, Mr Carter and Shaun. Then I see why Arkarian called. It's Jimmy – lying very still, half slumped against a log, blood pumping out from a deep wound to his thigh.

I run over and lift his fingers from the wound, running a hand over his sweat soaked face. A warrior approaches with his sword drawn. Shaun diverts his attention quickly, doing battle with two warriors at once. Immediately, I get to work on healing Jimmy. He's lost a lot of blood, and it takes me a few minutes to get started. Just as I think the task impossible, the cells will not repair, they begin to move at my will. I seal the exits first, saving what blood Jimmy has left, then repair his damaged tissues, muscles, tendons and blood vessels.

'Good work,' he says, regaining his strength with surprising speed. Leaning on me at first, he gets to his feet, tentatively trying out his newly repaired leg. It takes his full weight and he grins, nodding with relief. 'I owe you one, my girl!'

He takes his sword and gets straight back into the fighting. We are, of course, still severely outnumbered, two and sometimes three to one.

Shaun suddenly eliminates the pair he duels with and spins on Marduke, who still holds the torch threateningly near Matt's feet. 'Touch flame to that wood and I will slice your head completely off, as I should have done twelve years ago.'

Marduke only laughs, but tosses the flame to one of his warriors. I think he still resembles Lord Whitby. 'Hold this,' Marduke says. 'I'll be back to light it soon.' And to Shaun he says, 'It's about time we finally settled this score, *friend.*'

They begin to duel. This fight is unfair right from the start. Marduke is fresh, having fought no one yet, whereas Shaun has fought many already. This also is in Marduke's plan.

Matt suddenly groans and moves his head, as if slowly waking. What else can go wrong? I spin around in a mad circle, wondering how Ethan could possibly be taking so long. My attention is riveted to Shaun duelling with Marduke. This is the fight Shaun left the Guard to avoid. The others too have paused to watch, forming a rough circle so that they can keep an eye on each other as well.

Marduke has the upper hand right from the start. Shaun gives back as good as he gets, but it's obvious he's tiring. The battle just seems to go on and on, then Shaun's sword strikes Marduke's right shoulder, drawing blood.

Marduke shakes his head with a violent grunt, and comes back with a vengeance that leaves everyone stunned. Swords clash fiercely. Shaun is forced ever backwards. It's obvious now that Shaun is losing, but when the lethal strike comes, it happens so quickly it takes us all by surprise. Shaun falls to one knee. Terribly disadvantaged, he tries hard to regain his footing, but Marduke lunges his sword straight at Shaun's chest. It goes in swift and deep, piercing right through Shaun's protective armour.

Shaun gasps, his sword dropping with a clang to the ground. I run to him and, with Jimmy's help, withdraw Marduke's sword. Quickly, we remove the battered armour. I put my hands to Shaun's chest in an attempt to stem the massive blood flow while starting to work my healing skills. But I'm still weakened from healing Jimmy, and Shaun is fading fast.

Marduke stares down with a satisfied half-grin. 'At last,' he hisses.

Trying to ignore the hatred and bitterness emanating

from the heartless man towering over me, I press down hard on Shaun's chest and start visualising the enormous amount of healing that must take place to seal the wound first, then repair the heart and all the surrounding damaged areas.

But Marduke tries to distract me. He takes back the torch, calling my name, taunting me to watch him light the wood beneath my brother's feet.

A sudden commotion seizes my attention. Warriors move around the clearing. There's a new figure among them. Ethan! *Finally*, he makes an appearance. Where has he been? He doesn't even seem to be hurrying. Steadily, he approaches Marduke, ignoring everyone else, though as he passes near me he gives a lingering look at his father lying on his back beneath my hands, blood still oozing from his open heart-wound. In a flash, his eyes reveal the pain and torture of a child gripped by the certain knowledge that he could at any moment lose that which is most precious to him – his own parent.

'You're too late, it's almost over,' Marduke taunts, holding the torch mere centimetres from the wood.

'Ah, but not too late to show you this.' Keeping his eyes focused solely on Marduke, Ethan raises one hand and, in a dramatic show, moves it in a wide arch. Before our eyes a brilliant dome of light appears, the shape of a beautiful girl generating within. She looks up and around the dome, confusion on her delicate face.

'What game is this?' Marduke demands.

'Don't you think she looks a little familiar?' Ethan asks in a teasing voice.

Marduke takes the challenge by peering intently at

the girl. Suddenly, his head jerks backwards. 'It can't be!' he whispers.

'She is your daughter,' Ethan announces flamboyantly, bowing at the same time. '*Neriah.*'

Heal! I order myself to concentrate on repairing the damaged cells in Shaun's chest, visualising the sealing of vessels, blood returning to wounded tissue. As the healing takes shape, I wonder whether my efforts are too late, as Shaun's loss of blood is horrendous. I try hard to keep focused, but the torch at Matt's feet, the darkening of his bruised skin, and this unexpected shy-looking apparition have me mesmerised. I force myself to work on two levels: healing Shaun, which I do with an inner source of energy I'm normally unaware of; and observing the goings-on around me.

Marduke stares at Ethan, clearly unsettled. 'This is nothing but an illusion.'

Ethan wills a dagger from his boot to his hand, and in one fluid movement reaches within the dome and drags the girl into his arms. Forcing her back to his chest, he points the dagger to her throat.

Outside the dome the girl looks very real indeed. She squirms, her eyes widening with confusion and panic. Ethan tightens his grip. Drips of blood form across the girl's throat where the dagger has come too close. She screams.

'No!' Marduke commands with a surprising catch to his throat. 'Release her!'

'Only when you throw down the torch,' Ethan says, maintaining a steady front. I've never seen Ethan so controlled. What's happened to him? Where's the boy who generally acts before he thinks? He is wearing an air of calm-composure. 'If you don't do as I say, you will never know your own flesh again.'

Marduke lowers the torch just slightly. 'Where did you find her? I looked everywhere since that day, twelve years ago, when her mother snatched her from my arms.'

'She's been well cared for. You only had to wait. Obviously, she was going to be drawn to Veridian; it was simply a matter of time.'

'She is *Named*?' Marduke asks in a voice of disbelief and disgust. 'By the Guard?'

'She'll enter the Guard one day soon,' Arkarian announces.

Marduke suddenly laughs, his tone heavy with contempt. 'Do you think I will allow that?'

Arkarian shrugs. 'You won't have a choice.'

'These past twelve years I have seen another world and I have learned many things, old friend. I'll not confuse my loyalties again. My fealty is to the Goddess alone. She has made me very content.'

Ethan's arms stiffen as if unable to believe the heartlessness of the man before him. 'What are you saying?'

Marduke's eyes shift to Ethan's. 'What I'm saying, boy, is that I would not hesitate to kill my own daughter if that's what it takes to keep her from your hands.'

Ethan inhales sharply. 'I never did think of you as a man. All those years I was right.'

'So what am I?'

'In my dreams you were a monster. The reality is, you're far worse.'

Marduke looks at me while I work hard to save Shaun's life. 'You waste your strength on him, girl. One day perhaps you'll have the skill, but today you're far too inexperienced. He will die, as he should have done before he did this thing to me.' He raises a thick hand to the shattered side of his face where scars run in zigzag fashion from his hairline to the deep chasm of his chin.

And with those angry words Marduke throws the torch directly into the centre of the pile of wood beneath Matt's feet, simultaneously lunging for the girl still held in Ethan's arms.

Surprised by this sudden distracting move, Ethan lets his grip loosen, Marduke grabs the girl and holds her tightly. *'Neriah!'* he whispers close to her ear.

The fire ignites, causing chaos in the clearing, and my heart to racing. *'Noooo!'* I scream, losing my concentration altogether now, and make to run to Matt.

Arkarian pulls me back down, covering my hands with his own over the centre of Shaun's chest. 'Heal! For you're almost done, and a healer is what you are, Isabel.'

'But Matt?'

'Ethan and Jimmy will save him.'

I look up and see Ethan and Jimmy running to the fire. I glance down briefly at Shaun, his injured heart beneath my hands, wondering how close I really am to healing his wound. 'Marduke says I'm not strong enough to save Shaun.'

'Don't listen to the poison that flows from Marduke's mouth. Keep going, Isabel. Marduke forgot to mention what else he learned from the Order – to lie and cheat and deceive. If you believe in yourself, you can still heal this man. Without you he will surely die.'

But all thoughts of healing soon fly from my head when Ethan suddenly spins away from the burning flames without even trying to get Matt down. Shivers go through me as I watch him take his dagger, hold it tightly in his fist, then spin on Marduke as if possessed of a power and strength even Marduke would find intimidating. He rams into the big man with no apparent care for his own safety, the blow forcing Marduke to release the girl called Neriah. In the same instant Ethan grabs the girl, shoving her into the lighted dome. She falls into a heap on the floor and disappears.

Marduke looks at the spot where his daughter was and roars, his hands clawing the air angrily as if this action will somehow return her. Stunned, I can only stare as this huge man drops to all fours, digging away at the dirt where the last rays of Ethan's lighted dome are now disappearing.

Slowly, Marduke realises his daughter is gone. He staggers to his feet, his arms held wide, his misshapen face contorted. His eye searches for Ethan, and when he finds him, Marduke gives an earth-shattering roar, stretching his hands wide in front of him. To everyone's amazement Marduke's fingers start to glow with streaks of vivid blue light, as if his blood vessels have become luminous. And just like lightning, electric streaks flash from his fingertips with hissing, screeching sounds.

Arkarian calls out a sharp warning. But Ethan is one step ahead. Dagger drawn, Ethan charges Marduke, stabbing him deeply in the throat. Marduke screams, grabbing Ethan in a tight hold. But Ethan hangs on with all he has, stabbing Marduke again and again.

And while Marduke's life drains from his body, Jimmy and Mr Carter try their hardest to dismantle the burning timber to get to Matt. I try to keep my mind focused on the healing beneath my hands, sensing on some higher level that I'm close now, while still trying to see beyond the leaping and crackling flames. But they're just too strong. The wood must have been doused with something to make it ignite so viciously. The flames take a firm hold, stopping everyone from getting any closer to Matt.

'*Help him!*' I scream while still trying to continue working on Shaun.

Hands suddenly clasp over mine. I look down. They're Shaun's. Gently he pushes my hands away. 'You are truly gifted,' he says softly, apparently completely healed. 'Consider me always in your debt.'

Arkarian helps him to his feet, and I'm free now to run to the fire. But when I get there, everyone is just standing around looking at the place where Matt's scorched and murdered body should be hanging. They're staring, and now I understand why. Matt is not there. The tree is bare except for the flames leaping and dancing around its massive trunk.

Arkarian comes up behind me. 'Who did this?'

Ethan staggers over, as puzzled as the rest of us. 'I don't know, but Marduke is dead.'

'Are you sure?' Arkarian asks.

This question has everyone turn and look at the lifeless body lying in a widening pool of his own blood. As we stare, Marduke's body starts to disappear. 'He died out of his own time. What does this mean? He can't come back, can he?' I ask.

Ethan and Arkarian exchange a really weird look but don't say anything. Marduke's remaining warriors come over for a closer examination, but only blood-stained grass remains where their master's body lay but a few seconds earlier. They realise their master is dead and gone. Quickly, they back away, gather their dead and wounded, and disappear into the surrounding woods.

Shaun stands in the exact spot where Marduke's body disappeared and answers me. 'What this means, quite simply, is that our problems with this man are over. No one can come back from the dead, Isabel.'

Ethan finally drags his glance away from Arkarian and takes my hand, pointing it into the flames before us. 'You have to learn to trust more, Isabel.'

I think his words right now are insane. 'What are you talking about? Where's Matt? Where at least is his body?'

'Here … Here I am. But who the hell are you?' I spin around as Matt's laboured voice comes from somewhere behind me. He looks weary and beaten and bruised and greenish, but at least he's breathing. Jimmy and Mr Carter help him walk, taking most of his weight.

'How did you escape?' I ask, but quickly remind myself that as we're still in the past, Matt is seeing us as the strangers the Citadel created to keep our identities secret.

'Rochelle released me. She's gone now, said something about having to disappear for a while. I don't understand what's going on. Can someone please explain?'

I can't stop myself from screaming and jumping up and down in sheer relief. My brother is alive and safe, even though he resembles a corpse recently dragged from its grave. I run the short distance between us, throwing myself at him, giving him a fierce hug. Jimmy and Mr Carter have to hold him more firmly so my hug doesn't knock him backwards.

Matt labours to get a clear breath then pushes me slightly away. 'Do I know you?'

I stare straight into his eyes, brown like mine. He stares back. '*Isabel?*'

I nod and grin at him as speaking is too difficult.

He touches my long curls. 'What's with the red hair?' He peers at my face closely. 'And what are these? *Freckles?*'

'It's a long story and I'm not so sure you're supposed to hear it,' Ethan says, then glances at Arkarian.

'I wouldn't worry too much about that,' Arkarian says cryptically. 'But getting Matt's health back is our first priority.'

Matt stares hard at Arkarian and frowns. 'I know you. You're the one called Arkarian.'

'Yes,' Arkarian replies. 'But how do you know?'

'Your eyes are exactly as my sister described them in her sleep.'

Arkarian's eyes slide to mine, but my face is going hot so fast I think the freckles are all joining up. Quickly, I drop my gaze.

'Really?' Arkarian says in a curious tone. 'And what exactly did she say?'

'Ah,' I interrupt. 'This is hardly necessary. Matt's in pain. Shouldn't you do something?'

For once Matt doesn't argue. 'Do what you must, Arkarian, but first tell me what's going on.' He glances across at Ethan. 'I think I know you too.'

Ethan gives a little laugh. 'You do, friend, but you probably wish you didn't.'

'*Ethan?* Well, I should have guessed.' Matt takes in

Ethan's period dress, right down to his tight mail leggings. 'That's a good look on you. You should wear it more often.'

This conversation is driving me crazy. 'How much did you see, Matt? When did you regain consciousness?'

Matt glances at me with a look of compassion mixed with humour. 'I could put you out of your misery and tell you I only just came to when the flames started licking at my toes, but that would be a lie.'

'Oh?' My voice squeaks badly.

'I woke up when Rochelle started to work loose the ropes at the back of the tree. She warned me not to draw attention to myself, so I kept quiet, which got harder once Ethan made an appearance. By the way,' he says in an offhand manner, looking at Ethan. 'Where is that girl from the light? One second she's here, the next she disappears.'

'She's safe. Why?'

Matt frowns again. 'No reason. I just feel as if I've seen her before, or ...' He shrugs and groans, bending over with a sudden stab of pain. 'I don't know. I get the feeling, that's all, as if we know each other or something.' He turns to Jimmy first, then Mr Carter. 'Are you two people I should know as well?'

Arkarian pulls Matt out of their hands, taking most of Matt's weight on his own shoulder. 'We don't have time for any more guessing games. You need healing.'

Before Arkarian takes Matt away somewhere, I just have to ask, 'What's going to happen to Matt? He's seen us doing things.'

Arkarian calmly replies, 'We may just have to kill him.'

'*What!*'

But then he laughs and shakes his head at me.

'Your sense of humour needs work, Arkarian,' I snap at him, even though I know he's just trying to relieve the tension I'm still feeling.

He goes on to explain in a gentle voice, 'I have to take Matt to a special room in the Citadel for a while to heal his mortal body. But it's going to take some time. You'll have to work something out to tell your mother. Matt could be away for many weeks in the mortal measurement of time.'

'OK. But what's going to happen to him after he's healed?'

'The truth is, Isabel, after your incredible display of healing skills, I guarantee you'll no longer be anyone's Apprentice. And when Matt here is well again, no doubt he'll be initiated as Ethan's new trainee, for he too is Named.'

'Yes!' Ethan says, punching the air with a closed fist. But then his face drops, his eyes darkening as he recalls whatever it was he did to upset the Tribunal again. 'That's if I'm still in the Guard by then.'

Chapter Forty-one

Ethan

My trial is going to be brief. I've only been allocated an hour. At first, I don't get it as my breach was of the highest order – changing the past, *and* taking a mortal body and soul through time. But then I realise there's no need for a long trial; it'll be a quick disbarring. There are no character witnesses to testify in my favour. Carter won't be asked for an opinion on my maturity or level of responsibility – they already know what he thinks. The Tribunal will hand down its judgement, which is already a foregone conclusion.

Almost everyone is gathered here in the palace in Greece: Dad, Isabel, Carter, Jimmy and, of course, Arkarian. We're standing in the corridor outside the meeting chamber. Matt, who is soon to be an Apprentice, is still far from healed yet, recuperating in the Citadel's healing chamber. His first trip to Athens won't be made until after his first mission anyway. Marduke's daughter Neriah, who unknowingly was part of my illusion, remains unaware of her future with the Guard. She hasn't even come to Angel Falls yet, but her time is approaching, for she too will have her part to play. And as for Rochelle, she has apparently disappeared. People are already asking questions at school, especially as another student – Jade Myer – has gone missing as well. Rumours are spreading fast that both girls have taken off together. Jade was apparently a member of the Order who was killed during the battle. She will remain missing for ever. That Rochelle and Jade were both members of the Order is hard to comprehend. Who else of my peers, maybe even among my friends, support chaos and destruction? There's been no word on any of the others killed or injured; not all were from Angel Falls. But those who were will have their identities fiercely protected.

The doors now open inwards and Isabel throws me an encouraging smile before going inside with Carter and Jimmy. But it's to Arkarian that my thoughts shift right now. I just hope he doesn't cop any flak as a result of my disobedience. It wouldn't be fair.

Arkarian stands looking regal in his silver suit and full cloak, his blue hair loose around his shoulders. He waits to one side, while Dad takes my hand in both of his, locking it in a strong grip. 'I wish there was something I could say to make this trial easier for you, Ethan.'

'No. Don't say anything. It's all my own doing. But I do want to say something to you.' He waits while I gather my thoughts together. 'It's just that, well, I'm really glad you came back to finish this mission, Dad.'

'Thanks, son.'

'It was great seeing you … you know, in action and all that.'

'Yes …?' He senses there's more.

'But, I am sorry that I pushed you, and that I made

you feel you weren't good enough the way you were.'

He shakes his head and smiles at me. 'Don't be sorry, Ethan. You were right. I was only living half a life in my withdrawn state. I was hiding. And that was wrong. Perhaps now I can help your mother properly through her grief. It's time we moved through this pain, and together we'll be stronger.'

'Well, I'm glad we had this time to get to know each other in a different way. And I'm also glad Isabel was there to save your butt.'

Dad laughs, a wonderful sound, the first and probably the last laugh we'll share as Guardians of Time together. When I come out of this trial, my memory of the Guard will be erased. I'll wake up in my bed as though the past twelve adventure-filled years haven't happened. My chest contracts at the thought, tightening unbearably.

We go in, Dad first, finding himself a seat with the others. Arkarian walks with me to the centre of the circle, then he also joins the others.

I glance furtively around. The nine members of the Tribunal are all sitting in the same seats as the last time I stood here. Lorian is directly in front of me, next to Penbarin, who, while appearing to look my way, keeps his eyes cast down. To Penbarin's right I'm surprised to see a vacant chair, making the circle one not of nine but of ten, though this position remains empty. I quickly flick a look around the rest of the circle. Everyone else who should be here apparently is.

Lorian hushes everyone wordlessly and I find myself grateful for the stool provided. Lorian looks directly at me and I try to hold his powerful gaze, but as usual the immortal's aura overwhelms me and makes me want to hide. I force myself to stay put. 'Do you have anything you wish to say?' Lorian asks.

I take a deep, steadying breath. What can I say in my defence? *Uh, I don't know what made me do it?* For that is the only defence I have. Instead, I ask, 'How does King Richard fare?'

Lorian's head bows briefly, acknowledging my question. 'He is being healed in our specially sealed chambers. Do not worry for him, he is being looked after. Though the risk was enormous, he made it to the healing chamber in time. He will survive.' Lorian pauses. 'Is there anything else?'

'Yes, I'd like to know what's going to happen to Rochelle, and if you know where she is?'

'She is safe.'

The immortal appears as if there is nothing more to say, but murmurs break out among those watching. Everyone is wondering about her. They've heard how she saved Matt's life and, according to Isabel, Marduke used and tricked her into becoming one of them.

'She will be joining your group very soon.'

Carter stands and calls out, 'Is that wise? Will we ever be able to trust her? Will we ever feel safe enough in her company to turn our backs to her?'

Lorian appears annoyed with Carter's outburst. 'The question is, will Rochelle ever feel safe from your distrust?'

Suitably put down, Carter sits. Lorian's attention returns to me but I have nothing else to say. 'Stand, Ethan.'

I get to my feet on unsure legs. The immortal comes towards me and holds two hands above my head and a shower of white light unfolds around me from top to bottom. Everything I see through this light has a bright, yet slightly distorted appearance; even Lorian's words sound as if they come through a flexible barrier, lengthened and oddly out of proportion. 'Ethan Roberts, you have been charged with illegally using your position on the Guard to alter events of the past in strict opposition to the Guard's laws. How do you plead?'

My eyes close at these words. They might as well be a death sentence. 'Guilty.'

Lorian gives a little laugh. Do you give up so quickly?'

'I did it. I don't have a defence.'

The light surrounding me intensifies to a blinding glare for a moment. I cover my eyes until it eases. 'Instinct is your defence, Ethan.'

What is this immortal saying?

'Unknown to your own self, you were in fact acting under the power of the Prophecy.'

My eyes fly open at these words. *The Prophecy?*

'You risked your position on the Guard to answer the call of the Prophecy, which you recognised *instinctively*. It is one of your strengths, Ethan. You are fortunate in that you have a third skill.'

Lorian looks at me, and even though I don't meet the immortal's gaze, I feel warmth surge through the light. 'Following your instinct, you acted with complete and unconditional loyalty, doing what you knew in your heart was right. You risked your own future for your belief, and by doing so, you proved your honour.' Lorian pauses to allow these words to sink in. 'And so, you are completely exonerated of all wrongdoing.'

Before I have a chance to collapse in surprised relief, Lorian speaks again. 'Look to your right, Ethan.'

I do as commanded, and in the seat that was vacant there now sits a man. He looks familiar, but through the strange light his features appear distorted. The colour of his skin is a sickly dull green. I stare hard and long as I feel Lorian urging me to recognise this figure. Slowly, his features take clearer shape before my eyes and suddenly breath catches in my throat. 'It's King Richard.'

I feel Lorian smile. This time the warmth that fills the light permeates every cell of my body. 'In accordance with the Prophecy, from this day forth, King Richard II of England will be known as King of the House of Veridian.'

'The ancient city.'

'The city to which you belong, Ethan. You and the other eight members of the Guard whose identities are now revealed, five of whom have come today to witness this extraordinary event.' Lorian pauses, drawing my eyes upwards, and this time I can't resist the powerful pull. I lift my head and somehow, with the help of the distorted surrounding light, I'm able to hold the immortal's gaze.

Lorian looks down at me pleased. 'When King Richard is well enough, he will stand in the Tribunal circle for everyone to see, representing the House of Veridian, which he will rule. And his royal skills will be sorely required. Certain recent events have altered the Guard as we know it: Marduke's death, the revealing of the nine Named of Veridian, and the transformation of the ancient city into a noble House with King Richard at its head.' Lorian pauses to look around at the Tribunal circle and the others to the side. 'But our problems have not altered, nor has our reason for

332

being. Our greatest challenges are yet to come. Marduke was a mortal, but a warrior of high standing. The Goddess of Chaos will surely miss her traitorous commander. His death will not go unavenged.'

Lorian glances back down at me, making sure I understand the coming words. I sense they are meant especially for my ears. 'The Guard will not be weakened by the removal of one of its most talented and courageous members.'

It is the light, I realise, and the power radiating from Lorian's eyes that hold me upright. Nothing else. My limbs feel as if they've turned to water. I'm not to be punished after all. I was, in fact, supposed to set things right for King Richard II. He wasn't meant to die in that filthy prison like a gutter rat. My instinct, my gut feeling to release him, was correct. He too has a part to play in this Prophecy that shapes and protects our mortal world.

Lorian's hands move slightly, and the light changes around me from white to brilliant shimmering gold. Waves of power thunder through me, making my body tremble. Through the vibration and shuddering light I hear Lorian's voice again, distorted more than ever; but somehow the words unfold with crystal clarity within my head. The immortal says, 'For your trust in the Prophecy beyond logic, loyalty and recrimination, you are hereby awarded the responsibility and honour of the Guard's highest achievement: the power of flight.'

As the golden light enfolds tightly around me, and I receive my wings, a tumultuous cheer erupts.

old magic

marianne curley

a boy, a girl, a curse ... powerful chemistry!